Anton Chekhov – Neighbours & Other Short Stories

The short story is often viewed as an inferior relation to the Novel. But it is an art in itself. To take a story and distil its essence into fewer pages while keeping character and plot rounded and driven is not an easy task. Many try and many fail.

In this series we look at short stories from many of our most accomplished writers. Miniature masterpieces with a lot to say. In this volume we examine some of the short stories of Anton Chekhov.

Russian Literature is probably more known for the sheer length, scope and breadth of its novels. Chekhov was no exception to this with such masterpieces as War And Peace. But he also wrote such plays such as Uncle Vanya, The Cherry Orchard and The Seagull. But he also sits atop most literary critics as one of the greatest short story writers ever.

Born in 1860 Anton Chekhov was born on 29 January 1860, the third of six surviving children, in Taganrog, a port in the south of Russia.

Chekhov attended a school for Greek boys, followed by the Taganrog gymnasium, where he was kept down for a year at fifteen for failing a Greek exam. Despite having a religious background and education, he later on became an atheist.

In 1876, Chekhov's father was declared bankrupt after over-extending his finances building a new house. To avoid the debtor's prison he fled to Moscow, where his two eldest sons, Alexander and Nikolay, were attending university. The family lived in poverty in Moscow, Chekhov's mother physically and emotionally broken. Chekhov was left behind to sell the family possessions and finish his education.

In 1879, Chekhov completed his schooling and joined his family in Moscow, having gained admission to the medical school at Moscow University

Chekhov now assumed responsibility for the whole family. To support them and to pay his tuition fees, he wrote daily short, humorous sketches and vignettes of contemporary Russian life, many under pseudonyms. His prodigious output earned him a reputation as a satirical chronicler of Russian street life, and by 1882 he was writing for Oskolki (Fragments), owned by Nikolai Leykin, one of the leading publishers of the time.

In 1884, Chekhov qualified as a physician, which he considered his principal profession though he made little money from it and treated the poor free of charge.

In 1884 and 1885, Chekhov found himself coughing blood, and in 1886 the attacks worsened; but he would not admit tuberculosis to his family and friends

In the next twenty years his writing was to elevate him to that of a literary giant though he continued to practice medicine "Medicine is my lawful wife", he once said, "and literature is my mistress. When I get tired of one, I spend the night with the other"

One of the first to use the stream-of-consciousness technique, later adopted by the modernists, combined with a disavowal of the moral finality of traditional story structure. He made no apologies for the difficulties this posed to readers, insisting that the role of an artist was to ask questions, not to answer them.

But his health continued to deteriorate; he moved on doctors advice to a warmer climate at Yalta but yearned for Moscow and travel. Though the tuberculosis was to gradually worsen he kept working, his output prodigious but exemplary. But by May 1904, the outlook was terminal. Mikhail Chekhov recalled that "everyone who saw him secretly thought the end was not far off, but the nearer he was to the end, the less he seemed to realise it."

In 1908, Olga wrote this account of her husband's last moments: Anton sat up unusually straight and said loudly and clearly in German): Ich sterbe ("I'm dying"). The doctor calmed him, took a syringe, gave him an injection of camphor, and ordered champagne. Anton took a full glass, examined it, smiled at me and said: "It's a long time since I drank champagne." He drank it, lay quietly on his left side and died.

Chekhov's body was transported to Moscow in a refrigerated railway car for fresh oysters. Some of the thousands of mourners followed the funeral procession of a General Keller by mistake, to the accompaniment of a military band.

Chekhov was buried next to his father at the Novodevichy Cemetery.

Some of these stories are also available as an audiobook from our sister company Word Of Mouth. Many samples are at our youtube channel http://www.youtube.com/user/PortablePoetry?feature=mhee   The full volume can be purchased from iTunes, Amazon and other digital stores.

Index Of Stories

THE DUEL

I

It was eight o'clock in the morning—the time when the officers, the local officials, and the visitors usually took their morning dip in the sea after the hot, stifling night, and then went into the pavilion to drink tea or coffee. Ivan Andreitch Laevsky, a thin, fair young man of twenty-eight, wearing the cap of a clerk in the Ministry of Finance and with slippers on his feet, coming down to bathe, found a number of acquaintances on the beach, and among them his friend Samoylenko, the army doctor.

With his big cropped head, short neck, his red face, his big nose, his shaggy black eyebrows and grey whiskers, his stout puffy figure and his hoarse military bass, this Samoylenko made on every newcomer the unpleasant impression of a gruff bully; but two or three days after making his acquaintance, one began to think his face extraordinarily good-natured, kind, and even handsome. In spite of his clumsiness and rough manner, he was a peaceable man, of infinite kindliness and goodness of heart, always ready to be of use. He was on familiar terms with every one in the town, lent every one money, doctored every one, made matches, patched up quarrels, arranged picnics at which he cooked *shashlik* and an awfully good soup of grey mullets. He was always looking after other people's affairs and trying to interest some one on their behalf, and was always delighted about something. The general opinion about him was that he was without faults of character. He had only two weaknesses: he was ashamed of his own good nature, and tried to disguise it by a surly expression and an assumed gruffness; and he liked his assistants and his soldiers to call him "Your Excellency," although he was only a civil councillor.

"Answer one question for me, Alexandr Daviditch," Laevsky began, when both he and Samoylenko were in the water up to their shoulders. "Suppose you had loved a woman and had been living with her for two or three years, and then left off caring for her, as one does, and began to feel that you had nothing in common with her. How would you behave in that case?"

"It's very simple. 'You go where you please, madam'—and that would be the end of it."

"It's easy to say that! But if she has nowhere to go? A woman with no friends or relations, without a farthing, who can't work . . ."

"Well? Five hundred roubles down or an allowance of twenty-five roubles a month—and nothing more. It's very simple."

"Even supposing you have five hundred roubles and can pay twenty-five roubles a month, the woman I am speaking of is an educated woman and proud. Could you really bring yourself to offer her money? And how would you do it?"

Samoylenko was going to answer, but at that moment a big wave covered them both, then broke on the beach and rolled back noisily over the shingle. The friends got out and began dressing.

"Of course, it is difficult to live with a woman if you don't love her," said Samoylenko, shaking the sand out of his boots. "But one must look at the thing humanely, Vanya. If it were my case, I should never show a sign that I did not love her, and I should go on living with her till I died."

He was at once ashamed of his own words; he pulled himself up and said:

"But for aught I care, there might be no females at all. Let them all go to the devil!"

The friends dressed and went into the pavilion. There Samoylenko was quite at home, and even had a special cup and saucer. Every morning they brought him on a tray a cup of coffee, a tall cut glass of iced water, and a tiny glass of brandy. He would first drink the brandy, then the hot coffee, then the iced water, and this must have been very nice, for after drinking it his eyes looked moist with pleasure, he would stroke his whiskers with both hands, and say, looking at the sea:

"A wonderfully magnificent view!"

After a long night spent in cheerless, unprofitable thoughts which prevented him from sleeping, and seemed to intensify the darkness and sultriness of the night, Laevsky felt listless and shattered. He felt no better for the bathe and the coffee.

"Let us go on with our talk, Alexandr Daviditch," he said. "I won't make a secret of it; I'll speak to you openly as to a friend. Things are in a bad way with Nadyezhda Fyodorovna and me . . . a very bad way! Forgive me for forcing my private affairs upon you, but I must speak out."

Samoylenko, who had a misgiving of what he was going to speak about, dropped his eyes and drummed with his fingers on the table.

"I've lived with her for two years and have ceased to love her," Laevsky went on; "or, rather, I realised that I never had felt any love for her. . . . These two years have been a mistake."

It was Laevsky's habit as he talked to gaze attentively at the pink palms of his hands, to bite his nails, or to pinch his cuffs. And he did so now.

"I know very well you can't help me," he said. "But I tell you, because unsuccessful and superfluous people like me find their salvation in talking. I have to generalise about everything I do. I'm bound to look for an explanation and justification of my absurd existence in somebody else's theories, in literary types—in the idea that we, upper-class Russians, are degenerating, for instance, and so on. Last night, for example, I comforted myself by thinking all the time: 'Ah, how true Tolstoy is, how mercilessly true!' And that did me good. Yes, really, brother, he is a great writer, say what you like!"

Samoylenko, who had never read Tolstoy and was intending to do so every day of his life, was a little embarrassed, and said:

"Yes, all other authors write from imagination, but he writes straight from nature."

"My God!" sighed Laevsky; "how distorted we all are by civilisation! I fell in love with a married woman and she with me. . . . To begin with, we had kisses, and calm evenings, and vows, and Spencer, and ideals, and interests in common. . . . What a deception! We really ran away from her husband, but we lied to ourselves and made out that we ran away from the emptiness of the life of the educated class. We pictured our future like this: to begin with, in the Caucasus, while we were getting to know the people and the place, I would put on the Government uniform and enter the service; then at our leisure we would pick out a plot of ground, would toil in the sweat of our brow, would have a vineyard and a field, and so on. If you were in my place, or that zoologist of yours, Von Koren, you might live with Nadyezhda Fyodorovna for thirty years, perhaps, and might leave your heirs a rich vineyard and three thousand acres of maize; but I felt like a bankrupt from the first day. In the town you have insufferable heat, boredom, and no society; if you go out into the country, you fancy poisonous spiders, scorpions, or snakes lurking under every stone and behind every bush, and beyond the fields—mountains and the desert. Alien people, an alien country, a wretched form of civilisation—all that is not so easy, brother, as walking on the Nevsky Prospect in one's fur coat, arm-in-arm with Nadyezhda Fyodorovna, dreaming of the sunny South. What is needed here is a life and death struggle, and I'm not a fighting man. A wretched neurasthenic, an idle gentleman . . . . From the first day I knew that my dreams of a life of labour and of a vineyard were worthless. As for love, I ought to tell you that living with a woman who has read Spencer and has followed you to the ends of the earth is no more interesting than living with any Anfissa or Akulina. There's the same smell of ironing, of powder, and of medicines, the same curl-papers every morning, the same self-deception."

"You can't get on in the house without an iron," said Samoylenko, blushing at Laevsky's speaking to him so openly of a lady he knew. "You are out of humour to-day, Vanya, I notice. Nadyezhda Fyodorovna is a splendid woman, highly educated, and you are a man of the highest intellect. Of course, you are not married," Samoylenko went on, glancing round at the adjacent tables, "but that's not your fault; and besides . . . one ought to be above conventional prejudices and rise to the level of modern ideas. I believe in free love myself, yes. . . . But to my thinking, once you have settled together, you ought to go on living together all your life."

"Without love?"

"I will tell you directly," said Samoylenko. "Eight years ago there was an old fellow, an agent, here—a man of very great intelligence. Well, he used to say that the great thing in married life was patience. Do you hear, Vanya? Not love, but patience. Love cannot last long. You have lived two years in love, and now evidently your married life has reached the period when, in order to preserve equilibrium, so to speak, you ought to exercise all your patience. . . ."

"You believe in your old agent; to me his words are meaningless. Your old man could be a hypocrite; he could exercise himself in the virtue of patience, and, as he did so, look upon a person he did not love as an object indispensable for his moral exercises; but I have not yet fallen so low. If I want to exercise myself in patience, I will buy dumb-bells or a frisky horse, but I'll leave human beings alone."

Samoylenko asked for some white wine with ice. When they had drunk a glass each, Laevsky suddenly asked:

"Tell me, please, what is the meaning of softening of the brain?"

"How can I explain it to you? . . . It's a disease in which the brain becomes softer . . . as it were, dissolves."

"Is it curable?"

"Yes, if the disease is not neglected. Cold douches, blisters. . . .

Something internal, too."

"Oh! . . . Well, you see my position; I can't live with her: it is more than I can do. While I'm with you I can be philosophical about it and smile, but at home I lose heart completely; I am so utterly miserable, that if I were told, for instance, that I should have to live another month with her, I should blow out my brains. At the same time, parting with her is out of the question. She has no friends or relations; she cannot work, and neither she nor I have any money. . . . What could become of her? To whom could she go? There is nothing one can think of. . . . Come, tell me, what am I to do?"

"H'm! . . ." growled Samoylenko, not knowing what to answer. "Does she love you?"

"Yes, she loves me in so far as at her age and with her temperament she wants a man. It would be as difficult for her to do without me as to do without her powder or her curl-papers. I am for her an indispensable, integral part of her boudoir."

Samoylenko was embarrassed.

"You are out of humour to-day, Vanya," he said. "You must have had a bad night."

"Yes, I slept badly. . . . Altogether, I feel horribly out of sorts, brother. My head feels empty; there's a sinking at my heart, a weakness. . . . I must run away."

"Run where?"

"There, to the North. To the pines and the mushrooms, to people and ideas. . . . I'd give half my life to bathe now in some little stream in the province of Moscow or Tula; to feel chilly, you know, and then to stroll for three hours even with the feeblest student, and to talk and talk endlessly. . . . And the scent of the hay! Do you remember it? And in the evening, when one walks in the garden, sounds of the piano float from the house; one hears the train passing. . . ."

Laevsky laughed with pleasure; tears came into his eyes, and to cover them, without getting up, he stretched across the next table for the matches.

"I have not been in Russia for eighteen years," said Samoylenko. "I've forgotten what it is like. To my mind, there is not a country more splendid than the Caucasus."

"Vereshtchagin has a picture in which some men condemned to death are languishing at the bottom of a very deep well. Your magnificent Caucasus strikes me as just like that well. If I were offered the choice of a chimney-sweep in Petersburg or a prince in the Caucasus, I should choose the job of chimney-sweep."

Laevsky grew pensive. Looking at his stooping figure, at his eyes fixed dreamily at one spot, at his pale, perspiring face and sunken temples, at his bitten nails, at the slipper which had dropped off his heel, displaying a badly darned sock, Samoylenko was moved to pity, and probably because Laevsky reminded him of a helpless child, he asked:

"Is your mother living?"

"Yes, but we are on bad terms. She could not forgive me for this affair."

Samoylenko was fond of his friend. He looked upon Laevsky as a good-natured fellow, a student, a man with no nonsense about him, with whom one could drink, and laugh, and talk without reserve. What he understood in him he disliked extremely. Laevsky drank a great deal and at unsuitable times; he played cards, despised his work, lived beyond his means, frequently made use of unseemly expressions in conversation, walked about the streets in his slippers, and quarrelled with Nadyezhda Fyodorovna before other people—and Samoylenko did not like this. But the fact that Laevsky had once been a student in the Faculty of Arts, subscribed to two fat reviews, often talked so cleverly that only a few people understood him, was living with a well-educated woman—all this Samoylenko did not understand, and he liked this and respected Laevsky, thinking him superior to himself.

"There is another point," said Laevsky, shaking his head. "Only it is between ourselves. I'm concealing it from Nadyezhda Fyodorovna for the time. . . . Don't let it out before her. . . . I got a letter the day before yesterday, telling me that her husband has died from softening of the brain."

"The Kingdom of Heaven be his!" sighed Samoylenko. "Why are you concealing it from her?"

"To show her that letter would be equivalent to 'Come to church to be married.' And we should first have to make our relations clear. When she understands that we can't go on living together, I will show her the letter. Then there will be no danger in it."

"Do you know what, Vanya," said Samoylenko, and a sad and imploring expression came into his face, as though he were going to ask him about something very touching and were afraid of being refused. "Marry her, my dear boy!"

"Why?"

"Do your duty to that splendid woman! Her husband is dead, and so Providence itself shows you what to do!"

"But do understand, you queer fellow, that it is impossible. To marry without love is as base and unworthy of a man as to perform mass without believing in it."

"But it's your duty to."

"Why is it my duty?" Laevsky asked irritably.

"Because you took her away from her husband and made yourself responsible for her."

"But now I tell you in plain Russian, I don't love her!"

"Well, if you've no love, show her proper respect, consider her wishes. . . ."

"'Show her respect, consider her wishes,'" Laevsky mimicked him. "As though she were some Mother Superior! . . . You are a poor psychologist and physiologist if you think that living with a woman one can get off with nothing but respect and consideration. What a woman thinks most of is her bedroom."

"Vanya, Vanya!" said Samoylenko, overcome with confusion.

"You are an elderly child, a theorist, while I am an old man in spite of my years, and practical, and we shall never understand one another. We had better drop this conversation. Mustapha!" Laevsky shouted to the waiter. "What's our bill?"

"No, no . . ." the doctor cried in dismay, clutching Laevsky's arm. "It is for me to pay. I ordered it. Make it out to me," he cried to Mustapha.

The friends got up and walked in silence along the sea-front. When they reached the boulevard, they stopped and shook hands at parting.

"You are awfully spoilt, my friend!" Samoylenko sighed. "Fate has sent you a young, beautiful, cultured woman, and you refuse the gift, while if God were to give me a crooked old woman, how pleased I should be if only she were kind and affectionate! I would live with her in my vineyard and . . ."

Samoylenko caught himself up and said:

"And she might get the samovar ready for me there, the old hag."

After parting with Laevsky he walked along the boulevard. When, bulky and majestic, with a stern expression on his face, he walked along the boulevard in his snow-white tunic and superbly polished boots, squaring his chest, decorated with the Vladimir cross on a ribbon, he was very much pleased with himself, and it seemed as though the whole world were looking at him with pleasure. Without turning his head, he looked to each side and thought that the boulevard was extremely well laid out; that the young cypress-trees, the eucalyptuses, and the ugly, anemic palm-trees were very handsome and would in time give abundant shade; that the Circassians were an honest and hospitable people.

"It's strange that Laevsky does not like the Caucasus," he thought, "very strange."

Five soldiers, carrying rifles, met him and saluted him. On the right side of the boulevard the wife of a local official was walking along the pavement with her son, a schoolboy.

"Good-morning, Marya Konstantinovna," Samoylenko shouted to her with a pleasant smile. "Have you been to bathe? Ha, ha, ha! . . . My respects to Nikodim Alexandritch!"

And he went on, still smiling pleasantly, but seeing an assistant of the military hospital coming towards him, he suddenly frowned, stopped him, and asked:

"Is there any one in the hospital?"

"No one, Your Excellency."

"Eh?"

"No one, Your Excellency."

"Very well, run along. . . ."

Swaying majestically, he made for the lemonade stall, where sat a full-bosomed old Jewess, who gave herself out to be a Georgian, and said to her as loudly as though he were giving the word of command to a regiment:

"Be so good as to give me some soda-water!"

II

Laevsky's not loving Nadyezhda Fyodorovna showed itself chiefly in the fact that everything she said or did seemed to him a lie, or equivalent to a lie, and everything he read against women and love seemed to him to apply perfectly to himself, to Nadyezhda Fyodorovna and her husband. When he returned home, she was sitting at the window, dressed and with her hair done, and with a preoccupied face was drinking coffee and turning over the leaves of a fat magazine; and he thought the drinking of coffee was not such a remarkable event that she need put on a preoccupied expression over it, and that she had been wasting her time doing her hair in a fashionable style, as there was no one here to attract and no need to be attractive. And in the magazine he saw nothing but falsity. He thought she had dressed and done her hair so as to look handsomer, and was reading in order to seem clever.

"Will it be all right for me to go to bathe to-day?" she said.

"Why? There won't be an earthquake whether you go or not, I suppose . . . ."

"No, I only ask in case the doctor should be vexed."

"Well, ask the doctor, then; I'm not a doctor."

On this occasion what displeased Laevsky most in Nadyezhda Fyodorovna was her white open neck and the little curls at the back of her head. And he remembered that when Anna Karenin got tired of her husband, what she disliked most of all was his ears, and thought:

"How true it is, how true!"

Feeling weak and as though his head were perfectly empty, he went into his study, lay down on his sofa, and covered his face with a handkerchief that he might not be bothered by the flies. Despondent and oppressive thoughts always about the same thing trailed slowly across his brain like a long string of waggons on a gloomy autumn evening, and he sank into a state of drowsy oppression. It seemed to him that he had wronged Nadyezhda Fyodorovna and her husband, and that it was through his fault that her husband had died. It seemed to him that he had sinned against his own life, which he had ruined, against the world of lofty ideas, of learning, and of work, and he conceived that wonderful world as real and possible, not on this sea-front with hungry Turks and lazy mountaineers sauntering upon it, but there in the North, where there were operas, theatres, newspapers, and all kinds of intellectual activity. One could only there—not here—be honest, intelligent, lofty, and pure. He accused himself of having no ideal, no guiding principle in life, though he had a dim understanding now what it meant. Two years before, when he fell in love with Nadyezhda Fyodorovna, it seemed to him that he had only to go with her as his wife to the Caucasus, and he would be saved from vulgarity and emptiness; in the same way now, he was convinced that he had only to part from Nadyezhda Fyodorovna and to go to Petersburg, and he would get everything he wanted.

"Run away," he muttered to himself, sitting up and biting his nails.

"Run away!"

He pictured in his imagination how he would go aboard the steamer and then would have some lunch, would drink some cold beer, would talk on deck with ladies, then would get into the train at Sevastopol and set off. Hurrah for freedom! One station after another would flash by, the air would keep growing colder and keener, then the birches and the fir-trees, then Kursk, Moscow. . . . In the restaurants cabbage soup, mutton with kasha, sturgeon, beer, no more Asiaticism, but Russia, real Russia. The passengers in the train would talk about trade, new singers, the Franco-Russian *entente*; on all sides there would be the feeling of keen, cultured, intellectual, eager life. . . . Hasten on, on! At last Nevsky Prospect, and Great Morskaya Street, and then Kovensky Place, where he used to live at one time when he was a student, the dear grey sky, the drizzling rain, the drenched cabmen. . . .

"Ivan Andreitch!" some one called from the next room. "Are you at home?"

"I'm here," Laevsky responded. "What do you want?"

"Papers."

Laevsky got up languidly, feeling giddy, walked into the other room, yawning and shuffling with his slippers. There, at the open window that looked into the street, stood one of his young fellow-clerks, laying out some government documents on the window-sill.

"One minute, my dear fellow," Laevsky said softly, and he went to look for the ink; returning to the window, he signed the papers without looking at them, and said: "It's hot!"

"Yes. Are you coming to-day?"

"I don't think so. . . . I'm not quite well. Tell Sheshkovsky that I will come and see him after dinner."

The clerk went away. Laevsky lay down on his sofa again and began thinking:

"And so I must weigh all the circumstances and reflect on them. Before I go away from here I ought to pay up my debts. I owe about two thousand roubles. I have no money. . . . Of course, that's not important; I shall pay part now, somehow, and I shall send the rest, later, from Petersburg. The chief point is Nadyezhda Fyodorovna. . . . First of all we must define our relations. . . . Yes."

A little later he was considering whether it would not be better to go to Samoylenko for advice.

"I might go," he thought, "but what use would there be in it? I shall only say something inappropriate about boudoirs, about women, about what is honest or dishonest. What's the use of talking about what is honest or dishonest, if I must make haste to save my life, if I am suffocating in this cursed slavery and am killing myself? . . . One must realise at last that to go on leading the life I do is something so base and so cruel that everything else seems petty and trivial beside it. To run away," he muttered, sitting down, "to run away."

The deserted seashore, the insatiable heat, and the monotony of the smoky lilac mountains, ever the same and silent, everlastingly solitary, overwhelmed him with depression, and, as it were, made him drowsy and sapped his energy. He was perhaps very clever, talented, remarkably honest; perhaps if the sea and the mountains had not closed him in on all sides, he might have become an excellent Zemstvo leader, a statesman, an orator, a political writer, a saint. Who knows? If so, was it not stupid to argue whether it were honest or dishonest when a gifted and useful man—an artist or musician, for instance—to escape from prison, breaks a wall and deceives his jailers? Anything is honest when a man is in such a position.

At two o'clock Laevsky and Nadyezhda Fyodorovna sat down to dinner.

When the cook gave them rice and tomato soup, Laevsky said:

"The same thing every day. Why not have cabbage soup?"

"There are no cabbages."

"It's strange. Samoylenko has cabbage soup and Marya Konstantinovna has cabbage soup, and only I am obliged to eat this mawkish mess. We can't go on like this, darling."

As is common with the vast majority of husbands and wives, not a single dinner had in earlier days passed without scenes and fault-finding between Nadyezhda Fyodorovna and Laevsky; but ever since Laevsky had made up his mind that he did not love her, he had tried to give way to Nadyezhda Fyodorovna in everything, spoke to her gently and politely, smiled, and called her "darling."

"This soup tastes like liquorice," he said, smiling; he made an effort to control himself and seem amiable, but could not refrain from saying: "Nobody looks after the housekeeping. . . . If you are too ill or busy with reading, let me look after the cooking."

In earlier days she would have said to him, "Do by all means," or, "I see you want to turn me into a cook"; but now she only looked at him timidly and flushed crimson.

"Well, how do you feel to-day?" he asked kindly.

"I am all right to-day. There is nothing but a little weakness."

"You must take care of yourself, darling. I am awfully anxious about you."

Nadyezhda Fyodorovna was ill in some way. Samoylenko said she had intermittent fever, and gave her quinine; the other doctor, Ustimovitch, a tall, lean, unsociable man, who used to sit at home in the daytime, and in the evenings walk slowly up and down on the sea-front coughing, with his hands folded behind him and a cane stretched along his back, was of opinion that she had a female complaint, and prescribed warm compresses. In old days, when Laevsky loved her, Nadyezhda Fyodorovna's illness had excited his pity and terror; now he saw falsity even in her illness. Her yellow, sleepy face, her lustreless eyes, her apathetic expression, and the yawning that always followed her attacks of fever, and the fact that during them she lay under a shawl and looked more like a boy than a woman, and that it was close and stuffy in her room—all this, in his opinion, destroyed the illusion and was an argument against love and marriage.

The next dish given him was spinach with hard-boiled eggs, while Nadyezhda Fyodorovna, as an invalid, had jelly and milk. When with a preoccupied face she touched the jelly with a spoon and then began languidly eating it, sipping milk, and he heard her swallowing, he was possessed by such an overwhelming aversion that it made his head tingle. He recognised that such a feeling would be an insult even to a dog, but he was angry, not with himself but with Nadyezhda Fyodorovna, for arousing such a feeling, and he understood why lovers sometimes murder their mistresses. He would not murder her, of course, but if he had been on a jury now, he would have acquitted the murderer.

"Merci, darling," he said after dinner, and kissed Nadyezhda Fyodorovna on the forehead.

Going back into his study, he spent five minutes in walking to and fro, looking at his boots; then he sat down on his sofa and muttered:

"Run away, run away! We must define the position and run away!"

He lay down on the sofa and recalled again that Nadyezhda Fyodorovna's husband had died, perhaps, by his fault.

"To blame a man for loving a woman, or ceasing to love a woman, is stupid," he persuaded himself, lying down and raising his legs in order to put on his high boots. "Love and hatred are not under our control. As for her husband, maybe I was in an indirect way one of the causes of his death; but again, is it my fault that I fell in love with his wife and she with me?"

Then he got up, and finding his cap, set off to the lodgings of his colleague, Sheshkovsky, where the Government clerks met every day to play *vint* and drink beer.

"My indecision reminds me of Hamlet," thought Laevsky on the way.

"How truly Shakespeare describes it! Ah, how truly!"

III

For the sake of sociability and from sympathy for the hard plight of newcomers without families, who, as there was not an hotel in the town, had nowhere to dine, Dr. Samoylenko kept a sort of table d'hote. At this time there were only two men who habitually dined with him: a young zoologist called Von Koren, who had come for the summer to the Black Sea to study the embryology of the medusa, and a deacon called

Pobyedov, who had only just left the seminary and been sent to the town to take the duty of the old deacon who had gone away for a cure. Each of them paid twelve roubles a month for their dinner and supper, and Samoylenko made them promise to turn up at two o'clock punctually.

Von Koren was usually the first to appear. He sat down in the drawing-room in silence, and taking an album from the table, began attentively scrutinising the faded photographs of unknown men in full trousers and top-hats, and ladies in crinolines and caps. Samoylenko only remembered a few of them by name, and of those whom he had forgotten he said with a sigh: "A very fine fellow, remarkably intelligent!" When he had finished with the album, Von Koren took a pistol from the whatnot, and screwing up his left eye, took deliberate aim at the portrait of Prince Vorontsov, or stood still at the looking-glass and gazed a long time at his swarthy face, his big forehead, and his black hair, which curled like a negro's, and his shirt of dull-coloured cotton with big flowers on it like a Persian rug, and the broad leather belt he wore instead of a waistcoat. The contemplation of his own image seemed to afford him almost more satisfaction than looking at photographs or playing with the pistols. He was very well satisfied with his face, and his becomingly clipped beard, and the broad shoulders, which were unmistakable evidence of his excellent health and physical strength. He was satisfied, too, with his stylish get-up, from the cravat, which matched the colour of his shirt, down to his brown boots.

While he was looking at the album and standing before the glass, at that moment, in the kitchen and in the passage near, Samoylenko, without his coat and waistcoat, with his neck bare, excited and bathed in perspiration, was bustling about the tables, mixing the salad, or making some sauce, or preparing meat, cucumbers, and onion for the cold soup, while he glared fiercely at the orderly who was helping him, and brandished first a knife and then a spoon at him.

"Give me the vinegar!" he said. "That's not the vinegar—it's the salad oil!" he shouted, stamping. "Where are you off to, you brute?"

"To get the butter, Your Excellency," answered the flustered orderly in a cracked voice.

"Make haste; it's in the cupboard! And tell Daria to put some fennel in the jar with the cucumbers! Fennel! Cover the cream up, gaping laggard, or the flies will get into it!"

And the whole house seemed resounding with his shouts. When it was ten or fifteen minutes to two the deacon would come in; he was a lanky young man of twenty-two, with long hair, with no beard and a hardly perceptible moustache. Going into the drawing-room, he crossed himself before the ikon, smiled, and held out his hand to Von Koren.

"Good-morning," the zoologist said coldly. "Where have you been?"

"I've been catching sea-gudgeon in the harbour."

"Oh, of course. . . . Evidently, deacon, you will never be busy with work."

"Why not? Work is not like a bear; it doesn't run off into the woods," said the deacon, smiling and thrusting his hands into the very deep pockets of his white cassock.

"There's no one to whip you!" sighed the zoologist.

Another fifteen or twenty minutes passed and they were not called to dinner, and they could still hear the orderly running into the kitchen and back again, noisily treading with his boots, and Samoylenko shouting:

"Put it on the table! Where are your wits? Wash it first."

The famished deacon and Von Koren began tapping on the floor with their heels, expressing in this way their impatience like the audience at a theatre. At last the door opened and the harassed orderly announced that dinner was ready! In the dining-room they were met by Samoylenko, crimson in the face, wrathful, perspiring from the heat of the kitchen; he looked at them furiously, and with an expression of horror, took the lid off the soup tureen and helped each of them to a plateful; and only when he was convinced that they were eating it with relish and liked it, he gave a sigh of relief and settled himself in his deep arm-chair. His face looked blissful and his eyes grew moist. . . . He deliberately poured himself out a glass of vodka and said:

"To the health of the younger generation."

After his conversation with Laevsky, from early morning till dinner Samoylenko had been conscious of a load at his heart, although he was in the best of humours; he felt sorry for Laevsky and wanted to help him. After drinking a glass of vodka before the soup, he heaved a sigh and said:

"I saw Vanya Laevsky to-day. He is having a hard time of it, poor fellow! The material side of life is not encouraging for him, and the worst of it is all this psychology is too much for him. I'm sorry for the lad."

"Well, that is a person I am not sorry for," said Von Koren. "If that charming individual were drowning, I would push him under with a stick and say, 'Drown, brother, drown away.' . . ."

"That's untrue. You wouldn't do it."

"Why do you think that?" The zoologist shrugged his shoulders. "I'm just as capable of a good action as you are."

"Is drowning a man a good action?" asked the deacon, and he laughed.

"Laevsky? Yes."

"I think there is something amiss with the soup . . ." said Samoylenko, anxious to change the conversation.

"Laevsky is absolutely pernicious and is as dangerous to society as the cholera microbe," Von Koren went on. "To drown him would be a service."

"It does not do you credit to talk like that about your neighbour.

Tell us: what do you hate him for?"

"Don't talk nonsense, doctor. To hate and despise a microbe is stupid, but to look upon everybody one meets without distinction as one's neighbour, whatever happens—thanks very much, that is equivalent to giving up criticism, renouncing a straightforward attitude to people, washing one's hands of responsibility, in fact! I consider your Laevsky a blackguard; I do not conceal it, and I am perfectly conscientious in treating him as such. Well, you look upon him as your neighbour—and you may kiss him if you like: you look upon him as your neighbour, and that means that your attitude to him is the same as to me and to the deacon; that is no attitude at all. You are equally indifferent to all."

"To call a man a blackguard!" muttered Samoylenko, frowning with distaste—"that is so wrong that I can't find words for it!"

"People are judged by their actions," Von Koren continued. "Now you decide, deacon. . . . I am going to talk to you, deacon. Mr. Laevsky's career lies open before you, like a long Chinese puzzle, and you can read it from beginning to end. What has he been doing these two years that he has been living here? We will reckon his doings on our fingers. First, he has taught the inhabitants of the town to play *vint*: two years ago that game was unknown here; now they all play it from morning till late at night, even the women and the boys. Secondly, he has taught the residents to drink beer, which was not known here either; the inhabitants are indebted to him for the knowledge of various sorts of spirits, so that now they can distinguish Kospelov's vodka from Smirnov's No. 21, blindfold. Thirdly, in former days, people here made love to other men's wives in secret, from the same motives as thieves steal in secret and not openly; adultery was considered something they were ashamed to make a public display of. Laevsky has come as a pioneer in that line; he lives with another man's wife openly. . . . Fourthly . . ."

Von Koren hurriedly ate up his soup and gave his plate to the orderly.

"I understood Laevsky from the first month of our acquaintance," he went on, addressing the deacon. "We arrived here at the same time. Men like him are very fond of friendship, intimacy, solidarity, and all the rest of it, because they always want company for *vint*, drinking, and eating; besides, they are talkative and must have listeners. We made friends—that is, he turned up every day, hindered me working, and indulged in confidences in regard to his mistress. From the first he struck me by his exceptional falsity, which simply made me sick. As a friend I pitched into him, asking him why he drank too much, why he lived beyond his means and got into debt, why he did nothing and read nothing, why he had so little culture and so little knowledge; and in answer to all my questions he used to smile bitterly, sigh, and say: 'I am a failure, a superfluous man'; or: 'What do you expect, my dear fellow, from us, the debris of the serf-owning class?' or: 'We are degenerate. . . .' Or he would begin a long rigmarole about Onyegin, Petchorin, Byron's Cain, and Bazarov, of whom he would say: 'They are our fathers in flesh and in spirit.' So we are to understand that it was not his fault that Government envelopes lay unopened in his office for weeks together, and that he drank and taught others to drink, but Onyegin, Petchorin, and Turgenev, who had invented the failure and the superfluous man, were responsible for it. The cause of his extreme dissoluteness and unseemliness lies, do you see, not in himself, but somewhere outside in space. And so—an ingenious idea! it is not only he who is dissolute, false, and disgusting, but we . . . 'we men of the eighties,' 'we the spiritless, nervous offspring of the serf-owning class'; 'civilisation has crippled us' . . . in fact, we are to understand that such a great man as Laevsky is great even in his fall: that his dissoluteness, his lack of culture and of moral purity, is a phenomenon of natural history, sanctified by inevitability; that the causes of it are world-wide, elemental; and that we ought to hang up a lamp before Laevsky, since he is the fated victim of the age, of influences, of heredity, and so on. All the officials and their ladies were in ecstasies when they listened to him, and I could not make out for a long time what sort of man I had to deal with, a cynic or a clever rogue. Such types as he, on the surface intellectual with a smattering of education and a great deal of talk about their own nobility, are very clever in posing as exceptionally complex natures."

"Hold your tongue!" Samoylenko flared up. "I will not allow a splendid fellow to be spoken ill of in my presence!"

"Don't interrupt, Alexandr Daviditch," said Von Koren coldly; "I am just finishing. Laevsky is by no means a complex organism. Here is his moral skeleton: in the morning, slippers, a bathe, and coffee; then till dinner-time, slippers, a constitutional, and conversation; at two o'clock slippers, dinner, and wine; at five o'clock a bathe, tea and wine, then *vint* and lying; at ten o'clock supper and wine; and after midnight sleep and *la femme*. His existence is confined within this narrow programme like an egg within its shell. Whether he walks or sits, is angry, writes, rejoices, it may all be reduced to wine, cards, slippers, and women. Woman plays a fatal, overwhelming part in his life. He tells us himself that at thirteen he was in love; that when he was a student in his first year he was living with a lady who had a good influence over him, and to whom he was indebted for his musical education. In his second year he bought a prostitute from a brothel and raised her to his level—that is, took her as his kept mistress, and she lived with him for six months and then ran away back to the brothel-keeper, and her flight caused him much spiritual suffering. Alas! his sufferings were so great that he had to leave the university and spend two years at home doing nothing. But this was all for the best. At home he made friends with a widow who advised him to leave the Faculty of Jurisprudence and go into the Faculty of Arts. And so he did. When he had taken his degree, he fell passionately in love with his present . . . what's her name? . . . married lady, and was obliged to flee with her here to the Caucasus for the sake of his ideals, he would have us believe, seeing that . . . to-morrow, if not to-day, he will be tired of her and flee back again to Petersburg, and that, too, will be for the sake of his ideals."

"How do you know?" growled Samoylenko, looking angrily at the zoologist. "You had better eat your dinner."

The next course consisted of boiled mullet with Polish sauce. Samoylenko helped each of his companions to a whole mullet and poured out the sauce with his own hand. Two minutes passed in silence.

"Woman plays an essential part in the life of every man," said the deacon. "You can't help that."

"Yes, but to what degree? For each of us woman means mother, sister, wife, friend. To Laevsky she is everything, and at the same time nothing but a mistress. She—that is, cohabitation with her— is the happiness and object of his life; he is gay, sad, bored, disenchanted—on account of woman; his life grows disagreeable—woman is to blame; the dawn of a new life begins to glow, ideals turn up—and again look for the woman. . . . He only derives enjoyment from books and pictures in which there is woman. Our age is, to his thinking, poor and inferior to the forties and the sixties only because we do not know how to abandon ourselves obviously to the passion and ecstasy of love. These voluptuaries must have in their brains a special growth of the nature of sarcoma, which stifles the brain and directs their whole psychology. Watch Laevsky when he is sitting anywhere in company. You notice: when one raises any general question in his presence, for instance, about the cell or instinct, he sits apart, and neither speaks nor listens; he looks languid and disillusioned; nothing has any interest for him, everything is vulgar and trivial. But as soon as you speak of male and female—for instance, of the fact that the female spider, after fertilisation, devours the male—his eyes glow with curiosity, his face brightens, and the man revives, in fact. All his thoughts, however noble, lofty, or neutral they may be, they all have one point of resemblance. You walk along the street with him and meet a donkey, for instance. . . . 'Tell me, please,' he asks, 'what would happen if you mated a donkey with a camel?' And his dreams! Has he told you of his dreams? It is magnificent! First, he dreams that he is married to the moon, then that he is summoned before the police and ordered to live with a guitar . . ."

The deacon burst into resounding laughter; Samoylenko frowned and wrinkled up his face angrily so as not to laugh, but could not restrain himself, and laughed.

"And it's all nonsense!" he said, wiping his tears. "Yes, by Jove, it's nonsense!"

IV

The deacon was very easily amused, and laughed at every trifle till he got a stitch in his side, till he was helpless. It seemed as though he only liked to be in people's company because there was a ridiculous side to them, and because they might be given ridiculous nicknames. He had nicknamed Samoylenko "the tarantula," his orderly "the drake," and was in ecstasies when on one occasion Von Koren spoke of Laevsky and Nadyezhda Fyodorovna as "Japanese monkeys." He watched people's faces greedily, listened without blinking, and it could be seen that his eyes filled with laughter and his face was tense with expectation of the moment when he could let himself go and burst into laughter.

"He is a corrupt and depraved type," the zoologist continued, while the deacon kept his eyes riveted on his face, expecting he would say something funny. "It is not often one can meet with such a nonentity. In body he is inert, feeble, prematurely old, while in intellect he differs in no respect from a fat shopkeeper's wife who does nothing but eat, drink, and sleep on a feather-bed, and who keeps her coachman as a lover."

The deacon began guffawing again.

"Don't laugh, deacon," said Von Koren. "It grows stupid, at last. I should not have paid attention to his insignificance," he went on, after waiting till the deacon had left off laughing; "I should have passed him by if he were not so noxious and dangerous. His noxiousness lies first of all in the fact that he has great success with women, and so threatens to leave descendants—that is, to present the world with a dozen Laevskys as feeble and as depraved as himself. Secondly, he is in the highest degree contaminating. I have spoken to you already of *vint* and beer. In another year or two he will dominate the whole Caucasian coast. You know how the mass, especially its middle stratum, believe in intellectuality, in a university education, in gentlemanly manners, and in literary language. Whatever filthy thing he did, they would all believe that it was as it should be, since he is an intellectual man, of liberal ideas and university education. What is more, he is a failure, a superfluous man, a neurasthenic, a victim of the age, and that means he can do anything. He is a charming fellow, a regular good sort, he is so genuinely indulgent to human weaknesses; he is compliant, accommodating, easy and not proud; one can drink with him and gossip and talk evil of people. . . . The masses, always inclined to anthropomorphism in religion and morals, like best of all the little gods who have the same weaknesses as themselves. Only think what a wide field he has for contamination! Besides, he is not a bad actor and is a clever hypocrite, and knows very well how to twist things round. Only take his little shifts and dodges, his attitude to civilisation, for instance. He has scarcely sniffed at civilisation, yet: 'Ah, how we have been crippled by civilisation! Ah, how I envy those savages, those children of nature, who know nothing of civilisation!' We are to understand, you see, that at one time, in ancient days, he has been devoted to civilisation with his whole soul, has served it, has sounded it to its depths, but it has exhausted him, disillusioned him, deceived him; he is a Faust, do you see? a second Tolstoy. . . . As for Schopenhauer and Spencer, he treats them like small boys and slaps them on the shoulder in a fatherly way: 'Well, what do you say, old Spencer?' He has not read Spencer, of course, but how charming he is when with light, careless irony he says of his lady friend: 'She has read Spencer!' And they all listen to him, and no one cares to understand that this charlatan has not the right to kiss the sole of Spencer's foot, let alone speaking about him in that tone! Sapping the foundations of civilisation, of authority, of other people's altars, spattering them with filth, winking jocosely at them only to justify and conceal one's own rottenness and moral poverty is only possible for a very vain, base, and nasty creature."

"I don't know what it is you expect of him, Kolya," said Samoylenko, looking at the zoologist, not with anger now, but with a guilty air. "He is a man the same as every one else. Of course, he has his weaknesses, but he is abreast of modern ideas, is in the service, is of use to his country. Ten years ago there was an old fellow serving as agent here, a man of the greatest intelligence . . . and he used to say . . ."

"Nonsense, nonsense!" the zoologist interrupted. "You say he is in the service; but how does he serve? Do you mean to tell me that things have been done better because he is here, and the officials are more punctual, honest, and civil? On the contrary, he has only sanctioned their slackness by his prestige as an intellectual university man. He is only punctual on the 20th of the month, when he gets his salary; on the other days he lounges about at home in slippers and tries to look as if he were doing the Government a great service by living in the Caucasus. No, Alexandr Daviditch, don't stick up for him. You are insincere from beginning to end. If you really loved him and considered him your neighbour, you would above all not be indifferent to his weaknesses, you would not be indulgent to them, but for his own sake would try to make him innocuous."

"That is?"

"Innocuous. Since he is incorrigible, he can only be made innocuous in one way. . . ." Von Koren passed his finger round his throat. "Or he might be drowned . . .", he added. "In the interests of humanity and in their own interests, such people ought to be destroyed. They certainly ought."

"What are you saying?" muttered Samoylenko, getting up and looking with amazement at the zoologist's calm, cold face. "Deacon, what is he saying? Why—are you in your senses?"

"I don't insist on the death penalty," said Von Koren. "If it is proved that it is pernicious, devise something else. If we can't destroy Laevsky, why then, isolate him, make him harmless, send him to hard labour."

"What are you saying!" said Samoylenko in horror. "With pepper, with pepper," he cried in a voice of despair, seeing that the deacon was eating stuffed aubergines without pepper. "You with your great intellect, what are you saying! Send our friend, a proud intellectual man, to penal servitude!"

"Well, if he is proud and tries to resist, put him in fetters!"

Samoylenko could not utter a word, and only twiddled his fingers; the deacon looked at his flabbergasted and really absurd face, and laughed.

"Let us leave off talking of that," said the zoologist. "Only remember one thing, Alexandr Daviditch: primitive man was preserved from such as Laevsky by the struggle for existence and by natural selection; now our civilisation has considerably weakened the struggle and the selection, and we ought to look after the destruction of the rotten and worthless for ourselves; otherwise, when the Laevskys multiply, civilisation will perish and mankind will degenerate utterly. It will be our fault."

"If it depends on drowning and hanging," said Samoylenko, "damnation take your civilisation, damnation take your humanity! Damnation take it! I tell you what: you are a very learned and intelligent man and the pride of your country, but the Germans have ruined you. Yes, the Germans! The Germans!"

Since Samoylenko had left Dorpat, where he had studied medicine, he had rarely seen a German and had not read a single German book, but, in his opinion, every harmful idea in politics or science was due to the Germans. Where he had got this notion he could not have said himself, but he held it firmly.

"Yes, the Germans!" he repeated once more. "Come and have some tea."

All three stood up, and putting on their hats, went out into the little garden, and sat there under the shade of the light green maples, the pear-trees, and a chestnut-tree. The zoologist and the deacon sat on a bench by the table, while Samoylenko sank into a deep wicker chair with a sloping back. The orderly handed them tea, jam, and a bottle of syrup.

It was very hot, thirty degrees Reaumur in the shade. The sultry air was stagnant and motionless, and a long spider-web, stretching from the chestnut-tree to the ground, hung limply and did not stir.

The deacon took up the guitar, which was constantly lying on the ground near the table, tuned it, and began singing softly in a thin voice:

"'Gathered round the tavern were the seminary lads,'"

but instantly subsided, overcome by the heat, mopped his brow and glanced upwards at the blazing blue sky. Samoylenko grew drowsy; the sultry heat, the stillness and the delicious after-dinner languor, which quickly pervaded all his limbs, made him feel heavy and sleepy; his arms dropped at his sides, his eyes grew small, his head sank on his breast. He looked with almost tearful tenderness at Von Koren and the deacon, and muttered:

"The younger generation. . . A scientific star and a luminary of the Church. . . . I shouldn't wonder if the long-skirted alleluia will be shooting up into a bishop; I dare say I may come to kissing his hand. . . . Well . . . please God. . . ."

Soon a snore was heard. Von Koren and the deacon finished their tea and went out into the street.

"Are you going to the harbour again to catch sea-gudgeon?" asked the zoologist.

"No, it's too hot."

"Come and see me. You can pack up a parcel and copy something for me. By the way, we must have a talk about what you are to do. You must work, deacon. You can't go on like this."

"Your words are just and logical," said the deacon. "But my laziness finds an excuse in the circumstances of my present life. You know yourself that an uncertain position has a great tendency to make people apathetic. God only knows whether I have been sent here for a time or permanently. I am living here in uncertainty, while my wife is vegetating at her father's and is missing me. And I must confess my brain is melting with the heat."

"That's all nonsense," said the zoologist. "You can get used to the heat, and you can get used to being without the deaconess. You mustn't be slack; you must pull yourself together."

V

Nadyezhda Fyodorovna went to bathe in the morning, and her cook, Olga, followed her with a jug, a copper basin, towels, and a sponge. In the bay stood two unknown steamers with dirty white funnels, obviously foreign cargo vessels. Some men dressed in white and wearing white shoes were walking along the harbour, shouting loudly in French, and were answered from the steamers. The bells were ringing briskly in the little church of the town.

"To-day is Sunday!" Nadyezhda Fyodorovna remembered with pleasure.

She felt perfectly well, and was in a gay holiday humour. In a new loose-fitting dress of coarse thick tussore silk, and a big wide-brimmed straw hat which was bent down over her ears, so that her face looked out as though from a basket, she fancied she looked very charming. She thought that in the whole town there was only one young, pretty, intellectual woman, and that was herself, and that she was the only one who knew how to dress herself cheaply, elegantly, and with taste. That dress, for example, cost only twenty-two roubles, and yet how charming it was! In the whole town she was the only one who could be attractive, while there were numbers of men, so they must all, whether they would or not, be envious of Laevsky.

She was glad that of late Laevsky had been cold to her, reserved and polite, and at times even harsh and rude; in the past she had met all his outbursts, all his contemptuous, cold or strange incomprehensible glances, with tears, reproaches, and threats to leave him or to starve herself to death; now she only blushed, looked guiltily at him, and was glad he was not affectionate to her. If he had abused her, threatened her, it would have been better and pleasanter, since she felt hopelessly guilty towards him. She felt she was to blame, in the first place, for not sympathising with the dreams of a life of hard work, for the sake of which he had given up Petersburg and had come here to the Caucasus, and she was convinced that he had been angry with her of late for precisely that. When she was travelling to the Caucasus, it seemed that she would find here on the first day a cosy nook by the sea, a snug little garden with shade, with birds, with little brooks, where she could grow flowers and vegetables, rear ducks and hens, entertain her neighbours, doctor poor peasants and distribute little books amongst them. It had turned out that the Caucasus was nothing but bare mountains, forests, and huge valleys, where it took a long time and a great deal of effort to find anything and settle down; that there were no neighbours of any sort; that it was very hot and one might be robbed. Laevsky had been in no hurry to obtain a piece of land; she was glad of it, and they seemed to be in a tacit compact never to allude to a life of hard work. He was silent about it, she thought, because he was angry with her for being silent about it.

In the second place, she had without his knowledge during those two years bought various trifles to the value of three hundred roubles at Atchmianov's shop. She had bought the things by degrees, at one time materials, at another time silk or a parasol, and the debt had grown imperceptibly.

"I will tell him about it to-day . . .", she used to decide, but at once reflected that in Laevsky's present mood it would hardly be convenient to talk to him of debts.

Thirdly, she had on two occasions in Laevsky's absence received a visit from Kirilin, the police captain: once in the morning when Laevsky had gone to bathe, and another time at midnight when he was playing cards. Remembering this, Nadyezhda Fyodorovna flushed crimson, and looked round at the cook as though she might overhear her thoughts. The long, insufferably hot, wearisome days, beautiful languorous evenings and stifling nights, and the whole manner of living, when from morning to night one is at a loss to fill up the useless hours, and the persistent thought that she was the prettiest young woman in the town, and that her youth was passing and being wasted, and Laevsky himself, though honest and idealistic, always the same, always lounging about in his slippers, biting his nails, and wearying her with his caprices, led by degrees to her becoming possessed by desire, and as though she were mad, she thought of nothing else day and night. Breathing, looking, walking, she felt nothing but desire. The sound of the sea told her she must love; the darkness of evening—the same; the mountains—the same. . . . And when Kirilin began paying her attentions, she had neither the power nor the wish to resist, and surrendered to him. . . .

Now the foreign steamers and the men in white reminded her for some reason of a huge hall; together with the shouts of French she heard the strains of a waltz, and her bosom heaved with unaccountable delight. She longed to dance and talk French.

She reflected joyfully that there was nothing terrible about her infidelity. Her soul had no part in her infidelity; she still loved Laevsky, and that was proved by the fact that she was jealous of him, was sorry for him, and missed him when he was away. Kirilin had turned out to be very mediocre, rather coarse though handsome; everything was broken off with him already and there would never be anything more. What had happened was over; it had nothing to do with any one, and if Laevsky found it out he would not believe in it.

There was only one bathing-house for ladies on the sea-front; men bathed under the open sky. Going into the bathing-house, Nadyezhda Fyodorovna found there an elderly lady, Marya Konstantinovna Bityugov, and her daughter Katya, a schoolgirl of fifteen; both of them were sitting on a bench undressing. Marya Konstantinovna was a good-natured, enthusiastic, and genteel person, who talked in a drawling and pathetic voice. She had been a governess until she was thirty-two, and then had married Bityugov, a Government official—a bald little man with his hair combed on to his temples and with a very meek disposition. She was still in love with him, was jealous, blushed at the word "love," and told every one she was very happy.

"My dear," she cried enthusiastically, on seeing Nadyezhda Fyodorovna, assuming an expression which all her acquaintances called "almond-oily." "My dear, how delightful that you have come! We'll bathe together, that's enchanting!"

Olga quickly flung off her dress and chemise, and began undressing her mistress.

"It's not quite so hot to-day as yesterday?" said Nadyezhda Fyodorovna, shrinking at the coarse touch of the naked cook. "Yesterday I almost died of the heat."

"Oh, yes, my dear; I could hardly breathe myself. Would you believe it? I bathed yesterday three times! Just imagine, my dear, three times! Nikodim Alexandritch was quite uneasy."

"Is it possible to be so ugly?" thought Nadyezhda Fyodorovna, looking at Olga and the official's wife; she glanced at Katya and thought:

"The little girl's not badly made."

"Your Nikodim Alexandritch is very charming!" she said. "I'm simply in love with him."

"Ha, ha, ha!" cried Marya Konstantinovna, with a forced laugh;

"that's quite enchanting."

Free from her clothes, Nadyezhda Fyodorovna felt a desire to fly. And it seemed to her that if she were to wave her hands she would fly upwards. When she was undressed, she noticed that Olga looked scornfully at her white body. Olga, a young soldier's wife, was living with her lawful husband, and so considered herself superior to her mistress. Marya Konstantinovna and Katya were afraid of her, and did not respect her. This was disagreeable, and to raise herself in their opinion, Nadyezhda Fyodorovna said:

"At home, in Petersburg, summer villa life is at its height now.

My husband and I have so many friends! We ought to go and see them."

"I believe your husband is an engineer?" said Marya Konstantinovna timidly.

"I am speaking of Laevsky. He has a great many acquaintances. But unfortunately his mother is a proud aristocrat, not very intelligent. . . ."

Nadyezhda Fyodorovna threw herself into the water without finishing;

Marya Konstantinovna and Katya made their way in after her.

"There are so many conventional ideas in the world," Nadyezhda Fyodorovna went on, "and life is not so easy as it seems."

Marya Konstantinovna, who had been a governess in aristocratic families and who was an authority on social matters, said:

"Oh yes! Would you believe me, my dear, at the Garatynskys' I was expected to dress for lunch as well as for dinner, so that, like an actress, I received a special allowance for my wardrobe in addition to my salary."

She stood between Nadyezhda Fyodorovna and Katya as though to screen her daughter from the water that washed the former.

Through the open doors looking out to the sea they could see some one swimming a hundred paces from their bathing-place.

"Mother, it's our Kostya," said Katya.

"Ach, ach!" Marya Konstantinovna cackled in her dismay. "Ach, Kostya!" she shouted, "Come back! Kostya, come back!"

Kostya, a boy of fourteen, to show off his prowess before his mother and sister, dived and swam farther, but began to be exhausted and hurried back, and from his strained and serious face it could be seen that he could not trust his own strength.

"The trouble one has with these boys, my dear!" said Marya Konstantinovna, growing calmer. "Before you can turn round, he will break his neck. Ah, my dear, how sweet it is, and yet at the same time how difficult, to be a mother! One's afraid of everything."

Nadyezhda Fyodorovna put on her straw hat and dashed out into the open sea. She swam some thirty feet and then turned on her back. She could see the sea to the horizon, the steamers, the people on the sea-front, the town; and all this, together with the sultry heat and the soft, transparent waves, excited her and whispered that she must live, live. . . . A sailing-boat darted by her rapidly and vigorously, cleaving the waves and the air; the man sitting at the helm looked at her, and she liked being looked at. . . .

After bathing, the ladies dressed and went away together.

"I have fever every alternate day, and yet I don't get thin," said Nadyezhda Fyodorovna, licking her lips, which were salt from the bathe, and responding with a smile to the bows of her acquaintances. "I've always been plump, and now I believe I'm plumper than ever."

"That, my dear, is constitutional. If, like me, one has no constitutional tendency to stoutness, no diet is of any use. . . . But you've wetted your hat, my dear."

"It doesn't matter; it will dry."

Nadyezhda Fyodorovna saw again the men in white who were walking on the sea-front and talking French; and again she felt a sudden thrill of joy, and had a vague memory of some big hall in which she had once danced, or of which, perhaps, she had once dreamed. And something at the bottom of her soul dimly and obscurely whispered to her that she was a pretty, common, miserable, worthless woman. . . .

Marya Konstantinovna stopped at her gate and asked her to come in and sit down for a little while.

"Come in, my dear," she said in an imploring voice, and at the same time she looked at Nadyezhda Fyodorovna with anxiety and hope; perhaps she would refuse and not come in!

"With pleasure," said Nadyezhda Fyodorovna, accepting. "You know how I love being with you!"

And she went into the house. Marya Konstantinovna sat her down and gave her coffee, regaled her with milk rolls, then showed her photographs of her former pupils, the Garatynskys, who were by now married. She showed her, too, the examination reports of Kostya and Katya. The reports were very good, but to make them seem even better, she complained, with a sigh, how difficult the lessons at school were now. . . . She made much of her visitor, and was sorry for her, though at the same time she was harassed by the thought that Nadyezhda Fyodorovna might have a corrupting influence on the morals of Kostya and Katya, and was glad that her Nikodim Alexandritch was not at home. Seeing that in her opinion all men are fond of "women like that," Nadyezhda Fyodorovna might have a bad effect on Nikodim Alexandritch too.

As she talked to her visitor, Marya Konstantinovna kept remembering that they were to have a picnic that evening, and that Von Koren had particularly begged her to say nothing about it to the "Japanese monkeys"—that is, Laevsky and Nadyezhda

Fyodorovna; but she dropped a word about it unawares, crimsoned, and said in confusion:

"I hope you will come too!"

VI

It was agreed to drive about five miles out of town on the road to the south, to stop near a *duhan* at the junction of two streams the Black River and the Yellow River— and to cook fish soup.

They started out soon after five. Foremost of the party in a char-a-banc drove Samoylenko and Laevsky; they were followed by Marya Konstantinovna, Nadyezhda Fyodorovna, Katya and Kostya, in a coach with three horses, carrying with them the crockery and a basket with provisions. In the next carriage came the police captain, Kirilin, and the young Atchmianov, the son of the shopkeeper to whom Nadyezhda Fyodorovna owed three hundred roubles; opposite them, huddled up on the little seat with his feet tucked under him, sat Nikodim Alexandritch, a neat little man with hair combed on to his temples. Last of all came Von Koren and the deacon; at the deacon's feet stood a basket of fish.

"R-r-right!" Samoylenko shouted at the top of his voice when he met a cart or a mountaineer riding on a donkey.

"In two years' time, when I shall have the means and the people ready, I shall set off on an expedition," Von Koren was telling the deacon. "I shall go by the sea-coast from Vladivostok to the Behring Straits, and then from the Straits to the mouth of the Yenisei. We shall make the map, study the fauna and the flora, and make detailed geological, anthropological, and ethnographical researches. It depends upon you to go with me or not."

"It's impossible," said the deacon.

"Why?"

"I'm a man with ties and a family."

"Your wife will let you go; we will provide for her. Better still if you were to persuade her for the public benefit to go into a nunnery; that would make it possible for you to become a monk, too, and join the expedition as a priest. I can arrange it for you."

The deacon was silent.

"Do you know your theology well?" asked the zoologist.

"No, rather badly."

"H'm! . . . I can't give you any advice on that score, because I don't know much about theology myself. You give me a list of books you need, and I will send them to you from Petersburg in the winter. It will be necessary for you to read the notes of religious travellers, too; among them are some good ethnologists and Oriental scholars. When you are familiar with their methods, it will be easier for you to set to work. And you needn't waste your time till you get the books; come to me, and we will study the compass and go through a course of meteorology. All that's indispensable."

"To be sure . . ." muttered the deacon, and he laughed. "I was trying to get a place in Central Russia, and my uncle, the head priest, promised to help me. If I go with you I shall have troubled them for nothing."

"I don't understand your hesitation. If you go on being an ordinary deacon, who is only obliged to hold a service on holidays, and on the other days can rest from work, you will be exactly the same as you are now in ten years' time, and will have gained nothing but a beard and moustache; while on returning from this expedition in ten years' time you will be a different man, you will be enriched by the consciousness that something has been done by you."

From the ladies' carriage came shrieks of terror and delight. The carriages were driving along a road hollowed in a literally overhanging precipitous cliff, and it seemed to every one that they were galloping along a shelf on a steep wall, and that in a moment the carriages would drop into the abyss. On the right stretched the sea; on the left was a rough brown wall with black blotches and red veins and with climbing roots; while on the summit stood shaggy fir-trees bent over, as though looking down in terror and curiosity. A minute later there were shrieks and laughter again: they had to drive under a huge overhanging rock.

"I don't know why the devil I'm coming with you," said Laevsky. "How stupid and vulgar it is! I want to go to the North, to run away, to escape; but here I am, for some reason, going to this stupid picnic."

"But look, what a view!" said Samoylenko as the horses turned to the left, and the valley of the Yellow River came into sight and the stream itself gleamed in the sunlight, yellow, turbid, frantic.

"I see nothing fine in that, Sasha," answered Laevsky. "To be in continual ecstasies over nature shows poverty of imagination. In comparison with what my imagination can give me, all these streams and rocks are trash, and nothing else."

The carriages now were by the banks of the stream. The high mountain banks gradually grew closer, the valley shrank together and ended in a gorge; the rocky mountain round which they were driving had been piled together by nature out of huge rocks, pressing upon each other with such terrible weight, that Samoylenko could not help gasping every time he looked at them. The dark and beautiful mountain was cleft in places by narrow fissures and gorges from which came a breath of dewy moisture and mystery; through the gorges could be seen other mountains, brown, pink, lilac, smoky, or bathed in vivid sunlight. From time to time as they passed a gorge they caught the sound of water falling from the heights and splashing on the stones.

"Ach, the damned mountains!" sighed Laevsky. "How sick I am of them!"

At the place where the Black River falls into the Yellow, and the water black as ink stains the yellow and struggles with it, stood the Tatar Kerbalay's *duhan*, with the Russian flag on the roof and with an inscription written in chalk: "The Pleasant *duhan*." Near it was a little garden, enclosed in a hurdle fence, with tables and chairs set out in it, and in the midst of a thicket of wretched thornbushes stood a single solitary cypress, dark and beautiful.

Kerbalay, a nimble little Tatar in a blue shirt and a white apron, was standing in the road, and, holding his stomach, he bowed low to welcome the carriages, and smiled, showing his glistening white teeth.

"Good-evening, Kerbalay," shouted Samoylenko. "We are driving on a little further, and you take along the samovar and chairs! Look sharp!"

Kerbalay nodded his shaven head and muttered something, and only those sitting in the last carriage could hear: "We've got trout, your Excellency."

"Bring them, bring them!" said Von Koren.

Five hundred paces from the *duhan* the carriages stopped. Samoylenko selected a small meadow round which there were scattered stones convenient for sitting on, and a fallen tree blown down by the storm with roots overgrown by moss and dry yellow needles. Here there was a fragile wooden bridge over the stream, and just opposite on the other bank there was a little barn for drying maize, standing on four low piles, and looking like the hut on hen's legs in the fairy tale; a little ladder sloped from its door.

The first impression in all was a feeling that they would never get out of that place again. On all sides wherever they looked, the mountains rose up and towered above them, and the shadows of evening were stealing rapidly, rapidly from the *duhan* and dark cypress, making the narrow winding valley of the Black River narrower and the mountains higher. They could hear the river murmuring and the unceasing chirrup of the grasshoppers.

"Enchanting!" said Marya Konstantinovna, heaving deep sighs of ecstasy. "Children, look how fine! What peace!"

"Yes, it really is fine," assented Laevsky, who liked the view, and for some reason felt sad as he looked at the sky and then at the blue smoke rising from the chimney of the *duhan*. "Yes, it is fine," he repeated.

"Ivan Andreitch, describe this view," Marya Konstantinovna said tearfully.

"Why?" asked Laevsky. "The impression is better than any description. The wealth of sights and sounds which every one receives from nature by direct impression is ranted about by authors in a hideous and unrecognisable way."

"Really?" Von Koren asked coldly, choosing the biggest stone by the side of the water, and trying to clamber up and sit upon it. "Really?" he repeated, looking directly at Laevsky. "What of 'Romeo and Juliet'? Or, for instance, Pushkin's 'Night in the Ukraine'? Nature ought to come and bow down at their feet."

"Perhaps," said Laevsky, who was too lazy to think and oppose him. "Though what is 'Romeo and Juliet' after all?" he added after a short pause. "The beauty of poetry and holiness of love are simply the roses under which they try to hide its rottenness. Romeo is just the same sort of animal as all the rest of us."

"Whatever one talks to you about, you always bring it round to . . ." Von Koren glanced round at Katya and broke off.

"What do I bring it round to?" asked Laevsky.

"One tells you, for instance, how beautiful a bunch of grapes is, and you answer: 'Yes, but how ugly it is when it is chewed and digested in one's stomach!' Why say that? It's not new, and . . . altogether it is a queer habit."

Laevsky knew that Von Koren did not like him, and so was afraid of him, and felt in his presence as though every one were constrained and some one were standing behind his back. He made no answer and walked away, feeling sorry he had come.

"Gentlemen, quick march for brushwood for the fire!" commanded Samoylenko.

They all wandered off in different directions, and no one was left but Kirilin, Atchmianov, and Nikodim Alexandritch. Kerbalay brought chairs, spread a rug on the ground, and set a few bottles of wine.

The police captain, Kirilin, a tall, good-looking man, who in all weathers wore his great-coat over his tunic, with his haughty deportment, stately carriage, and thick, rather hoarse voice, looked like a young provincial chief of police; his expression was mournful and sleepy, as though he had just been waked against his will.

"What have you brought this for, you brute?" he asked Kerbalay, deliberately articulating each word. "I ordered you to give us *kvarel*, and what have you brought, you ugly Tatar? Eh? What?"

"We have plenty of wine of our own, Yegor Alekseitch," Nikodim Alexandritch observed, timidly and politely.

"What? But I want us to have my wine, too; I'm taking part in the picnic and I imagine I have full right to contribute my share. I im-ma-gine so! Bring ten bottles of *kvarel*."

"Why so many?" asked Nikodim Alexandritch, in wonder, knowing Kirilin had no money.

"Twenty bottles! Thirty!" shouted Kirilin.

"Never mind, let him," Atchmianov whispered to Nikodim Alexandritch;

"I'll pay."

Nadyezhda Fyodorovna was in a light-hearted, mischievous mood; she wanted to skip and jump, to laugh, to shout, to tease, to flirt. In her cheap cotton dress with blue pansies on it, in her red shoes and the same straw hat, she seemed to herself, little, simple, light, ethereal as a butterfly. She ran over the rickety bridge and looked for a minute into the water, in order to feel giddy; then, shrieking and laughing, ran to the other side to the drying-shed, and she fancied that all the men were admiring her, even Kerbalay. When in the rapidly falling darkness the trees began to melt into the mountains and the horses into the carriages, and a light gleamed in the windows of the *duhan*, she climbed up the mountain by the little path which zigzagged between stones and thorn-bushes and sat on a stone. Down below, the camp-fire was burning. Near the fire, with his sleeves tucked up, the deacon was moving to and fro, and his long black shadow kept describing a circle round it; he put on wood, and with a spoon tied to a long stick he stirred the cauldron. Samoylenko, with a copper-red face, was fussing round the fire just as though he were in his own kitchen, shouting furiously:

"Where's the salt, gentlemen? I bet you've forgotten it. Why are you all sitting about like lords while I do the work?"

Laevsky and Nikodim Alexandritch were sitting side by side on the fallen tree looking pensively at the fire. Marya Konstantinovna, Katya, and Kostya were taking the cups, saucers, and plates out of the baskets. Von Koren, with his arms folded and one foot on a stone, was standing on a bank at the very edge of the water, thinking about something. Patches of red light from the fire moved together with the shadows over the ground near the dark human figures, and quivered on the mountain, on the trees, on the bridge, on the drying-shed; on the other side the steep, scooped-out bank was all lighted up and glimmering in the stream, and the rushing turbid water broke its reflection into little bits.

The deacon went for the fish which Kerbalay was cleaning and washing on the bank, but he stood still half-way and looked about him.

"My God, how nice it is!" he thought. "People, rocks, the fire, the twilight, a monstrous tree—nothing more, and yet how fine it is!"

On the further bank some unknown persons made their appearance near the drying-shed. The flickering light and the smoke from the camp-fire puffing in that direction made it impossible to get a full view of them all at once, but glimpses were caught now of a shaggy hat and a grey beard, now of a blue shirt, now of a figure, ragged from shoulder to knee, with a dagger across the body; then a swarthy young face with black eyebrows, as thick and bold as though they had been drawn in charcoal. Five of them sat in a circle on the ground, and the other five went into the drying-shed. One was standing at the door with his back to the fire, and with his hands behind his back was telling something, which must have been very interesting, for when Samoylenko threw on twigs and the fire flared up, and scattered sparks and threw a glaring light on the shed, two calm countenances with an expression on them of deep attention could be seen, looking out of the door, while those who were sitting in a circle turned round and began listening to the speaker. Soon after, those sitting in a circle began softly singing something slow and melodious, that sounded like Lenten Church music. . . . Listening to them, the deacon imagined how it would be with him in ten years' time, when he would come back from the expedition: he would be a young priest and monk, an author with a name and a splendid past; he would be consecrated an archimandrite, then a bishop; and he would serve mass in the cathedral; in a golden mitre he would come out into the body of the church with the ikon on his breast, and blessing the mass of the people with the triple and the double candelabra, would proclaim: "Look down from Heaven, O God, behold and visit this vineyard which Thy Hand has planted," and the children with their angel voices would sing in response: "Holy God. . ."

"Deacon, where is that fish?" he heard Samoylenko's voice.

As he went back to the fire, the deacon imagined the Church procession going along a dusty road on a hot July day; in front the peasants carrying the banners and the women and children the ikons, then the boy choristers and the sacristan with his face tied up and a straw in his hair, then in due order himself, the deacon, and behind him the priest wearing his *calotte* and carrying a cross, and behind them, tramping in the dust, a crowd of peasants—men, women, and children; in the crowd his wife and the priest's wife with kerchiefs on their heads. The choristers sing, the babies cry, the corncrakes call, the lark carols. . . . Then they make a stand and sprinkle the herd with holy water. . . . They go on again, and then kneeling pray for rain. Then lunch and talk. . . .

"And that's nice too . . ." thought the deacon.

VII

Kirilin and Atchmianov climbed up the mountain by the path. Atchmianov dropped behind and stopped, while Kirilin went up to Nadyezhda Fyodorovna.

"Good-evening," he said, touching his cap.

"Good-evening."

"Yes!" said Kirilin, looking at the sky and pondering.

"Why 'yes'?" asked Nadyezhda Fyodorovna after a brief pause, noticing that Atchmianov was watching them both.

"And so it seems," said the officer, slowly, "that our love has withered before it has blossomed, so to speak. How do you wish me to understand it? Is it a sort of coquetry on your part, or do you look upon me as a nincompoop who can be treated as you choose."

"It was a mistake! Leave me alone!" Nadyezhda Fyodorovna said sharply, on that beautiful, marvellous evening, looking at him with terror and asking herself with bewilderment, could there really have been a moment when that man attracted her and had been near to her?

"So that's it!" said Kirilin; he thought in silence for a few minutes and said: "Well, I'll wait till you are in a better humour, and meanwhile I venture to assure you I am a gentleman, and I don't allow any one to doubt it. Adieu!"

He touched his cap again and walked off, making his way between the bushes. After a short interval Atchmianov approached hesitatingly.

"What a fine evening!" he said with a slight Armenian accent.

He was nice-looking, fashionably dressed, and behaved unaffectedly like a well-bred youth, but Nadyezhda Fyodorovna did not like him because she owed his father three hundred roubles; it was displeasing to her, too, that a shopkeeper had been asked to the picnic, and she was vexed at his coming up to her that evening when her heart felt so pure.

"The picnic is a success altogether," he said, after a pause.

"Yes," she agreed, and as though suddenly remembering her debt, she said carelessly: "Oh, tell them in your shop that Ivan Andreitch will come round in a day or two and will pay three hundred roubles . . . . I don't remember exactly what it is."

"I would give another three hundred if you would not mention that debt every day. Why be prosaic?"

Nadyezhda Fyodorovna laughed; the amusing idea occurred to her that if she had been willing and sufficiently immoral she might in one minute be free from her debt. If she, for instance, were to turn the head of this handsome young fool! How amusing, absurd, wild it would be really! And she suddenly felt a longing to make him love her, to plunder him, throw him over, and then to see what would come of it.

"Allow me to give you one piece of advice," Atchmianov said timidly. "I beg you to beware of Kirilin. He says horrible things about you everywhere."

"It doesn't interest me to know what every fool says of me," Nadyezhda Fyodorovna said coldly, and the amusing thought of playing with handsome young Atchmianov suddenly lost its charm.

"We must go down," she said; "they're calling us."

The fish soup was ready by now. They were ladling it out by platefuls, and eating it with the religious solemnity with which this is only done at a picnic; and every one thought the fish soup very good, and thought that at home they had never eaten anything so nice. As is always the case at picnics, in the mass of dinner napkins, parcels, useless greasy papers fluttering in the wind, no one knew where was his glass or where his bread. They poured the wine on the carpet and on their own knees, spilt the salt, while it was dark all round them and the fire burnt more dimly, and every one was too lazy to get up and put wood on. They all drank wine, and even gave Kostya and Katya half a glass each. Nadyezhda Fyodorovna drank one glass and then another, got a little drunk and forgot about Kirilin.

"A splendid picnic, an enchanting evening," said Laevsky, growing lively with the wine. "But I should prefer a fine winter to all this. 'His beaver collar is silver with hoar-frost.'"

"Every one to his taste," observed Von Koren.

Laevsky felt uncomfortable; the heat of the campfire was beating upon his back, and the hatred of Von Koren upon his breast and face: this hatred on the part of a decent, clever man, a feeling in which there probably lay hid a well-grounded reason, humiliated him and enervated him, and unable to stand up against it, he said in a propitiatory tone:

"I am passionately fond of nature, and I regret that I'm not a naturalist. I envy you."

"Well, I don't envy you, and don't regret it," said Nadyezhda Fyodorovna. "I don't understand how any one can seriously interest himself in beetles and ladybirds while the people are suffering."

Laevsky shared her opinion. He was absolutely ignorant of natural science, and so could never reconcile himself to the authoritative tone and the learned and profound air of the people who devoted themselves to the whiskers of ants and the claws of beetles, and he always felt vexed that these people, relying on these whiskers, claws, and something they called protoplasm (he always imagined it in the form of an oyster), should undertake to decide questions involving the origin and life of man. But in Nadyezhda Fyodorovna's words he heard a note of falsity, and simply to contradict her he said: "The point is not the ladybirds, but the deductions made from them."

VIII

It was late, eleven o'clock, when they began to get into the carriages to go home. They took their seats, and the only ones missing were Nadyezhda Fyodorovna and Atchmianov, who were running after one another, laughing, the other side of the stream.

"Make haste, my friends," shouted Samoylenko.

"You oughtn't to give ladies wine," said Von Koren in a low voice.

Laevsky, exhausted by the picnic, by the hatred of Von Koren, and by his own thoughts, went to meet Nadyezhda Fyodorovna, and when, gay and happy, feeling light as a feather, breathless and laughing, she took him by both hands and laid her head on his breast, he stepped back and said dryly:

"You are behaving like a . . . cocotte."

It sounded horribly coarse, so that he felt sorry for her at once. On his angry, exhausted face she read hatred, pity and vexation with himself, and her heart sank at once. She realised instantly that she had gone too far, had been too free and easy in her behaviour, and overcome with misery, feeling herself heavy, stout, coarse, and drunk, she got into the first empty carriage together with Atchmianov. Laevsky got in with Kirilin, the zoologist with Samoylenko, the deacon with the ladies, and the party set off.

"You see what the Japanese monkeys are like," Von Koren began, rolling himself up in his cloak and shutting his eyes. "You heard she doesn't care to take an interest in beetles and ladybirds because the people are suffering. That's how all the Japanese monkeys look upon people like us. They're a slavish, cunning race, terrified by the whip and the fist for ten generations; they tremble and burn incense only before violence; but let the monkey into a free state where there's no one to take it by the collar, and it relaxes at once and shows itself in its true colours. Look how bold they are in picture galleries, in museums, in theatres, or when they talk of science: they puff themselves out and get excited, they are abusive and critical . . . they are bound to criticise—it's the sign of the slave. You listen: men of the liberal professions are more often sworn at than pickpockets—that's because three-quarters of society are made up of slaves, of just such monkeys. It never happens that a slave holds out his hand to you and sincerely says 'Thank you' to you for your work."

"I don't know what you want," said Samoylenko, yawning; "the poor thing, in the simplicity of her heart, wanted to talk to you of scientific subjects, and you draw a conclusion from that. You're cross with him for something or other, and with her, too, to keep him company. She's a splendid woman."

"Ah, nonsense! An ordinary kept woman, depraved and vulgar. Listen, Alexandr Daviditch; when you meet a simple peasant woman, who isn't living with her husband, who does nothing but giggle, you tell her to go and work. Why are you timid in this case and afraid to tell the truth? Simply because Nadyezhda Fyodorovna is kept, not by a sailor, but by an official."

"What am I to do with her?" said Samoylenko, getting angry. "Beat her or what?

"Not flatter vice. We curse vice only behind its back, and that's like making a long nose at it round a corner. I am a zoologist or a sociologist, which is the same thing; you are a doctor; society believes in us; we ought to point out the terrible harm which threatens it and the next generation from the existence of ladies like Nadyezhda Ivanovna."

"Fyodorovna," Samoylenko corrected. "But what ought society to do?"

"Society? That's its affair. To my thinking the surest and most direct method is—compulsion. *Manu militari* she ought to be returned to her husband; and if her husband won't take her in, then she ought to be sent to penal servitude or some house of correction."

"Ouf!" sighed Samoylenko. He paused and asked quietly: "You said the other day that people like Laevsky ought to be destroyed. . . . Tell me, if you . . . if the State or society commissioned you to destroy him, could you . . . bring yourself to it?"

"My hand would not tremble."

IX

When they got home, Laevsky and Nadyezhda Fyodorovna went into their dark, stuffy, dull rooms. Both were silent. Laevsky lighted a candle, while Nadyezhda Fyodorovna sat down, and without taking off her cloak and hat, lifted her melancholy, guilty eyes to him.

He knew that she expected an explanation from him, but an explanation would be wearisome, useless and exhausting, and his heart was heavy because he had lost control over himself and been rude to her. He chanced to feel in his pocket the letter which he had been intending every day to read to her, and thought if he were to show her that letter now, it would turn her thoughts in another direction.

"It is time to define our relations," he thought. "I will give it her; what is to be will be."

He took out the letter and gave it her.

"Read it. It concerns you."

Saying this, he went into his own room and lay down on the sofa in the dark without a pillow. Nadyezhda Fyodorovna read the letter, and it seemed to her as though the ceiling were falling and the walls were closing in on her. It seemed suddenly dark and shut in and terrible. She crossed herself quickly three times and said:

"Give him peace, O Lord . . . give him peace. . . ."

And she began crying.

"Vanya," she called. "Ivan Andreitch!"

There was no answer. Thinking that Laevsky had come in and was standing behind her chair, she sobbed like a child, and said:

"Why did you not tell me before that he was dead? I wouldn't have gone to the picnic; I shouldn't have laughed so horribly. . . . The men said horrid things to me. What a sin, what a sin! Save me, Vanya, save me. . . . I have been mad. . . . I am lost. . . ."

Laevsky heard her sobs. He felt stifled and his heart was beating violently. In his misery he got up, stood in the middle of the room, groped his way in the dark to an easy-chair by the table, and sat down.

"This is a prison . . ." he thought. "I must get away . . . I can't bear it."

It was too late to go and play cards; there were no restaurants in the town. He lay down again and covered his ears that he might not hear her sobbing, and he suddenly remembered that he could go to Samoylenko. To avoid going near Nadyezhda Fyodorovna, he got out of the window into the garden, climbed over the garden fence and went along the street. It was dark. A steamer, judging by its lights, a big passenger one, had just come in. He heard the clank of the anchor chain. A red light was moving rapidly from the shore in the direction of the steamer: it was the Customs boat going out to it.

"The passengers are asleep in their cabins . . ." thought Laevsky, and he envied the peace of mind of other people.

The windows in Samoylenko's house were open. Laevsky looked in at one of them, then in at another; it was dark and still in the rooms.

"Alexandr Daviditch, are you asleep?" he called. "Alexandr Daviditch!"

He heard a cough and an uneasy shout:

"Who's there? What the devil?"

"It is I, Alexandr Daviditch; excuse me."

A little later the door opened; there was a glow of soft light from the lamp, and Samoylenko's huge figure appeared all in white, with a white nightcap on his head.

"What now?" he asked, scratching himself and breathing hard from sleepiness. "Wait a minute; I'll open the door directly."

"Don't trouble; I'll get in at the window. . . ."

Laevsky climbed in at the window, and when he reached Samoylenko, seized him by the hand.

"Alexandr Daviditch," he said in a shaking voice, "save me! I beseech you, I implore you. Understand me! My position is agonising. If it goes on for another two days I shall strangle myself like . . . like a dog."

"Wait a bit. . . . What are you talking about exactly?"

"Light a candle."

"Oh . . . oh! . . ." sighed Samoylenko, lighting a candle. "My God!

My God! . . . Why, it's past one, brother."

"Excuse me, but I can't stay at home," said Laevsky, feeling great comfort from the light and the presence of Samoylenko. "You are my best, my only friend, Alexandr Daviditch. . . . You are my only hope. For God's sake, come to my rescue, whether you want to or not. I must get away from here, come what may! . . . Lend me the money!"

"Oh, my God, my God! . . ." sighed Samoylenko, scratching himself. "I was dropping asleep and I hear the whistle of the steamer, and now you . . . Do you want much?"

"Three hundred roubles at least. I must leave her a hundred, and I need two hundred for the journey. . . . I owe you about four hundred already, but I will send it you all . . . all. . . ."

Samoylenko took hold of both his whiskers in one hand, and standing with his legs wide apart, pondered.

"Yes . . ." he muttered, musing. "Three hundred. . . . Yes. . . .

But I haven't got so much. I shall have to borrow it from some one."

"Borrow it, for God's sake!" said Laevsky, seeing from Samoylenko's face that he wanted to lend him the money and certainly would lend it. "Borrow it, and I'll be sure to pay you back. I will send it from Petersburg as soon as I get there. You can set your mind at rest about that. I'll tell you what, Sasha," he said, growing more animated; "let us have some wine."

"Yes . . . we can have some wine, too."

They both went into the dining-room.

"And how about Nadyezhda Fyodorovna?" asked Samoylenko, setting three bottles and a plate of peaches on the table. "Surely she's not remaining?"

"I will arrange it all, I will arrange it all," said Laevsky, feeling an unexpected rush of joy. "I will send her the money afterwards and she will join me. . . . Then we will define our relations. To your health, friend."

"Wait a bit," said Samoylenko. "Drink this first. . . . This is from my vineyard. This bottle is from Navaridze's vineyard and this one is from Ahatulov's. . . . Try all three kinds and tell me candidly. . . . There seems a little acidity about mine. Eh? Don't you taste it?"

"Yes. You have comforted me, Alexandr Daviditch. Thank you. . . .
I feel better."

"Is there any acidity?"

"Goodness only knows, I don't know. But you are a splendid, wonderful man!"

Looking at his pale, excited, good-natured face, Samoylenko remembered Von Koren's view that men like that ought to be destroyed, and Laevsky seemed to him a weak, defenceless child, whom any one could injure and destroy.

"And when you go, make it up with your mother," he said. "It's not right."

"Yes, yes; I certainly shall."

They were silent for a while. When they had emptied the first bottle, Samoylenko said:

"You ought to make it up with Von Koren too. You are both such splendid, clever fellows, and you glare at each other like wolves."

"Yes, he's a fine, very intelligent fellow," Laevsky assented, ready now to praise and forgive every one. "He's a remarkable man, but it's impossible for me to get on with him. No! Our natures are too different. I'm an indolent, weak, submissive nature. Perhaps in a good minute I might hold out my hand to him, but he would turn away from me . . . with contempt."

Laevsky took a sip of wine, walked from corner to corner and went on, standing in the middle of the room:

"I understand Von Koren very well. His is a resolute, strong, despotic nature. You have heard him continually talking of 'the expedition,' and it's not mere talk. He wants the wilderness, the moonlit night: all around in little tents, under the open sky, lie sleeping his sick and hungry Cossacks, guides, porters, doctor, priest, all exhausted with their weary marches, while only he is awake, sitting like Stanley on a camp-stool, feeling himself the monarch of the desert and the master of these men. He goes on and on and on, his men groan and die, one after another, and he goes on and on, and in the end perishes himself, but still is monarch and ruler of the desert, since the cross upon his tomb can be seen by the caravans for thirty or forty miles over the desert. I am sorry the man is not in the army. He would have made a splendid military genius. He would not have hesitated to drown his cavalry in the river and make a bridge out of dead bodies. And such hardihood is more needed in war than any kind of fortification or strategy. Oh, I understand him perfectly! Tell me: why is he wasting his substance here? What does he want here?"

"He is studying the marine fauna."

"No, no, brother, no!" Laevsky sighed. "A scientific man who was on the steamer told me the Black Sea was poor in animal life, and that in its depths, thanks to the abundance of sulphuric hydrogen, organic life was impossible. All the serious zoologists work at the biological station at Naples or Villefranche. But Von Koren is independent and obstinate: he works on the Black Sea because nobody else is working there; he is at loggerheads with the university, does not care to know his comrades and other scientific men because he is first of all a despot and only secondly a zoologist. And you'll see he'll do something. He is already dreaming that when he comes back from his expedition he will purify our universities from intrigue and mediocrity, and will make the scientific men mind their p's and q's. Despotism is just as strong in science as in the army. And he is spending his second summer in this stinking little town because he would rather be first in a village than second in a town. Here he is a king and an eagle; he keeps all the inhabitants under his thumb and oppresses them with his authority. He has appropriated every one, he meddles in other people's affairs; everything is of use to him, and every one is afraid of him. I am slipping out of his clutches, he feels that and hates me. Hasn't he told you that I ought to be destroyed or sent to hard labour?"

"Yes," laughed Samoylenko.

Laevsky laughed too, and drank some wine.

"His ideals are despotic too," he said, laughing, and biting a peach. "Ordinary mortals think of their neighbour—me, you, man in fact—if they work for the common weal. To Von Koren men are puppets and nonentities, too trivial to be the object of his life. He works, will go for his expedition and break his neck there, not for the sake of love for his neighbour, but for the sake of such abstractions as humanity, future generations, an ideal race of men. He exerts himself for the improvement of the human race, and we are in his eyes only slaves, food for the cannon, beasts of burden; some he would destroy or stow away in Siberia, others he would break by discipline, would, like Araktcheev, force them to get up and go to bed to the sound of the drum; would appoint eunuchs to preserve our chastity and morality, would order them to fire at any one who steps out of the circle of our narrow conservative morality; and all this in the name of the improvement of the human race. . . . And what is the human race? Illusion, mirage . . . despots have always been illusionists. I understand him very well, brother. I appreciate him and don't deny his importance; this world rests on men like him, and if the world were left only to such men as us, for all our good-nature and good intentions, we should make as great a mess of it as the flies have of that picture. Yes."

Laevsky sat down beside Samoylenko, and said with genuine feeling:

"I'm a foolish, worthless, depraved man. The air I breathe, this wine, love, life in fact—for all that, I have given nothing in exchange so far but lying, idleness, and cowardice. Till now I have deceived myself and other people; I have been miserable about it, and my misery was cheap and common. I bow my back humbly before Von Koren's hatred because at times I hate and despise myself."

Laevsky began again pacing from one end of the room to the other in excitement, and said:

"I'm glad I see my faults clearly and am conscious of them. That will help me to reform and become a different man. My dear fellow, if only you knew how passionately, with what anguish, I long for such a change. And I swear to you I'll be a man! I will! I don't know whether it is the wine that is speaking in me, or whether it really is so, but it seems to me that it is long since I have spent such pure and lucid moments as I have just now with you."

"It's time to sleep, brother," said Samoylenko.

"Yes, yes. . . . Excuse me; I'll go directly."

Laevsky moved hurriedly about the furniture and windows, looking for his cap.

"Thank you," he muttered, sighing. "Thank you. . . . Kind and friendly words are better than charity. You have given me new life."

He found his cap, stopped, and looked guiltily at Samoylenko.

"Alexandr Daviditch," he said in an imploring voice.

"What is it?"

"Let me stay the night with you, my dear fellow!"

"Certainly. . . . Why not?"

Laevsky lay down on the sofa, and went on talking to the doctor for a long time.

X

Three days after the picnic, Marya Konstantinovna unexpectedly called on Nadyezhda Fyodorovna, and without greeting her or taking off her hat, seized her by both hands, pressed them to her breast and said in great excitement:

"My dear, I am deeply touched and moved: our dear kind-hearted doctor told my Nikodim Alexandritch yesterday that your husband was dead. Tell me, my dear . . . tell me, is it true?

"Yes, it's true; he is dead," answered Nadyezhda Fyodorovna.

"That is awful, awful, my dear! But there's no evil without some compensation; your husband was no doubt a noble, wonderful, holy man, and such are more needed in Heaven than on earth."

Every line and feature in Marya Konstantinovna's face began quivering as though little needles were jumping up and down under her skin; she gave an almond-oily smile and said, breathlessly, enthusiastically:

"And so you are free, my dear. You can hold your head high now, and look people boldly in the face. Henceforth God and man will bless your union with Ivan Andreitch. It's enchanting. I am trembling with joy, I can find no words. My dear, I will give you away. . . . Nikodim Alexandritch and I have been so fond of you, you will allow us to give our blessing to your pure, lawful union. When, when do you think of being married?"

"I haven't thought of it," said Nadyezhda Fyodorovna, freeing her hands.

"That's impossible, my dear. You have thought of it, you have."

"Upon my word, I haven't," said Nadyezhda Fyodorovna, laughing. "What should we be married for? I see no necessity for it. We'll go on living as we have lived."

"What are you saying!" cried Marya Konstantinovna in horror. "For God's sake, what are you saying!"

"Our getting married won't make things any better. On the contrary, it will make them even worse. We shall lose our freedom."

"My dear, my dear, what are you saying!" exclaimed Marya Konstantinovna, stepping back and flinging up her hands. "You are talking wildly! Think what you are saying. You must settle down!"

"'Settle down.' How do you mean? I have not lived yet, and you tell me to settle down."

Nadyezhda Fyodorovna reflected that she really had not lived. She had finished her studies in a boarding-school and had been married to a man she did not love; then she had thrown in her lot with Laevsky, and had spent all her time with him on this empty, desolate coast, always expecting something better. Was that life?

"I ought to be married though," she thought, but remembering Kirilin and Atchmianov she flushed and said:

"No, it's impossible. Even if Ivan Andreitch begged me to on his knees—even then I would refuse."

Marya Konstantinovna sat on the sofa for a minute in silence, grave and mournful, gazing fixedly into space; then she got up and said coldly:

"Good-bye, my dear! Forgive me for having troubled you. Though it's not easy for me, it's my duty to tell you that from this day all is over between us, and, in spite of my profound respect for Ivan Andreitch, the door of my house is closed to you henceforth."

She uttered these words with great solemnity and was herself overwhelmed by her solemn tone. Her face began quivering again; it assumed a soft almond-oily expression. She held out both hands to Nadyezhda Fyodorovna, who was overcome with alarm and confusion, and said in an imploring voice:

"My dear, allow me if only for a moment to be a mother or an elder sister to you! I will be as frank with you as a mother."

Nadyezhda Fyodorovna felt in her bosom warmth, gladness, and pity for herself, as though her own mother had really risen up and were standing before her. She impulsively embraced Marya Konstantinovna and pressed her face to her shoulder. Both of them shed tears. They sat down on the sofa and for a few minutes sobbed without looking at one another or being able to utter a word.

"My dear child," began Marya Konstantinovna, "I will tell you some harsh truths, without sparing you."

"For God's sake, for God's sake, do!

"Trust me, my dear. You remember of all the ladies here, I was the only one to receive you. You horrified me from the very first day, but I had not the heart to treat you with disdain like all the rest. I grieved over dear, good Ivan Andreitch as though he were my son, a young man in a strange place, inexperienced, weak, with no mother; and I was worried, dreadfully worried. . . . My husband was opposed to our making his acquaintance, but I talked him over . . . persuaded him. . . . We began receiving Ivan Andreitch, and with him, of course, you. If we had not, he would have been insulted. I have a daughter, a son. . . . You understand the tender mind, the pure heart of childhood . . . 'who so offendeth one of these little ones.' . . . I received you into my house and trembled for my children. Oh, when you become a mother, you will understand my fears. And every one was surprised at my receiving you, excuse my saying so, as a respectable woman, and hinted to me . . . well, of course, slanders, suppositions. . . . At the bottom of my heart I blamed you, but you were unhappy, flighty, to be pitied, and my heart was wrung with pity for you."

"But why, why?" asked Nadyezhda Fyodorovna, trembling all over.

"What harm have I done any one?"

"You are a terrible sinner. You broke the vow you made your husband at the altar. You seduced a fine young man, who perhaps had he not met you might have taken a lawful partner for life from a good family in his own circle, and would have been like every one else now. You have ruined his youth. Don't speak, don't speak, my dear! I never believe that man is to blame for our sins. It is always the woman's fault. Men are frivolous in domestic life; they are guided by their minds, and not by their hearts. There's a great deal they don't understand; woman understands it all. Everything depends on her. To her much is given and from her much will be required. Oh, my dear, if she had been more foolish or weaker than man on that side, God would not have entrusted her with the education of boys and girls. And then, my dear, you entered on the path of vice, forgetting all modesty; any other woman in your place would have hidden herself from people, would have sat shut up at home, and would only have been seen in the temple of God, pale, dressed all in black and weeping, and every one would have said in genuine compassion: 'O Lord, this erring angel is coming back again to Thee . . . .' But you, my dear, have forgotten all discretion; have lived openly, extravagantly; have seemed to be proud of your sin; you have been gay and laughing, and I, looking at you, shuddered with horror, and have been afraid that thunder from Heaven would strike our house while you were sitting with us. My dear, don't speak, don't speak," cried Marya Konstantinovna, observing that Nadyezhda Fyodorovna wanted to speak. "Trust me, I will not deceive you, I will not hide one truth from the eyes of your soul. Listen to me, my dear. . . . God marks great sinners, and you have been marked-out: only think—your costumes have always been appalling."

Nadyezhda Fyodorovna, who had always had the highest opinion of her costumes, left off crying and looked at her with surprise.

"Yes, appalling," Marya Konstantinovna went on. "Any one could judge of your behaviour from the elaboration and gaudiness of your attire. People laughed and shrugged their shoulders as they looked at you, and I grieved, I grieved. . . . And forgive me, my dear; you are not nice in your person! When we met in the bathing-place, you made me tremble. Your outer clothing was decent enough, but your petticoat, your chemise. . . . My dear, I blushed! Poor Ivan Andreitch! No one ever ties his cravat properly, and from his linen and his boots, poor fellow! one can see he has no one at home to look after him. And he is always hungry, my darling, and of course, if there is no one at home to think of the samovar and the coffee, one is forced to spend half one's salary at the pavilion. And it's simply awful, awful in your home! No one else in the town has flies, but there's no getting rid of them in your rooms: all the plates and dishes are black with them. If you look at the windows and the chairs, there's nothing but dust, dead flies, and glasses. . . . What do you want glasses standing about for? And, my dear, the table's not cleared till this time in the day. And one's ashamed to go into your bedroom: underclothes flung about everywhere, india-rubber tubes hanging on the walls, pails and basins standing about. . . . My dear! A husband ought to know nothing, and his wife ought to be as neat as a little angel in his presence. I wake up every morning before it is light, and wash my face with cold water that my Nikodim Alexandritch may not see me looking drowsy."

"That's all nonsense," Nadyezhda Fyodorovna sobbed. "If only I were happy, but I am so unhappy!"

"Yes, yes; you are very unhappy!" Marya Konstantinovna sighed, hardly able to restrain herself from weeping. "And there's terrible grief in store for you in the future!

A solitary old age, ill-health; and then you will have to answer at the dread judgment seat. . . It's awful, awful. Now fate itself holds out to you a helping hand, and you madly thrust it from you. Be married, make haste and be married!"

"Yes, we must, we must," said Nadyezhda Fyodorovna; "but it's impossible!"

"Why?"

"It's impossible. Oh, if only you knew!"

Nadyezhda Fyodorovna had an impulse to tell her about Kirilin, and how the evening before she had met handsome young Atchmianov at the harbour, and how the mad, ridiculous idea had occurred to her of cancelling her debt for three hundred; it had amused her very much, and she returned home late in the evening feeling that she had sold herself and was irrevocably lost. She did not know herself how it had happened. And she longed to swear to Marya Konstantinovna that she would certainly pay that debt, but sobs and shame prevented her from speaking.

"I am going away," she said. "Ivan Andreitch may stay, but I am going."

"Where?"

"To Russia."

"But how will you live there? Why, you have nothing."

"I will do translation, or . . . or I will open a library . . . ."

"Don't let your fancy run away with you, my dear. You must have money for a library. Well, I will leave you now, and you calm yourself and think things over, and to-morrow come and see me, bright and happy. That will be enchanting! Well, good-bye, my angel. Let me kiss you."

Marya Konstantinovna kissed Nadyezhda Fyodorovna on the forehead, made the sign of the cross over her, and softly withdrew. It was getting dark, and Olga lighted up in the kitchen. Still crying, Nadyezhda Fyodorovna went into the bedroom and lay down on the bed. She began to be very feverish. She undressed without getting up, crumpled up her clothes at her feet, and curled herself up under the bedclothes. She was thirsty, and there was no one to give her something to drink.

"I'll pay it back!" she said to herself, and it seemed to her in delirium that she was sitting beside some sick woman, and recognised her as herself. "I'll pay it back. It would be stupid to imagine that it was for money I . . . I will go away and send him the money from Petersburg. At first a hundred . . . then another hundred . . . and then the third hundred. . . ."

It was late at night when Laevsky came in.

"At first a hundred . . ." Nadyezhda Fyodorovna said to him, "then another hundred . . ."

"You ought to take some quinine," he said, and thought, "To-morrow is Wednesday; the steamer goes and I am not going in it. So I shall have to go on living here till Saturday."

Nadyezhda Fyodorovna knelt up in bed.

"I didn't say anything just now, did I?" she asked, smiling and screwing up her eyes at the light.

"No, nothing. We shall have to send for the doctor to-morrow morning.

Go to sleep."

He took his pillow and went to the door. Ever since he had finally made up his mind to go away and leave Nadyezhda Fyodorovna, she had begun to raise in him pity and a sense of guilt; he felt a little ashamed in her presence, as though in the presence of a sick or old horse whom one has decided to kill. He stopped in the doorway and looked round at her.

"I was out of humour at the picnic and said something rude to you.

Forgive me, for God's sake!"

Saying this, he went off to his study, lay down, and for a long while could not get to sleep.

Next morning when Samoylenko, attired, as it was a holiday, in full-dress uniform with epaulettes on his shoulders and decorations on his breast, came out of the bedroom after feeling Nadyezhda Fyodorovna's pulse and looking at her tongue, Laevsky, who was standing in the doorway, asked him anxiously: "Well? Well?"

There was an expression of terror, of extreme uneasiness, and of hope on his face.

"Don't worry yourself; there's nothing dangerous," said Samoylenko;

"it's the usual fever."

"I don't mean that." Laevsky frowned impatiently. "Have you got the money?"

"My dear soul, forgive me," he whispered, looking round at the door and overcome with confusion.

"For God's sake, forgive me! No one has anything to spare, and I've only been able to collect by five- and by ten-rouble notes. . . . Only a hundred and ten in all. To-day I'll speak to some one else.

Have patience."

"But Saturday is the latest date," whispered Laevsky, trembling with impatience. "By all that's sacred, get it by Saturday! If I don't get away by Saturday, nothing's any use, nothing! I can't understand how a doctor can be without money!"

"Lord have mercy on us!" Samoylenko whispered rapidly and intensely, and there was positively a breaking note in his throat. "I've been stripped of everything; I am owed seven thousand, and I'm in debt all round. Is it my fault?"

"Then you'll get it by Saturday? Yes?"

"I'll try."

"I implore you, my dear fellow! So that the money may be in my hands by Friday morning!"

Samoylenko sat down and prescribed solution of quinine and kalii bromati and tincture of rhubarb, tincturae gentianae, aquae foeniculi , all in one mixture, added some pink syrup to sweeten it, and went away.

XI

"You look as though you were coming to arrest me," said Von Koren, seeing Samoylenko coming in, in his full-dress uniform.

"I was passing by and thought: 'Suppose I go in and pay my respects to zoology,'" said Samoylenko, sitting down at the big table, knocked together by the zoologist himself out of plain boards. "Good-morning, holy father," he said to the deacon, who was sitting in the window, copying something. "I'll stay a minute and then run home to see about dinner. It's time. . . . I'm not hindering you?"

"Not in the least," answered the zoologist, laying out over the table slips of paper covered with small writing. "We are busy copying."

"Ah! . . . Oh, my goodness, my goodness! . . ." sighed Samoylenko. He cautiously took up from the table a dusty book on which there was lying a dead dried spider, and said: "Only fancy, though; some little green beetle is going about its business, when suddenly a monster like this swoops down upon it. I can fancy its terror."

"Yes, I suppose so."

"Is poison given it to protect it from its enemies?"

"Yes, to protect it and enable it to attack."

"To be sure, to be sure. . . . And everything in nature, my dear fellows, is consistent and can be explained," sighed Samoylenko;

"only I tell you what I don't understand. You're a man of very great intellect, so explain it to me, please. There are, you know, little beasts no bigger than rats, rather handsome to look at, but nasty and immoral in the extreme, let me tell you. Suppose such a little beast is running in the woods. He sees a bird; he catches it and devours it. He goes on and sees in the grass a nest of eggs; he does not want to eat them—he is not hungry, but yet he tastes one egg and scatters the others out of the nest with his paw. Then he meets a frog and begins to play with it; when he has tormented the frog he goes on licking himself and meets a beetle; he crushes the beetle with his paw . . . and so he spoils and destroys everything on his way. . . . He creeps into other beasts' holes, tears up the anthills, cracks the snail's shell. If he meets a rat, he fights with it; if he meets a snake or a mouse, he must strangle it; and so the whole day long. Come, tell me: what is the use of a beast like that? Why was he created?"

"I don't know what animal you are talking of," said Von Koren; "most likely one of the insectivora. Well, he got hold of the bird because it was incautious; he broke the nest of eggs because the bird was not skilful, had made the nest badly and did not know how to conceal it. The frog probably had some defect in its colouring or he would not have seen it, and so on. Your little beast only destroys the weak, the unskilful, the careless—in fact, those who have defects which nature does not think fit to hand on to posterity. Only the cleverer, the stronger, the more careful and developed survive; and so your little beast, without suspecting it, is serving the great ends of perfecting creation."

"Yes, yes, yes. . . . By the way, brother," said Samoylenko carelessly, "lend me a hundred roubles."

"Very good. There are some very interesting types among the insectivorous mammals. For instance, the mole is said to be useful because he devours noxious insects. There is a story that some German sent William I. a fur coat made of moleskins, and the Emperor ordered him to be reproved for having destroyed so great a number of useful animals. And yet the mole is not a bit less cruel than your little beast, and is very mischievous besides, as he spoils meadows terribly."

Von Koren opened a box and took out a hundred-rouble note.

"The mole has a powerful thorax, just like the bat," he went on, shutting the box; "the bones and muscles are tremendously developed, the mouth is extraordinarily powerfully furnished. If it had the proportions of an elephant, it would be an all-destructive, invincible animal. It is interesting when two moles meet underground; they begin at once as though by agreement digging a little platform; they need the platform in order to have a battle more conveniently. When they have made it they enter upon a ferocious struggle and fight till the weaker one falls. Take the hundred roubles," said Von Koren, dropping his voice, "but only on condition that you're not borrowing it for Laevsky."

"And if it were for Laevsky," cried Samoylenko, flaring up, "what is that to you?"

"I can't give it to you for Laevsky. I know you like lending people money. You would give it to Kerim, the brigand, if he were to ask you; but, excuse me, I can't assist you in that direction."

"Yes, it is for Laevsky I am asking it," said Samoylenko, standing up and waving his right arm. "Yes! For Laevsky! And no one, fiend or devil, has a right to dictate to me how to dispose of my own money. It doesn't suit you to lend it me? No?"

The deacon began laughing.

"Don't get excited, but be reasonable," said the zoologist. "To shower benefits on Mr. Laevsky is, to my thinking, as senseless as to water weeds or to feed locusts."

"To my thinking, it is our duty to help our neighbours!" cried Samoylenko.

"In that case, help that hungry Turk who is lying under the fence!

He is a workman and more useful and indispensable than your Laevsky. Give him that hundred-rouble note! Or subscribe a hundred roubles to my expedition!"

"Will you give me the money or not? I ask you!"

"Tell me openly: what does he want money for?

"It's not a secret; he wants to go to Petersburg on Saturday."

"So that is it!" Von Koren drawled out. "Aha! . . . We understand.

And is she going with him, or how is it to be?"

"She's staying here for the time. He'll arrange his affairs in Petersburg and send her the money, and then she'll go."

"That's smart!" said the zoologist, and he gave a short tenor laugh.

"Smart, well planned."

He went rapidly up to Samoylenko, and standing face to face with him, and looking him in the eyes, asked: "Tell me now honestly: is he tired of her? Yes? tell me: is he tired of her? Yes?"

"Yes," Samoylenko articulated, beginning to perspire.

"How repulsive it is!" said Von Koren, and from his face it could be seen that he felt repulsion. "One of two things, Alexandr Daviditch: either you are in the plot with him, or, excuse my saying so, you are a simpleton. Surely you must see that he is taking you in like a child in the most shameless way? Why, it's as clear as day that he wants to get rid of her and abandon her here. She'll be left a burden on you. It is as clear as day that you will have to send her to Petersburg at your expense. Surely your fine friend can't have so blinded you by his dazzling qualities that you can't see the simplest thing?"

"That's all supposition," said Samoylenko, sitting down.

"Supposition? But why is he going alone instead of taking her with him? And ask him why he doesn't send her off first. The sly beast!"

Overcome with sudden doubts and suspicions about his friend, Samoylenko weakened and took a humbler tone.

"But it's impossible," he said, recalling the night Laevsky had spent at his house. "He is so unhappy!"

"What of that? Thieves and incendiaries are unhappy too!"

"Even supposing you are right . . ." said Samoylenko, hesitating. "Let us admit it. . . . Still, he's a young man in a strange place . . . a student. We have been students, too, and there is no one but us to come to his assistance."

"To help him to do abominable things, because he and you at different times have been at universities, and neither of you did anything there! What nonsense!"

"Stop; let us talk it over coolly. I imagine it will be possible to make some arrangement. . . ." Samoylenko reflected, twiddling his fingers. "I'll give him the money, you see, but make him promise on his honour that within a week he'll send Nadyezhda Fyodorovna the money for the journey."

"And he'll give you his word of honour—in fact, he'll shed tears and believe in it himself; but what's his word of honour worth? He won't keep it, and when in a year or two you meet him on the Nevsky Prospect with a new mistress on his arm, he'll excuse himself on the ground that he has been crippled by civilisation, and that he is made after the pattern of Rudin. Drop him, for God's sake! Keep away from the filth; don't stir it up with both hands!"

Samoylenko thought for a minute and said resolutely:

"But I shall give him the money all the same. As you please. I can't bring myself to refuse a man simply on an assumption."

"Very fine, too. You can kiss him if you like."

"Give me the hundred roubles, then," Samoylenko asked timidly.

"I won't."

A silence followed. Samoylenko was quite crushed; his face wore a guilty, abashed, and ingratiating expression, and it was strange to see this pitiful, childish, shamefaced countenance on a huge man wearing epaulettes and orders of merit.

"The bishop here goes the round of his diocese on horseback instead of in a carriage," said the deacon, laying down his pen. "It's extremely touching to see him sit on his horse. His simplicity and humility are full of Biblical grandeur."

"Is he a good man?" asked Von Koren, who was glad to change the conversation.

"Of course! If he hadn't been a good man, do you suppose he would have been consecrated a bishop?"

"Among the bishops are to be found good and gifted men," said Von Koren. "The only drawback is that some of them have the weakness to imagine themselves statesmen. One busies himself with Russification, another criticises the sciences. That's not their business. They had much better look into their consistory a little."

"A layman cannot judge of bishops."

"Why so, deacon? A bishop is a man just the same as you or I."

"The same, but not the same." The deacon was offended and took up his pen. "If you had been the same, the Divine Grace would have rested upon you, and you would have been bishop yourself; and since you are not bishop, it follows you are not the same."

"Don't talk nonsense, deacon," said Samoylenko dejectedly. "Listen to what I suggest," he said, turning to Von Koren. "Don't give me that hundred roubles. You'll be having your dinners with me for three months before the winter, so let me have the money beforehand for three months."

"I won't."

Samoylenko blinked and turned crimson; he mechanically drew towards him the book with the spider on it and looked at it, then he got up and took his hat.

Von Koren felt sorry for him.

"What it is to have to live and do with people like this," said the zoologist, and he kicked a paper into the corner with indignation. "You must understand that this is not kindness, it is not love, but cowardice, slackness, poison! What's gained by reason is lost by your flabby good-for-nothing hearts! When I was ill with typhoid as a schoolboy, my aunt in her sympathy gave me pickled mushrooms to eat, and I very nearly died. You, and my aunt too, must understand that love for man is not to be found in the heart or the stomach or the bowels, but here!"

Von Koren slapped himself on the forehead.

"Take it," he said, and thrust a hundred-rouble note into his hand.

"You've no need to be angry, Kolya," said Samoylenko mildly, folding up the note. "I quite understand you, but . . . you must put yourself in my place."

"You are an old woman, that's what you are."

The deacon burst out laughing.

"Hear my last request, Alexandr Daviditch," said Von Koren hotly. "When you give that scoundrel the money, make it a condition that he takes his lady with him, or sends her on ahead, and don't give it him without. There's no need to stand on ceremony with him. Tell him so, or, if you don't, I give you my word I'll go to his office and kick him downstairs, and I'll break off all acquaintance with you. So you'd better know it."

"Well! To go with her or send her on beforehand will be more convenient for him," said Samoylenko. "He'll be delighted indeed. Well, goodbye."

He said good-bye affectionately and went out, but before shutting the door after him, he looked round at Von Koren and, with a ferocious face, said:

"It's the Germans who have ruined you, brother! Yes! The Germans!"

XII

Next day, Thursday, Marya Konstantinovna was celebrating the birthday of her Kostya. All were invited to come at midday and eat pies, and in the evening to drink chocolate. When Laevsky and Nadyezhda Fyodorovna arrived in the evening, the zoologist, who was already sitting in the drawing-room, drinking chocolate, asked Samoylenko:

"Have you talked to him?"

"Not yet."

"Mind now, don't stand on ceremony. I can't understand the insolence of these people! Why, they know perfectly well the view taken by this family of their cohabitation, and yet they force themselves in here."

"If one is to pay attention to every prejudice," said Samoylenko, "one could go nowhere."

"Do you mean to say that the repugnance felt by the masses for illicit love and moral laxity is a prejudice?"

"Of course it is. It's prejudice and hate. When the soldiers see a girl of light behaviour, they laugh and whistle; but just ask them what they are themselves."

"It's not for nothing they whistle. The fact that girls strangle their illegitimate children and go to prison for it, and that Anna Karenin flung herself under the train, and that in the villages they smear the gates with tar, and that you and I, without knowing why, are pleased by Katya's purity, and that every one of us feels a vague craving for pure love, though he knows there is no such love—is all that prejudice? That is the one thing, brother, which has survived intact from natural selection, and, if it were not for that obscure force regulating the relations of the sexes, the Laevskys would have it all their own way, and mankind would degenerate in two years."

Laevsky came into the drawing-room, greeted every one, and shaking hands with Von Koren, smiled ingratiatingly. He waited for a favourable moment and said to Samoylenko:

"Excuse me, Alexandr Daviditch, I must say two words to you."

Samoylenko got up, put his arm round Laevsky's waist, and both of them went into Nikodim Alexandritch's study.

"To-morrow's Friday," said Laevsky, biting his nails. "Have you got what you promised?"

"I've only got two hundred. I'll get the rest to-day or to-morrow.

Don't worry yourself."

"Thank God . . ." sighed Laevsky, and his hands began trembling with joy. "You are saving me, Alexandr Daviditch, and I swear to you by God, by my happiness and anything you like, I'll send you the money as soon as I arrive. And I'll send you my old debt too."

"Look here, Vanya . . ." said Samoylenko, turning crimson and taking him by the button. "You must forgive my meddling in your private affairs, but . . . why shouldn't you take Nadyezhda Fyodorovna with you?"

"You queer fellow. How is that possible? One of us must stay, or our creditors will raise an outcry. You see, I owe seven hundred or more to the shops. Only wait, and I will send them the money. I'll stop their mouths, and then she can come away."

"I see. . . . But why shouldn't you send her on first?"

"My goodness, as though that were possible!" Laevsky was horrified. "Why, she's a woman; what would she do there alone? What does she know about it? That would only be a loss of time and a useless waste of money."

"That's reasonable . . ." thought Samoylenko, but remembering his conversation with Von Koren, he looked down and said sullenly: "I can't agree with you. Either go with her or send her first; otherwise . . . otherwise I won't give you the money. Those are my last words. . ."

He staggered back, lurched backwards against the door, and went into the drawing-room, crimson, and overcome with confusion.

"Friday . . . Friday," thought Laevsky, going back into the drawing-room. "Friday. . . ."

He was handed a cup of chocolate; he burnt his lips and tongue with the scalding chocolate and thought: "Friday . . . Friday. . . ."

For some reason he could not get the word "Friday" out of his head; he could think of nothing but Friday, and the only thing that was clear to him, not in his brain but somewhere in his heart, was that he would not get off on Saturday. Before him stood Nikodim Alexandritch, very neat, with his hair combed over his temples, saying:

"Please take something to eat. . . ."

Marya Konstantinovna showed the visitors Katya's school report and said, drawling:

"It's very, very difficult to do well at school nowadays! So much is expected . . ."

"Mamma!" groaned Katya, not knowing where to hide her confusion at the praises of the company.

Laevsky, too, looked at the report and praised it. Scripture, Russian language, conduct, fives and fours, danced before his eyes, and all this, mixed with the haunting refrain of "Friday," with the carefully combed locks of Nikodim Alexandritch and the red cheeks of Katya, produced on him a sensation of such immense overwhelming boredom that he almost shrieked with despair and asked himself: "Is it possible, is it possible I shall not get away?"

They put two card tables side by side and sat down to play post.

Laevsky sat down too.

"Friday . . . Friday . . ." he kept thinking, as he smiled and took a pencil out of his pocket. "Friday. . . ."

He wanted to think over his position, and was afraid to think. It was terrible to him to realise that the doctor had detected him in the deception which he had so long and carefully concealed from himself. Every time he thought of his future he would not let his thoughts have full rein. He would get into the train and set off, and thereby the problem of his life would be solved, and he did not let his thoughts go farther. Like a far-away dim light in the fields, the thought sometimes flickered in his mind that in one of the side-streets of Petersburg, in the remote future, he would have to have recourse to a tiny lie in order to get rid of Nadyezhda Fyodorovna and pay his debts; he would tell a lie only once, and then a completely new life would begin. And that was right: at the price of a small lie he would win so much truth.

Now when by his blunt refusal the doctor had crudely hinted at his deception, he began to understand that he would need deception not only in the remote future, but to-day, and to-morrow, and in a month's time, and perhaps up to the very end of his life. In fact, in order to get away he would have to lie to Nadyezhda Fyodorovna, to his creditors, and to his superiors in the Service; then, in order to get money in Petersburg, he would have to lie to his mother, to tell her that he had already broken with Nadyezhda Fyodorovna; and his mother would not give him more than five hundred roubles, so he had already deceived the doctor, as he would not be in a position to pay him back the money within a short time. Afterwards, when Nadyezhda Fyodorovna came to Petersburg, he would have to resort to a regular series of deceptions, little and big, in order to get free of her; and again there would be tears, boredom, a disgusting existence, remorse, and so there would be no new life. Deception and nothing more. A whole mountain of lies rose before Laevsky's imagination. To leap over it at one bound and not to do his lying piecemeal, he would have to bring himself to stern, uncompromising action; for instance, to getting up without saying a word, putting on his hat, and at once setting off without money and without explanation. But Laevsky felt that was impossible for him.

"Friday, Friday . . ." he thought. "Friday. . . ."

They wrote little notes, folded them in two, and put them in Nikodim Alexandritch's old top-hat. When there were a sufficient heap of notes, Kostya, who acted the part of postman, walked round the table and delivered them. The deacon, Katya, and Kostya, who received amusing notes and tried to write as funnily as they could, were highly delighted.

"We must have a little talk," Nadyezhda Fyodorovna read in a little note; she glanced at Marya Konstantinovna, who gave her an almond-oily smile and nodded.

"Talk of what?" thought Nadyezhda Fyodorovna. "If one can't tell the whole, it's no use talking."

Before going out for the evening she had tied Laevsky's cravat for him, and that simple action filled her soul with tenderness and sorrow. The anxiety in his face, his absent-minded looks, his pallor, and the incomprehensible change that had taken place in him of late, and the fact that she had a terrible revolting secret from him, and the fact that her hands trembled when she tied his cravat—all this seemed to tell her that they had not long left to be together. She looked at him as though he were an ikon, with terror and penitence, and thought: "Forgive, forgive."

Opposite her was sitting Atchmianov, and he never took his black, love-sick eyes off her. She was stirred by passion; she was ashamed of herself, and afraid that even her misery and sorrow would not prevent her from yielding to impure desire to-morrow, if not to-day and that, like a drunkard, she would not have the strength to stop herself.

She made up her mind to go away that she might not continue this life, shameful for herself, and humiliating for Laevsky. She would beseech him with tears to let her go;

and if he opposed her, she would go away secretly. She would not tell him what had happened; let him keep a pure memory of her.

"I love you, I love you, I love you," she read. It was from Atchmianov.

She would live in some far remote place, would work and send Laevsky, "anonymously," money, embroidered shirts, and tobacco, and would return to him only in old age or if he were dangerously ill and needed a nurse. When in his old age he learned what were her reasons for leaving him and refusing to be his wife, he would appreciate her sacrifice and forgive.

"You've got a long nose." That must be from the deacon or Kostya.

Nadyezhda Fyodorovna imagined how, parting from Laevsky, she would embrace him warmly, would kiss his hand, and would swear to love him all her life, all her life, and then, living in obscurity among strangers, she would every day think that somewhere she had a friend, some one she loved—a pure, noble, lofty man who kept a pure memory of her.

"If you don't give me an interview to-day, I shall take measures, I assure you on my word of honour. You can't treat decent people like this; you must understand that." That was from Kirilin.

XIII

Laevsky received two notes; he opened one and read: "Don't go away, my darling."

"Who could have written that?" he thought. "Not Samoylenko, of course. And not the deacon, for he doesn't know I want to go away. Von Koren, perhaps?"

The zoologist bent over the table and drew a pyramid. Laevsky fancied that his eyes were smiling.

"Most likely Samoylenko . . . has been gossiping," thought Laevsky.

In the other note, in the same disguised angular handwriting with long tails to the letters, was written: "Somebody won't go away on Saturday."

"A stupid gibe," thought Laevsky. "Friday, Friday. . . ."

Something rose in his throat. He touched his collar and coughed, but instead of a cough a laugh broke from his throat.

"Ha-ha-ha!" he laughed. "Ha-ha-ha! What am I laughing at? Ha-ha-ha!"

He tried to restrain himself, covered his mouth with his hand, but the laugh choked his chest and throat, and his hand could not cover his mouth.

"How stupid it is!" he thought, rolling with laughter. "Have I gone out of my mind?"

The laugh grew shriller and shriller, and became something like the bark of a lap-dog. Laevsky tried to get up from the table, but his legs would not obey him and his right hand was strangely, without his volition, dancing on the table, convulsively clutching and crumpling up the bits of paper. He saw looks of wonder, Samoylenko's grave, frightened face, and the eyes of the zoologist full of cold irony and disgust, and realised that he was in hysterics.

"How hideous, how shameful!" he thought, feeling the warmth of tears on his face. ". . . Oh, oh, what a disgrace! It has never happened to me. . . ."

They took him under his arms, and supporting his head from behind, led him away; a glass gleamed before his eyes and knocked against his teeth, and the water was spilt on his breast; he was in a little room, with two beds in the middle, side by side, covered by two snow-white quilts. He dropped on one of the beds and sobbed.

"It's nothing, it's nothing," Samoylenko kept saying; "it does happen . . . it does happen. . . ."

Chill with horror, trembling all over and dreading something awful, Nadyezhda Fyodorovna stood by the bedside and kept asking:

"What is it? What is it? For God's sake, tell me."

"Can Kirilin have written him something?" she thought.

"It's nothing," said Laevsky, laughing and crying; "go away, darling."

His face expressed neither hatred nor repulsion: so he knew nothing;

Nadyezhda Fyodorovna was somewhat reassured, and she went into the drawing-room.

"Don't agitate yourself, my dear!" said Marya Konstantinovna, sitting down beside her and taking her hand. "It will pass. Men are just as weak as we poor sinners. You are both going through a crisis. . . . One can so well understand it! Well, my dear, I am waiting for an answer. Let us have a little talk."

"No, we are not going to talk," said Nadyezhda Fyodorovna, listening to Laevsky's sobs. "I feel depressed. . . . You must allow me to go home."

"What do you mean, what do you mean, my dear?" cried Marya Konstantinovna in alarm. "Do you think I could let you go without supper? We will have something to eat, and then you may go with my blessing."

"I feel miserable . . ." whispered Nadyezhda Fyodorovna, and she caught at the arm of the chair with both hands to avoid falling.

"He's got a touch of hysterics," said Von Koren gaily, coming into the drawing-room, but seeing Nadyezhda Fyodorovna, he was taken aback and retreated.

When the attack was over, Laevsky sat on the strange bed and thought.

"Disgraceful! I've been howling like some wretched girl! I must have been absurd and disgusting. I will go away by the back stairs . . . . But that would seem as though I took my hysterics too seriously. I ought to take it as a joke. . . ."

He looked in the looking-glass, sat there for some time, and went back into the drawing-room.

"Here I am," he said, smiling; he felt agonisingly ashamed, and he felt others were ashamed in his presence. "Fancy such a thing happening," he said, sitting down. "I was sitting here, and all of a sudden, do you know, I felt a terrible piercing pain in my side . . . unendurable, my nerves could not stand it, and . . . and it led to this silly performance. This is the age of nerves; there is no help for it."

At supper he drank some wine, and, from time to time, with an abrupt sigh rubbed his side as though to suggest that he still felt the pain. And no one, except Nadyezhda Fyodorovna, believed him, and he saw that.

After nine o'clock they went for a walk on the boulevard. Nadyezhda Fyodorovna, afraid that Kirilin would speak to her, did her best to keep all the time beside Marya Konstantinovna and the children. She felt weak with fear and misery, and felt she was going to be feverish; she was exhausted and her legs would hardly move, but she did not go home, because she felt sure that she would be followed by Kirilin or Atchmianov or both at once. Kirilin walked behind her with Nikodim Alexandritch, and kept humming in an undertone:

"I don't al-low people to play with me! I don't al-low it."

From the boulevard they went back to the pavilion and walked along the beach, and looked for a long time at the phosphorescence on the water. Von Koren began telling them why it looked phosphorescent.

XIV

"It's time I went to my *vint*. . . . They will be waiting for me," said Laevsky. "Good-bye, my friends."

"I'll come with you; wait a minute," said Nadyezhda Fyodorovna, and she took his arm.

They said good-bye to the company and went away. Kirilin took leave too, and saying that he was going the same way, went along beside them.

"What will be, will be," thought Nadyezhda Fyodorovna. "So be it. . . ."

And it seemed to her that all the evil memories in her head had taken shape and were walking beside her in the darkness, breathing heavily, while she, like a fly that had fallen into the inkpot, was crawling painfully along the pavement and smirching Laevsky's side and arm with blackness.

If Kirilin should do anything horrid, she thought, not he but she would be to blame for it. There was a time when no man would have talked to her as Kirilin had done, and she had torn up her security like a thread and destroyed it irrevocably—who was to blame for it? Intoxicated by her passions she had smiled at a complete stranger, probably just because he was tall and a fine figure. After two meetings she was weary of him, had thrown him over, and did not that, she thought now, give him the right to treat her as he chose?

"Here I'll say good-bye to you, darling," said Laevsky. "Ilya Mihalitch will see you home."

He nodded to Kirilin, and, quickly crossing the boulevard, walked along the street to Sheshkovsky's, where there were lights in the windows, and then they heard the gate bang as he went in.

"Allow me to have an explanation with you," said Kirilin. "I'm not a boy, not some Atchkasov or Latchkasov, Zatchkasov. . . . I demand serious attention."

Nadyezhda Fyodorovna's heart began beating violently. She made no reply.

"The abrupt change in your behaviour to me I put down at first to coquetry," Kirilin went on; "now I see that you don't know how to behave with gentlemanly people. You simply wanted to play with me, as you are playing with that wretched Armenian boy; but I'm a gentleman and I insist on being treated like a gentleman. And so I am at your service. . . ."

"I'm miserable," said Nadyezhda Fyodorovna beginning to cry, and to hide her tears she turned away.

"I'm miserable too," said Kirilin, "but what of that?"

Kirilin was silent for a space, then he said distinctly and emphatically:

"I repeat, madam, that if you do not give me an interview this evening, I'll make a scandal this very evening."

"Let me off this evening," said Nadyezhda Fyodorovna, and she did not recognise her own voice, it was so weak and pitiful.

"I must give you a lesson. . . . Excuse me for the roughness of my tone, but it's necessary to give you a lesson. Yes, I regret to say I must give you a lesson. I insist on two interviews—to-day and to-morrow. After to-morrow you are perfectly free and can go wherever you like with any one you choose. To-day and to-morrow."

Nadyezhda Fyodorovna went up to her gate and stopped.

"Let me go," she murmured, trembling all over and seeing nothing before her in the darkness but his white tunic. "You're right: I'm a horrible woman. . . . I'm to blame, but let me go . . . I beg you." She touched his cold hand and shuddered. "I beseech you. . . ."

"Alas!" sighed Kirilin, "alas! it's not part of my plan to let you go; I only mean to give you a lesson and make you realise. And what's more, madam, I've too little faith in women."

"I'm miserable. . . ."

Nadyezhda Fyodorovna listened to the even splash of the sea, looked at the sky studded with stars, and longed to make haste and end it all, and get away from the cursed sensation of life, with its sea, stars, men, fever.

"Only not in my home," she said coldly. "Take me somewhere else."

"Come to Muridov's. That's better."

"Where's that?"

"Near the old wall."

She walked quickly along the street and then turned into the side-street that led towards the mountains. It was dark. There were pale streaks of light here and there on the pavement, from the lighted windows, and it seemed to her that, like a fly, she kept falling into the ink and crawling out into the light again. At one point he stumbled, almost fell down and burst out laughing.

"He's drunk," thought Nadyezhda Fyodorovna. "Never mind. . . . Never mind. . . . So be it."

Atchmianov, too, soon took leave of the party and followed Nadyezhda Fyodorovna to ask her to go for a row. He went to her house and looked over the fence: the windows were wide open, there were no lights.

"Nadyezhda Fyodorovna!" he called.

A moment passed, he called again.

"Who's there?" he heard Olga's voice.

"Is Nadyezhda Fyodorovna at home?"

"No, she has not come in yet."

"Strange . . . very strange," thought Atchmianov, feeling very uneasy. "She went home. . . ."

He walked along the boulevard, then along the street, and glanced in at the windows of Sheshkovsky's. Laevsky was sitting at the table without his coat on, looking attentively at his cards.

"Strange, strange," muttered Atchmianov, and remembering Laevsky's hysterics, he felt ashamed. "If she is not at home, where is she?"

He went to Nadyezhda Fyodorovna's lodgings again, and looked at the dark windows.

"It's a cheat, a cheat . . ." he thought, remembering that, meeting him at midday at Marya Konstantinovna's, she had promised to go in a boat with him that evening.

The windows of the house where Kirilin lived were dark, and there was a policeman sitting asleep on a little bench at the gate. Everything was clear to Atchmianov when he looked at the windows and the policeman. He made up his mind to go home, and set off in that direction, but somehow found himself near Nadyezhda Fyodorovna's lodgings again. He sat down on the bench near the gate and took off his hat, feeling that his head was burning with jealousy and resentment.

The clock in the town church only struck twice in the twenty-four hours—at midday and midnight. Soon after it struck midnight he heard hurried footsteps.

"To-morrow evening, then, again at Muridov's," Atchmianov heard, and he recognised Kirilin's voice. "At eight o'clock; good-bye!"

Nadyezhda Fyodorovna made her appearance near the garden. Without noticing that Atchmianov was sitting on the bench, she passed beside him like a shadow, opened the gate, and leaving it open, went into the house. In her own room she lighted the candle and quickly undressed, but instead of getting into bed, she sank on her knees before a chair, flung her arms round it, and rested her head on it.

It was past two when Laevsky came home.

XV

Having made up his mind to lie, not all at once but piecemeal, Laevsky went soon after one o'clock next day to Samoylenko to ask for the money that he might be sure to get off on Saturday. After his hysterical attack, which had added an acute feeling of shame to his depressed state of mind, it was unthinkable to remain in the town. If Samoylenko should insist on his conditions, he thought it would be possible to agree to them and take the money, and next day, just as he was starting, to say that Nadyezhda Fyodorovna refused to go. He would be able to persuade her that evening that the whole arrangement would be for her benefit. If Samoylenko, who was obviously under the influence of Von Koren, should refuse the money altogether or make fresh conditions, then he, Laevsky, would go off that very evening in a cargo vessel, or even in a sailing-boat, to Novy Athon or Novorossiisk, would send from there an humiliating telegram, and would stay there till his mother sent him the money for the journey.

When he went into Samoylenko's, he found Von Koren in the drawing-room. The zoologist had just arrived for dinner, and, as usual, was turning over the album and scrutinising the gentlemen in top-hats and the ladies in caps.

"How very unlucky!" thought Laevsky, seeing him. "He may be in the way. Good-morning."

"Good-morning," answered Von Koren, without looking at him.

"Is Alexandr Daviditch at home?"

"Yes, in the kitchen."

Laevsky went into the kitchen, but seeing from the door that Samoylenko was busy over the salad, he went back into the drawing-room and sat down. He always had a feeling of awkwardness in the zoologist's presence, and now he was afraid there would be talk about his attack of hysterics. There was more than a minute of silence. Von Koren suddenly raised his eyes to Laevsky and asked:

"How do you feel after yesterday?"

"Very well indeed," said Laevsky, flushing. "It really was nothing much. . . ."

"Until yesterday I thought it was only ladies who had hysterics, and so at first I thought you had St. Vitus's dance."

Laevsky smiled ingratiatingly, and thought:

"How indelicate on his part! He knows quite well how unpleasant it is for me. . . ."

"Yes, it was a ridiculous performance," he said, still smiling. "I've been laughing over it the whole morning. What's so curious in an attack of hysterics is that you know it is absurd, and are laughing at it in your heart, and at the same time you sob. In our neurotic age we are the slaves of our nerves; they are our masters and do as they like with us. Civilisation has done us a bad turn in that way. . . ."

As Laevsky talked, he felt it disagreeable that Von Koren listened to him gravely, and looked at him steadily and attentively as though studying him; and he was vexed with himself that in spite of his dislike of Von Koren, he could not banish the ingratiating smile from his face.

"I must admit, though," he added, "that there were immediate causes for the attack, and quite sufficient ones too. My health has been terribly shaky of late. To which one must add boredom, constantly being hard up . . . the absence of people and general interests . . . . My position is worse than a governor's."

"Yes, your position is a hopeless one," answered Von Koren.

These calm, cold words, implying something between a jeer and an uninvited prediction, offended Laevsky. He recalled the zoologist's eyes the evening before, full of mockery and disgust. He was silent for a space and then asked, no longer smiling:

"How do you know anything of my position?"

"You were only just speaking of it yourself. Besides, your friends take such a warm interest in you, that I am hearing about you all day long."

"What friends? Samoylenko, I suppose?"

"Yes, he too."

"I would ask Alexandr Daviditch and my friends in general not to trouble so much about me."

"Here is Samoylenko; you had better ask him not to trouble so much about you."

"I don't understand your tone," Laevsky muttered, suddenly feeling as though he had only just realised that the zoologist hated and despised him, and was jeering at him, and was his bitterest and most inveterate enemy.

"Keep that tone for some one else," he said softly, unable to speak aloud for the hatred with which his chest and throat were choking, as they had been the night before with laughter.

Samoylenko came in in his shirt-sleeves, crimson and perspiring from the stifling kitchen.

"Ah, you here?" he said. "Good-morning, my dear boy. Have you had dinner? Don't stand on ceremony. Have you had dinner?"

"Alexandr Daviditch," said Laevsky, standing up, "though I did appeal to you to help me in a private matter, it did not follow that I released you from the obligation of discretion and respect for other people's private affairs."

"What's this?" asked Samoylenko, in astonishment.

"If you have no money," Laevsky went on, raising his voice and shifting from one foot to the other in his excitement, "don't give it; refuse it. But why spread abroad in every back street that my position is hopeless, and all the rest of it? I can't endure such benevolence and friend's assistance where there's a shilling-worth of talk for a ha'p'orth of help! You can boast of your benevolence as much as you please, but no one has given you the right to gossip about my private affairs!"

"What private affairs?" asked Samoylenko, puzzled and beginning to be angry. "If you've come here to be abusive, you had better clear out. You can come again afterwards!"

He remembered the rule that when one is angry with one's neighbour, one must begin to count a hundred, and one will grow calm again; and he began rapidly counting.

"I beg you not to trouble yourself about me," Laevsky went on. "Don't pay any attention to me, and whose business is it what I do and how I live? Yes, I want to go away. Yes, I get into debt, I drink, I am living with another man's wife, I'm hysterical, I'm ordinary. I am not so profound as some people, but whose business is that? Respect other people's privacy."

"Excuse me, brother," said Samoylenko, who had counted up to thirty-five, "but . . . ."

"Respect other people's individuality!" interrupted Laevsky. "This continual gossip about other people's affairs, this sighing and groaning and everlasting prying, this eavesdropping, this friendly sympathy . . . damn it all! They lend me money and make conditions as though I were a schoolboy! I am treated as the devil knows what! I don't want anything," shouted Laevsky, staggering with excitement and afraid that it might end in another attack of hysterics. "I shan't get away on Saturday, then," flashed through his mind. "I want nothing. All I ask of you is to spare me your protecting care. I'm not a boy, and I'm not mad, and I beg you to leave off looking after me."

The deacon came in, and seeing Laevsky pale and gesticulating, addressing his strange speech to the portrait of Prince Vorontsov, stood still by the door as though petrified.

"This continual prying into my soul," Laevsky went on, "is insulting to my human dignity, and I beg these volunteer detectives to give up their spying! Enough!"

"What's that . . . what did you say?" said Samoylenko, who had counted up to a hundred. He turned crimson and went up to Laevsky.

"It's enough," said Laevsky, breathing hard and snatching up his cap.

"I'm a Russian doctor, a nobleman by birth, and a civil councillor," said Samoylenko emphatically. "I've never been a spy, and I allow no one to insult me!" he shouted in a breaking voice, emphasising the last word. "Hold your tongue!"

The deacon, who had never seen the doctor so majestic, so swelling with dignity, so crimson and so ferocious, shut his mouth, ran out into the entry and there exploded with laughter.

As though through a fog, Laevsky saw Von Koren get up and, putting his hands in his trouser-pockets, stand still in an attitude of expectancy, as though waiting to see what would happen. This calm attitude struck Laevsky as insolent and insulting to the last degree.

"Kindly take back your words," shouted Samoylenko.

Laevsky, who did not by now remember what his words were, answered:

"Leave me alone! I ask for nothing. All I ask is that you and German upstarts of Jewish origin should let me alone! Or I shall take steps to make you! I will fight you!"

"Now we understand," said Von Koren, coming from behind the table.
"Mr. Laevsky wants to amuse himself with a duel before he goes away.
I can give him that pleasure. Mr. Laevsky, I accept your challenge."
"A challenge," said Laevsky, in a low voice, going up to the zoologist and looking with hatred at his swarthy brow and curly hair. "A challenge? By all means! I hate you! I hate you!"

"Delighted. To-morrow morning early near Kerbalay's. I leave all details to your taste. And now, clear out!"

"I hate you," Laevsky said softly, breathing hard. "I have hated you a long while! A duel! Yes!"

"Get rid of him, Alexandr Daviditch, or else I'm going," said Von Koren. "He'll bite me."

Von Koren's cool tone calmed the doctor; he seemed suddenly to come to himself, to recover his reason; he put both arms round Laevsky's waist, and, leading him away from the zoologist, muttered in a friendly voice that shook with emotion:

"My friends . . . dear, good . . . you've lost your tempers and that's enough . . . and that's enough, my friends."

Hearing his soft, friendly voice, Laevsky felt that something unheard of, monstrous, had just happened to him, as though he had been nearly run over by a train; he almost burst into tears, waved his hand, and ran out of the room.

"To feel that one is hated, to expose oneself before the man who hates one, in the most pitiful, contemptible, helpless state. My God, how hard it is!" he thought a little while afterwards as he sat in the pavilion, feeling as though his body were scarred by the hatred of which he had just been the object.

"How coarse it is, my God!"

Cold water with brandy in it revived him. He vividly pictured Von Koren's calm, haughty face; his eyes the day before, his shirt like a rug, his voice, his white hand; and heavy, passionate, hungry hatred rankled in his breast and clamoured for satisfaction. In his thoughts he felled Von Koren to the ground, and trampled him underfoot. He remembered to the minutest detail all that had happened, and wondered how he could have smiled ingratiatingly to that insignificant man, and how he could care for the opinion of wretched petty people whom nobody knew, living in a miserable little town which was not, it seemed, even on the map, and of which not one decent person in Petersburg had heard. If this wretched little town suddenly fell into ruins or caught fire, the telegram with the news would be read in Russia with no more interest than an advertisement of the sale of second-hand furniture. Whether he killed Von Koren next day or left him alive, it would be just the same, equally useless and uninteresting. Better to shoot him in the leg or hand, wound him, then laugh at him, and let him, like an insect with a broken leg lost in the grass—let him be lost with his obscure sufferings in the crowd of insignificant people like himself.

Laevsky went to Sheshkovsky, told him all about it, and asked him to be his second; then they both went to the superintendent of the postal telegraph department, and asked him, too, to be a second, and stayed to dinner with him. At dinner there was a great deal of joking and laughing. Laevsky made jests at his own expense, saying he hardly knew how to fire off a pistol, calling himself a royal archer and William Tell.

"We must give this gentleman a lesson . . ." he said.

After dinner they sat down to cards. Laevsky played, drank wine, and thought that duelling was stupid and senseless, as it did not decide the question but only complicated it, but that it was sometimes impossible to get on without it. In the given case, for instance, one could not, of course, bring an action against Von Koren. And this duel was so far good in that it made it impossible for Laevsky to remain in the town afterwards. He got a little drunk and interested in the game, and felt at ease.

But when the sun had set and it grew dark, he was possessed by a feeling of uneasiness. It was not fear at the thought of death, because while he was dining and playing cards, he had for some reason a confident belief that the duel would end in nothing; it was dread at the thought of something unknown which was to happen next morning for the first time in his life, and dread of the coming night. . . . He knew that the night would be long and sleepless, and that he would have to think not only of Von Koren and his hatred, but also of the mountain of lies which he had to get through, and which he had not strength or ability to dispense with. It was as though he had been taken suddenly ill; all at once he lost all interest in the cards and in people, grew restless, and began asking them to let him go home. He was eager to get into bed, to lie without moving, and to prepare his thoughts for the night. Sheshkovsky and the postal superintendent saw him home and went on to Von Koren's to arrange about the duel.

Near his lodgings Laevsky met Atchmianov. The young man was breathless and excited.

"I am looking for you, Ivan Andreitch," he said. "I beg you to come quickly. . . ."

"Where?"

"Some one wants to see you, some one you don't know, about very important business; he earnestly begs you to come for a minute. He wants to speak to you of something. . . . For him it's a question of life and death. . . ." In his excitement Atchmianov spoke in a strong Armenian accent.

"Who is it?" asked Laevsky.

"He asked me not to tell you his name."

"Tell him I'm busy; to-morrow, if he likes. . . ."

"How can you!" Atchmianov was aghast. "He wants to tell you something very important for you . . . very important! If you don't come, something dreadful will happen."

"Strange . . ." muttered Laevsky, unable to understand why Atchmianov was so excited and what mysteries there could be in this dull, useless little town.

"Strange," he repeated in hesitation. "Come along, though; I don't care."

Atchmianov walked rapidly on ahead and Laevsky followed him. They walked down a street, then turned into an alley.

"What a bore this is!" said Laevsky.

"One minute, one minute . . . it's near."

Near the old rampart they went down a narrow alley between two empty enclosures, then they came into a sort of large yard and went towards a small house.

"That's Muridov's, isn't it?" asked Laevsky.

"Yes."

"But why we've come by the back yards I don't understand. We might have come by the street; it's nearer. . . ."

"Never mind, never mind. . . ."

It struck Laevsky as strange, too, that Atchmianov led him to a back entrance, and motioned to him as though bidding him go quietly and hold his tongue.

"This way, this way . . ." said Atchmianov, cautiously opening the door and going into the passage on tiptoe. "Quietly, quietly, I beg you . . . they may hear."

He listened, drew a deep breath and said in a whisper:

"Open that door, and go in . . . don't be afraid."

Laevsky, puzzled, opened the door and went into a room with a low ceiling and curtained windows.

There was a candle on the table.

"What do you want?" asked some one in the next room. "Is it you, Muridov?"

Laevsky turned into that room and saw Kirilin, and beside him Nadyezhda Fyodorovna.

He didn't hear what was said to him; he staggered back, and did not know how he found himself in the street. His hatred for Von Koren and his uneasiness—all had vanished from his soul. As he went home he waved his right arm awkwardly and looked carefully at the ground under his feet, trying to step where it was smooth. At home in his study he walked backwards and forwards, rubbing his hands, and awkwardly shrugging his shoulders and neck, as though his jacket and shirt were too tight; then he lighted a candle and sat down to the table. . . .

XVI

"The 'humane studies' of which you speak will only satisfy human thought when, as they advance, they meet the exact sciences and progress side by side with them. Whether they will meet under a new microscope, or in the monologues of a new Hamlet, or in a new religion, I do not know, but I expect the earth will be covered with a crust of ice before it comes to pass. Of all humane learning the most durable and living is, of course, the teaching of Christ; but look how differently even that is interpreted! Some teach that we must love all our neighbours but make an exception of soldiers, criminals, and lunatics. They allow the first to be killed in war, the second to be isolated or executed, and the third they forbid to marry. Other interpreters teach that we must love all our neighbours without exception, with no distinction of *plus* or *minus*. According to their teaching, if a consumptive or a murderer or an epileptic asks your daughter in marriage, you must let him have her. If *cretins* go to war against the physically and mentally healthy, don't defend yourselves. This advocacy of love for love's sake, like art for art's sake, if it could have power, would bring mankind in the long run to complete extinction, and so would become the vastest crime that has ever been committed upon earth. There are very many interpretations, and since there are many of them, serious thought is not satisfied by any one of them, and hastens to add its own individual interpretation to the mass. For that reason you should never put a question on a philosophical or so-called Christian basis; by so doing you only remove the question further from solution."

The deacon listened to the zoologist attentively, thought a little, and asked:

"Have the philosophers invented the moral law which is innate in every man, or did God create it together with the body?"

"I don't know. But that law is so universal among all peoples and all ages that I fancy we ought to recognise it as organically connected with man. It is not invented, but exists and will exist. I don't tell you that one day it will be seen under the microscope, but its organic connection is shown, indeed, by evidence: serious affections of the brain and all so-called mental diseases, to the best of my belief, show themselves first of all in the perversion of the moral law."

"Good. So then, just as our stomach bids us eat, our moral sense bids us love our neighbours. Is that it? But our natural man through self-love opposes the voice of conscience and reason, and this gives rise to many brain-racking questions. To whom ought we to turn for the solution of those questions if you forbid us to put them on the philosophic basis?"

"Turn to what little exact science we have. Trust to evidence and the logic of facts. It is true it is but little, but, on the other hand, it is less fluid and shifting than philosophy. The moral law, let us suppose, demands that you love your neighbour. Well? Love ought to show itself in the removal of everything which in one way or another is injurious to men and threatens them with danger in the present or in the future. Our knowledge and the evidence tells us that the morally and physically abnormal are a menace to humanity. If so you must struggle against the abnormal; if you are not able to raise them to the normal standard you must have strength and ability to render them harmless—that is, to destroy them."

"So love consists in the strong overcoming the weak."

"Undoubtedly."

"But you know the strong crucified our Lord Jesus Christ," said the deacon hotly.

"The fact is that those who crucified Him were not the strong but the weak. Human culture weakens and strives to nullify the struggle for existence and natural selection; hence the rapid advancement of the weak and their predominance over the strong. Imagine that you succeeded in instilling into bees humanitarian ideas in their crude and elementary form. What would come of it? The drones who ought to be killed would remain alive, would devour the honey, would corrupt and stifle the bees, resulting in the predominance of the weak over the strong and the degeneration of the latter. The same process is taking place now with humanity; the weak are oppressing the strong. Among savages untouched by civilisation the strongest, cleverest, and most moral takes the lead; he is the chief and the master. But we civilised men have crucified Christ, and we go on crucifying Him, so there is something lacking in us. . . . And that something one ought to raise up in ourselves, or there will be no end to these errors."

"But what criterion have you to distinguish the strong from the weak?"

"Knowledge and evidence. The tuberculous and the scrofulous are recognised by their diseases, and the insane and the immoral by their actions."

"But mistakes may be made!"

"Yes, but it's no use to be afraid of getting your feet wet when you are threatened with the deluge!"

"That's philosophy," laughed the deacon.

"Not a bit of it. You are so corrupted by your seminary philosophy that you want to see nothing but fog in everything. The abstract studies with which your youthful head is stuffed are called abstract just because they abstract your minds from what is obvious. Look the devil straight in the eye, and if he's the devil, tell him he's the devil, and don't go calling to Kant or Hegel for explanations."

The zoologist paused and went on:

"Twice two's four, and a stone's a stone. Here to-morrow we have a duel. You and I will say it's stupid and absurd, that the duel is out of date, that there is no real difference between the aristocratic duel and the drunken brawl in the pot-house, and yet we shall not stop, we shall go there and fight. So there is some force stronger than our reasoning. We shout that war is plunder, robbery, atrocity, fratricide; we cannot look upon blood without fainting; but the French or the Germans have only to insult us for us to feel at once an exaltation of spirit; in the most genuine way we shout 'Hurrah!' and rush to attack the foe. You will invoke the blessing of God on our weapons, and our valour will arouse universal and general enthusiasm. Again it follows that there is a force, if not higher, at any rate stronger, than us and our philosophy. We can no more stop it than that cloud which is moving upwards over the sea. Don't be hypocritical, don't make a long nose at it on the sly; and don't say, 'Ah, old-fashioned, stupid! Ah, it's inconsistent with Scripture!' but look it straight in the face, recognise its rational lawfulness, and when, for instance, it wants to destroy a rotten, scrofulous, corrupt race, don't hinder it with your pilules and misunderstood quotations from the Gospel. Leskov has a story of a conscientious Danila who found a leper outside the town, and fed and warmed him in the name of love and of Christ. If that Danila had really loved humanity, he would have dragged the leper as far as possible from the town, and would have flung him in a pit, and would have gone to save the healthy. Christ, I hope, taught us a rational, intelligent, practical love."

"What a fellow you are!" laughed the deacon. "You don't believe in Christ. Why do you mention His name so often?"

"Yes, I do believe in Him. Only, of course, in my own way, not in yours. Oh, deacon, deacon!" laughed the zoologist; he put his arm round the deacon's waist, and said gaily: "Well? Are you coming with us to the duel to-morrow?"

"My orders don't allow it, or else I should come."

"What do you mean by 'orders'?"

"I have been consecrated. I am in a state of grace."

"Oh, deacon, deacon," repeated Von Koren, laughing, "I love talking to you."

"You say you have faith," said the deacon. "What sort of faith is it? Why, I have an uncle, a priest, and he believes so that when in time of drought he goes out into the fields to pray for rain, he takes his umbrella and leather overcoat for fear of getting wet through on his way home. That's faith! When he speaks of Christ, his face is full of radiance, and all the peasants, men and women, weep floods of tears. He would stop that cloud and put all those forces you talk about to flight. Yes . . . faith moves mountains."

The deacon laughed and slapped the zoologist on the shoulder.

"Yes . . ." he went on; "here you are teaching all the time, fathoming the depths of the ocean, dividing the weak and the strong, writing books and challenging to duels—and everything remains as it is; but, behold! some feeble old man will mutter just one word with a holy spirit, or a new Mahomet, with a sword, will gallop from Arabia, and everything will be topsy-turvy, and in Europe not one stone will be left standing upon another."

"Well, deacon, that's on the knees of the gods."

"Faith without works is dead, but works without faith are worse still—mere waste of time and nothing more."

The doctor came into sight on the sea-front. He saw the deacon and the zoologist, and went up to them.

"I believe everything is ready," he said, breathing hard. "Govorovsky and Boyko will be the seconds. They will start at five o'clock in the morning. How it has clouded over," he said, looking at the sky. "One can see nothing; there will be rain directly."

"I hope you are coming with us?" said the zoologist.

"No, God preserve me; I'm worried enough as it is. Ustimovitch is going instead of me. I've spoken to him already."

Far over the sea was a flash of lightning, followed by a hollow roll of thunder.

"How stifling it is before a storm!" said Von Koren. "I bet you've been to Laevsky already and have been weeping on his bosom."

"Why should I go to him?" answered the doctor in confusion. "What next?"

Before sunset he had walked several times along the boulevard and the street in the hope of meeting Laevsky. He was ashamed of his hastiness and the sudden outburst of friendliness which had followed it. He wanted to apologise to Laevsky in a joking tone, to give him a good talking to, to soothe him and to tell him that the duel was a survival of mediaeval barbarism, but that Providence itself had brought them to the duel as a means of reconciliation; that the next day, both being splendid and highly intelligent people, they would, after exchanging shots, appreciate each other's noble qualities and would become friends. But he could not come across Laevsky.

"What should I go and see him for?" repeated Samoylenko. "I did not insult him; he insulted me. Tell me, please, why he attacked me. What harm had I done him? I go into the drawing-room, and, all of a sudden, without the least provocation: 'Spy!' There's a nice thing! Tell me, how did it begin? What did you say to him?"

"I told him his position was hopeless. And I was right. It is only honest men or scoundrels who can find an escape from any position, but one who wants to be at the same time an honest man and a scoundrel, it is a hopeless position. But it's eleven o'clock, gentlemen, and we have to be up early to-morrow."

There was a sudden gust of wind; it blew up the dust on the sea-front, whirled it round in eddies, with a howl that drowned the roar of the sea.

"A squall," said the deacon. "We must go in, our eyes are getting full of dust."

As they went, Samoylenko sighed and, holding his hat, said:

"I suppose I shan't sleep to-night."

"Don't you agitate yourself," laughed the zoologist. "You can set your mind at rest; the duel will end in nothing. Laevsky will magnanimously fire into the air—he can do nothing else; and I daresay I shall not fire at all. To be arrested and lose my time on Laevsky's account—the game's not worth the candle. By the way, what is the punishment for duelling?"

"Arrest, and in the case of the death of your opponent a maximum of three years' imprisonment in the fortress."

"The fortress of St. Peter and St. Paul?"

"No, in a military fortress, I believe."

"Though this fine gentleman ought to have a lesson!"

Behind them on the sea, there was a flash of lightning, which for an instant lighted up the roofs of the houses and the mountains. The friends parted near the boulevard. When the doctor disappeared in the darkness and his steps had died away, Von Koren shouted to him:

"I only hope the weather won't interfere with us to-morrow!"

"Very likely it will! Please God it may!"

"Good-night!"

"What about the night? What do you say?"

In the roar of the wind and the sea and the crashes of thunder, it was difficult to hear.

"It's nothing," shouted the zoologist, and hurried home.

XVII

"Upon my mind, weighed down with woe, Crowd thoughts, a heavy multitude:

In silence memory unfolds
Her long, long scroll before my eyes.
Loathing and shuddering I curse
And bitterly lament in vain,
And bitter though the tears I weep
I do not wash those lines away."

PUSHKIN.

Whether they killed him next morning, or mocked at him—that is, left him his life—he was ruined, anyway. Whether this disgraced woman killed herself in her shame and despair, or dragged on her pitiful existence, she was ruined anyway.

So thought Laevsky as he sat at the table late in the evening, still rubbing his hands. The windows suddenly blew open with a bang; a violent gust of wind burst into the room, and the papers fluttered from the table. Laevsky closed the windows and bent down to pick up the papers. He was aware of something new in his body, a sort of awkwardness he had not felt before, and his movements were strange to him. He moved timidly, jerking with his elbows and shrugging his shoulders; and when he sat down to the table again, he again began rubbing his hands. His body had lost its suppleness.

On the eve of death one ought to write to one's nearest relation. Laevsky thought of this. He took a pen and wrote with a tremulous hand:

"Mother!"

He wanted to write to beg his mother, for the sake of the merciful God in whom she believed, that she would give shelter and bring a little warmth and kindness into the life of the unhappy woman who, by his doing, had been disgraced and was in solitude, poverty, and weakness, that she would forgive and forget everything, everything, everything, and by her sacrifice atone to some extent for her son's terrible sin. But he remembered how his mother, a stout, heavily-built old woman in a lace cap, used to go out into the garden in the morning, followed by her companion with the lap-dog; how she used to shout in a peremptory way to the gardener and the servants, and how proud and haughty her face was—he remembered all this and scratched out the word he had written.

There was a vivid flash of lightning at all three windows, and it was followed by a prolonged, deafening roll of thunder, beginning with a hollow rumble and ending with a crash so violent that all the window-panes rattled. Laevsky got up, went to the window, and pressed his forehead against the pane. There was a fierce, magnificent storm. On the horizon lightning-flashes were flung in white streams from the storm-clouds into the sea, lighting up the high, dark waves over the far-away expanse. And to right and to left, and, no doubt, over the house too, the lightning flashed.

"The storm!" whispered Laevsky; he had a longing to pray to some one or to something, if only to the lightning or the storm-clouds. "Dear storm!"

He remembered how as a boy he used to run out into the garden without a hat on when there was a storm, and how two fair-haired girls with blue eyes used to run after him, and how they got wet through with the rain; they laughed with delight, but when there was a loud peal of thunder, the girls used to nestle up to the boy confidingly, while he crossed himself and made haste to repeat: "Holy, holy, holy. . . ." Oh, where had they vanished to! In what sea were they drowned, those dawning days of pure, fair life? He had no fear of the storm, no love of nature now; he had no God. All the confiding girls he had ever known had by now been ruined by him and those like him. All his life he had not planted one tree in his own garden, nor grown one blade of grass; and living among the living, he had not saved one fly; he had done nothing but destroy and ruin, and lie, lie. . . .

"What in my past was not vice?" he asked himself, trying to clutch at some bright memory as a man falling down a precipice clutches at the bushes.

School? The university? But that was a sham. He had neglected his work and forgotten what he had learnt. The service of his country? That, too, was a sham, for he did nothing in the Service, took a salary for doing nothing, and it was an abominable swindling of the State for which one was not punished.

He had no craving for truth, and had not sought it; spellbound by vice and lying, his conscience had slept or been silent. Like a stranger, like an alien from another planet, he had taken no part in the common life of men, had been indifferent to their sufferings, their ideas, their religion, their sciences, their strivings, and their struggles. He had not said one good word, not written one line that was not useless and vulgar; he had not done his fellows one ha'p'orth of service, but had eaten their bread, drunk their wine, seduced their wives, lived on their thoughts, and to justify his contemptible, parasitic life in their eyes and in his own, he had always tried to assume an air of being higher and better than they. Lies, lies, lies. . . .

He vividly remembered what he had seen that evening at Muridov's, and he was in an insufferable anguish of loathing and misery. Kirilin and Atchmianov were loathsome, but they were only continuing what he had begun; they were his accomplices and his disciples. This young weak woman had trusted him more than a brother, and he had deprived her of her husband, of her friends and of her country, and had brought her here—to the heat, to fever, and to boredom; and from day to day she was bound to reflect, like a mirror, his idleness, his viciousness and falsity—and that was all she had had to fill her weak, listless, pitiable life. Then he had grown sick of her, had begun to hate her, but had not had the pluck to abandon her, and he had tried to entangle her more and more closely in a web of lies. . . . These men had done the rest.

Laevsky sat at the table, then got up and went to the window; at one minute he put out the candle and then he lighted it again. He cursed himself aloud, wept and wailed, and asked forgiveness; several times he ran to the table in despair, and wrote:

"Mother!"

Except his mother, he had no relations or near friends; but how could his mother help him? And where was she? He had an impulse to run to Nadyezhda Fyodorovna, to fall at her feet, to kiss her hands and feet, to beg her forgiveness; but she was his victim, and he was afraid of her as though she were dead.

"My life is ruined," he repeated, rubbing his hands. "Why am I still alive, my God!"

He had cast out of heaven his dim star; it had fallen, and its track was lost in the darkness of night. It would never return to the sky again, because life was given only once and never came a second time. If he could have turned back the days and years of the past, he would have replaced the falsity with truth, the idleness with work, the boredom with happiness; he would have given back purity to those whom he had robbed of it. He would have found God and goodness, but that was as impossible as to put back the fallen star into the sky, and because it was impossible he was in despair.

When the storm was over, he sat by the open window and thought calmly of what was before him. Von Koren would most likely kill him. The man's clear, cold theory of life justified the destruction of the rotten and the useless; if it changed at the crucial moment, it would be the hatred and the repugnance that Laevsky inspired in him that would save him. If he missed his aim or, in mockery of his hated opponent, only wounded him, or fired in the air, what could he do then? Where could he go?

"Go to Petersburg?" Laevsky asked himself. But that would mean beginning over again the old life which he cursed. And the man who seeks salvation in change of place like a migrating bird would find nothing anywhere, for all the world is alike to him. Seek salvation in men? In whom and how? Samoylenko's kindness and generosity could no more save him than the deacon's laughter or Von Koren's hatred. He must look for salvation in himself alone, and if there were no finding it, why waste time? He must kill himself, that was all. . . .

He heard the sound of a carriage. It was getting light. The carriage passed by, turned, and crunching on the wet sand, stopped near the house. There were two men in the carriage.

"Wait a minute; I'm coming directly," Laevsky said to them out of the window. "I'm not asleep. Surely it's not time yet?"

"Yes, it's four o'clock. By the time we get there . . . ."

Laevsky put on his overcoat and cap, put some cigarettes in his pocket, and stood still hesitating. He felt as though there was something else he must do. In the street the seconds talked in low voices and the horses snorted, and this sound in the damp, early morning, when everybody was asleep and light was hardly dawning in the sky, filled Laevsky's soul with a disconsolate feeling which was like a presentiment of evil. He stood for a little, hesitating, and went into the bedroom.

Nadyezhda Fyodorovna was lying stretched out on the bed, wrapped from head to foot in a rug. She did not stir, and her whole appearance, especially her head, suggested an Egyptian mummy. Looking at her in silence, Laevsky mentally asked her forgiveness, and thought that if the heavens were not empty and there really were a God, then He would save her; if there were no God, then she had better perish—there was nothing for her to live for.

All at once she jumped up, and sat up in bed. Lifting her pale face and looking with horror at Laevsky, she asked:

"Is it you? Is the storm over?"

"Yes."

She remembered; put both hands to her head and shuddered all over.

"How miserable I am!" she said. "If only you knew how miserable I am! I expected," she went on, half closing her eyes, "that you would kill me or turn me out of the house into the rain and storm, but you delay . . . delay . . ."

Warmly and impulsively he put his arms round her and covered her knees and hands with kisses. Then when she muttered something and shuddered with the thought of the past, he stroked her hair, and looking into her face, realised that this unhappy, sinful woman was the one creature near and dear to him, whom no one could replace.

When he went out of the house and got into the carriage he wanted to return home alive.

XVIII

The deacon got up, dressed, took his thick, gnarled stick and slipped quietly out of the house. It was dark, and for the first minute when he went into the street, he could not even see his white stick. There was not a single star in the sky, and it looked as though there would be rain again. There was a smell of wet sand and sea.

"It's to be hoped that the mountaineers won't attack us," thought the deacon, hearing the tap of the stick on the pavement, and noticing how loud and lonely the taps sounded in the stillness of the night.

When he got out of town, he began to see both the road and his stick. Here and there in the black sky there were dark cloudy patches, and soon a star peeped out and timidly blinked its one eye. The deacon walked along the high rocky coast and did not see the sea; it was slumbering below, and its unseen waves broke languidly and heavily on the shore, as though sighing "Ouf!" and how slowly! One wave broke— the deacon had time to count eight steps; then another broke, and six steps; later a third. As before, nothing could be seen, and in the darkness one could hear the languid, drowsy drone of the sea. One could hear the infinitely faraway, inconceivable time when God moved above chaos.

The deacon felt uncanny. He hoped God would not punish him for keeping company with infidels, and even going to look at their duels. The duel would be nonsensical, bloodless, absurd, but however that might be, it was a heathen spectacle, and it was altogether unseemly for an ecclesiastical person to be present at it. He stopped and wondered—should he go back? But an intense, restless curiosity triumphed over his doubts, and he went on.

"Though they are infidels they are good people, and will be saved," he assured himself. "They are sure to be saved," he said aloud, lighting a cigarette.

By what standard must one measure men's qualities, to judge rightly of them? The deacon remembered his enemy, the inspector of the clerical school, who believed in God, lived in chastity, and did not fight duels; but he used to feed the deacon on bread with sand in it, and on one occasion almost pulled off the deacon's ear. If human life was so artlessly constructed that every one respected this cruel and dishonest inspector who stole the Government flour, and his health and salvation were prayed for in the schools, was it just to shun such men as Von Koren and Laevsky, simply because they were unbelievers? The deacon was weighing this question, but he recalled how absurd Samoylenko had looked yesterday, and that broke the thread of his ideas. What fun they would have next day! The deacon imagined how he would sit under a bush and look on, and when Von Koren began boasting next day at dinner, he, the deacon, would begin laughing and telling him all the details of the duel.

"How do you know all about it?" the zoologist would ask.

"Well, there you are! I stayed at home, but I know all about it."

It would be nice to write a comic description of the duel. His father-in-law would read it and laugh. A good story, told or written, was more than meat and drink to his father-in-law.

The valley of the Yellow River opened before him. The stream was broader and fiercer for the rain, and instead of murmuring as before, it was raging. It began to get light. The grey, dingy morning, and the clouds racing towards the west to overtake the storm-clouds, the mountains girt with mist, and the wet trees, all struck the deacon as ugly and sinister. He washed at the brook, repeated his morning prayer, and felt a longing for tea and hot rolls, with sour cream, which were served every morning at his father-in-law's. He remembered his wife and the "Days past Recall," which she played on the piano. What sort of woman was she? His wife had been introduced, betrothed, and married to him all in one week: he had lived with her less than a month when he was ordered here, so that he had not had time to find out what she was like. All the same, he rather missed her.

"I must write her a nice letter . . ." he thought. The flag on the *duhan* hung limp, soaked by the rain, and the *duhan* itself with its wet roof seemed darker and lower than it had been before. Near the door was standing a cart; Kerbalay, with two mountaineers and a young Tatar woman in trousers—no doubt Kerbalay's wife or daughter—were bringing sacks of something out of the *duhan*, and putting them on maize straw in the cart.

Near the cart stood a pair of asses hanging their heads. When they had put in all the sacks, the mountaineers and the Tatar woman began covering them over with straw, while Kerbalay began hurriedly harnessing the asses.

"Smuggling, perhaps," thought the deacon.

Here was the fallen tree with the dried pine-needles, here was the blackened patch from the fire. He remembered the picnic and all its incidents, the fire, the singing of the mountaineers, his sweet dreams of becoming a bishop, and of the Church procession. . . . The Black River had grown blacker and broader with the rain. The deacon walked cautiously over the narrow bridge, which by now was reached by the topmost crests of the dirty water, and went up through the little copse to the drying-shed.

"A splendid head," he thought, stretching himself on the straw, and thinking of Von Koren. "A fine head—God grant him health; only there is cruelty in him. . . ."

Why did he hate Laevsky and Laevsky hate him? Why were they going to fight a duel? If from their childhood they had known poverty as the deacon had; if they had been brought up among ignorant, hard-hearted, grasping, coarse and ill-mannered people who grudged you a crust of bread, who spat on the floor and hiccoughed at dinner and at prayers; if they had not been spoilt from childhood by the pleasant surroundings and the select circle of friends they lived in—how they would have rushed at each other, how readily they would have overlooked each other's shortcomings and would have prized each other's strong points! Why, how few even outwardly decent people there were in the world! It was true that Laevsky was flighty, dissipated, queer, but he did not steal, did not spit loudly on the floor; he did not abuse his wife and say, "You'll eat till you burst, but you don't want to work;" he would not beat a child with reins, or give his servants stinking meat to eat— surely this was reason enough to be indulgent to him? Besides, he was the chief sufferer from his failings, like a sick man from his sores. Instead of being led by boredom and some sort of misunderstanding to look for degeneracy, extinction, heredity, and other such incomprehensible things in each other, would they not do better to stoop a little lower and turn their hatred and anger where whole streets resounded with moanings from coarse ignorance, greed, scolding, impurity, swearing, the shrieks of women. . . .

The sound of a carriage interrupted the deacon's thoughts. He glanced out of the door and saw a carriage and in it three persons: Laevsky, Sheshkovsky, and the superintendent of the post-office.

"Stop!" said Sheshkovsky.

All three got out of the carriage and looked at one another.

"They are not here yet," said Sheshkovsky, shaking the mud off. "Well? Till the show begins, let us go and find a suitable spot; there's not room to turn round here."

They went further up the river and soon vanished from sight. The Tatar driver sat in the carriage with his head resting on his shoulder and fell asleep. After waiting ten minutes the deacon came out of the drying-shed, and taking off his black hat that he might not be noticed, he began threading his way among the bushes and strips of maize along the bank, crouching and looking about him. The grass and maize were wet, and big drops fell on his head from the trees and bushes. "Disgraceful!" he muttered, picking up his wet and muddy skirt. "Had I realised it, I would not have come."

Soon he heard voices and caught sight of them. Laevsky was walking rapidly to and fro in the small glade with bowed back and hands thrust in his sleeves; his seconds were standing at the water's edge, rolling cigarettes.

"Strange," thought the deacon, not recognising Laevsky's walk; "he looks like an old man. . . ."

"How rude it is of them!" said the superintendent of the post-office, looking at his watch. "It may be learned manners to be late, but to my thinking it's hoggish."

Sheshkovsky, a stout man with a black beard, listened and said:

"They're coming!"

XIX

"It's the first time in my life I've seen it! How glorious!" said Von Koren, pointing to the glade and stretching out his hands to the east. "Look: green rays!"

In the east behind the mountains rose two green streaks of light, and it really was beautiful. The sun was rising.

"Good-morning!" the zoologist went on, nodding to Laevsky's seconds.

"I'm not late, am I?"

He was followed by his seconds, Boyko and Govorovsky, two very young officers of the same height, wearing white tunics, and Ustimovitch, the thin, unsociable doctor; in one hand he had a bag of some sort, and in the other hand, as usual, a cane which he held behind him. Laying the bag on the ground and greeting no one, he put the other hand, too, behind his back and began pacing up and down the glade.

Laevsky felt the exhaustion and awkwardness of a man who is soon perhaps to die, and is for that reason an object of general attention. He wanted to be killed as soon as possible or taken home. He saw the sunrise now for the first time in his life; the early morning, the green rays of light, the dampness, and the men in wet boots, seemed to him to have nothing to do with his life, to be superfluous and embarrassing. All this had no connection with the night he had been through, with his thoughts and his feeling of guilt, and so he would have gladly gone away without waiting for the duel.

Von Koren was noticeably excited and tried to conceal it, pretending that he was more interested in the green light than anything. The seconds were confused, and looked at one another as though wondering why they were here and what they were to do.

"I imagine, gentlemen, there is no need for us to go further," said Sheshkovsky. "This place will do."

"Yes, of course," Von Koren agreed.

A silence followed. Ustimovitch, pacing to and fro, suddenly turned sharply to Laevsky and said in a low voice, breathing into his face:

"They have very likely not told you my terms yet. Each side is to pay me fifteen roubles, and in the case of the death of one party, the survivor is to pay thirty."

Laevsky was already acquainted with the man, but now for the first time he had a distinct view of his lustreless eyes, his stiff moustaches, and wasted, consumptive neck; he was a money-grubber, not a doctor; his breath had an unpleasant smell of beef.

"What people there are in the world!" thought Laevsky, and answered:

"Very good."

The doctor nodded and began pacing to and fro again, and it was evident he did not need the money at all, but simply asked for it from hatred. Every one felt it was time to begin, or to end what had been begun, but instead of beginning or ending, they stood about, moved to and fro and smoked. The young officers, who were present at a duel for the first time in their lives, and even now hardly believed in this civilian and, to their thinking, unnecessary duel, looked critically at their tunics and stroked their sleeves. Sheshkovsky went up to them and said softly: "Gentlemen, we must use every effort to prevent this duel; they ought to be reconciled."

He flushed crimson and added:

"Kirilin was at my rooms last night complaining that Laevsky had found him with Nadyezhda Fyodorovna, and all that sort of thing."

"Yes, we know that too," said Boyko.

"Well, you see, then . . . Laevsky's hands are trembling and all that sort of thing . . . he can scarcely hold a pistol now. To fight with him is as inhuman as to fight a man who is drunk or who has typhoid. If a reconciliation cannot be arranged, we ought to put off the duel, gentlemen, or something. . . . It's such a sickening business, I can't bear to see it.

"Talk to Von Koren."

"I don't know the rules of duelling, damnation take them, and I don't want to either; perhaps he'll imagine Laevsky funks it and has sent me to him, but he can think what he likes—I'll speak to him."

Sheshkovsky hesitatingly walked up to Von Koren with a slight limp, as though his leg had gone to sleep; and as he went towards him, clearing his throat, his whole figure was a picture of indolence.

"There's something I must say to you, sir," he began, carefully scrutinising the flowers on the zoologist's shirt. "It's confidential. I don't know the rules of duelling, damnation take them, and I don't want to, and I look on the matter not as a second and that sort of thing, but as a man, and that's all about it."

"Yes. Well?"

"When seconds suggest reconciliation they are usually not listened to; it is looked upon as a formality. *Amour propre* and all that. But I humbly beg you to look carefully at Ivan Andreitch. He's not in a normal state, so to speak, to-day—not in his right mind, and a pitiable object. He has had a misfortune. I can't endure gossip. . . ."

Sheshkovsky flushed crimson and looked round.

"But in view of the duel, I think it necessary to inform you, Laevsky found his madam last night at Muridov's with . . . another gentleman."

"How disgusting!" muttered the zoologist; he turned pale, frowned, and spat loudly. "Tfoo!"

His lower lip quivered, he walked away from Sheshkovsky, unwilling to hear more, and as though he had accidentally tasted something bitter, spat loudly again, and for the first time that morning looked with hatred at Laevsky. His excitement and awkwardness passed off; he tossed his head and said aloud:

"Gentlemen, what are we waiting for, I should like to know? Why don't we begin?"

Sheshkovsky glanced at the officers and shrugged his shoulders.

"Gentlemen," he said aloud, addressing no one in particular.

"Gentlemen, we propose that you should be reconciled."

"Let us make haste and get the formalities over," said Von Koren. "Reconciliation has been discussed already. What is the next formality? Make haste, gentlemen, time won't wait for us."

"But we insist on reconciliation all the same," said Sheshkovsky in a guilty voice, as a man compelled to interfere in another man's business; he flushed, laid his hand on his heart, and went on:

"Gentlemen, we see no grounds for associating the offence with the duel. There's nothing in common between duelling and offences against one another of which we are sometimes guilty through human weakness. You are university men and men of culture, and no doubt you see in the duel nothing but a foolish and out-of-date formality, and all that sort of thing. That's how we look at it ourselves, or we shouldn't have come, for we cannot allow that in our presence men should fire at one another, and all that." Sheshkovsky wiped the perspiration off his face and went on: "Make an end to your misunderstanding, gentlemen; shake hands, and let us go home and drink to peace. Upon my honour, gentlemen!"

Von Koren did not speak. Laevsky, seeing that they were looking at him, said:

"I have nothing against Nikolay Vassilitch; if he considers I'm to blame, I'm ready to apologise to him."

Von Koren was offended.

"It is evident, gentlemen," he said, "you want Mr. Laevsky to return home a magnanimous and chivalrous figure, but I cannot give you and him that satisfaction. And there was no need to get up early and drive eight miles out of town simply to drink to peace, to have breakfast, and to explain to me that the duel is an out-of-date formality. A duel is a duel, and there is no need to make it more false and stupid than it is in reality. I want to fight!"

A silence followed. Boyko took a pair of pistols out of a box; one was given to Von Koren and one to Laevsky, and then there followed a difficulty which afforded a brief amusement to the zoologist and the seconds. It appeared that of all the people present not one had ever in his life been at a duel, and no one knew precisely how they ought to stand, and what the seconds ought to say and do. But then Boyko remembered and began, with a smile, to explain.

"Gentlemen, who remembers the description in Lermontov?" asked Von Koren, laughing. "In Turgenev, too, Bazarov had a duel with some one. . . ."

"There's no need to remember," said Ustimovitch impatiently. "Measure the distance, that's all."

And he took three steps as though to show how to measure it. Boyko counted out the steps while his companion drew his sabre and scratched the earth at the extreme points to mark the barrier. In complete silence the opponents took their places.

"Moles," the deacon thought, sitting in the bushes.

Sheshkovsky said something, Boyko explained something again, but Laevsky did not hear—or rather heard, but did not understand. He cocked his pistol when the time came to do so, and raised the cold, heavy weapon with the barrel upwards. He forgot to unbutton his overcoat, and it felt very tight over his shoulder and under his arm, and his arm rose as awkwardly as though the sleeve had been cut out of tin. He remembered the hatred he had felt the night before for the swarthy brow and curly hair, and felt that even yesterday at the moment of intense hatred and anger he could not have shot a man. Fearing that the bullet might somehow hit Von Koren by accident, he raised the pistol higher and higher, and felt that this too obvious magnanimity was indelicate and anything but magnanimous, but he did not know how else to do and could do nothing else. Looking at the pale, ironically smiling face of Von Koren, who evidently had been convinced from the beginning that his opponent would fire in the air, Laevsky thought that, thank God, everything would be over directly, and all that he had to do was to press the trigger rather hard. . . .

He felt a violent shock on the shoulder; there was the sound of a shot and an answering echo in the mountains: ping-ting!

Von Koren cocked his pistol and looked at Ustimovitch, who was pacing as before with his hands behind his back, taking no notice of any one.

"Doctor," said the zoologist, "be so good as not to move to and fro like a pendulum. You make me dizzy."

The doctor stood still. Von Koren began to take aim at Laevsky.

"It's all over!" thought Laevsky.

The barrel of the pistol aimed straight at his face, the expression of hatred and contempt in Von Koren's attitude and whole figure, and the murder just about to be committed by a decent man in broad daylight, in the presence of decent men, and the stillness and the unknown force that compelled Laevsky to stand still and not to run, how mysterious it all was, how incomprehensible and terrible!

The moment while Von Koren was taking aim seemed to Laevsky longer than a night: he glanced imploringly at the seconds; they were pale and did not stir.

"Make haste and fire," thought Laevsky, and felt that his pale, quivering, and pitiful face must arouse even greater hatred in Von Koren.

"I'll kill him directly," thought Von Koren, aiming at his forehead, with his finger already on the catch. "Yes, of course I'll kill him."

"He'll kill him!" A despairing shout was suddenly heard somewhere very close at hand.

A shot rang out at once. Seeing that Laevsky remained standing where he was and did not fall, they all looked in the direction from which the shout had come, and saw the deacon. With pale face and wet hair sticking to his forehead and his cheeks, wet through and muddy, he was standing in the maize on the further bank, smiling rather queerly and waving his wet hat. Sheshkovsky laughed with joy, burst into tears, and moved away. . . .

XX

A little while afterwards, Von Koren and the deacon met near the little bridge. The deacon was excited; he breathed hard, and avoided looking in people's faces. He felt ashamed both of his terror and his muddy, wet garments.

"I thought you meant to kill him . . ." he muttered. "How contrary to human nature it is! How utterly unnatural it is!"

"But how did you come here?" asked the zoologist.

"Don't ask," said the deacon, waving his hand. "The evil one tempted me, saying: 'Go, go. . . .' So I went and almost died of fright in the maize. But now, thank God, thank God. . . . I am awfully pleased with you," muttered the deacon. "Old Grandad Tarantula will be glad . . . . It's funny, it's too funny! Only I beg of you most earnestly don't tell anybody I was there, or I may get into hot water with the authorities. They will say: 'The deacon was a second.'"

"Gentlemen," said Von Koren, "the deacon asks you not to tell any one you've seen him here. He might get into trouble."

"How contrary to human nature it is!" sighed the deacon. "Excuse my saying so, but your face was so dreadful that I thought you were going to kill him."

"I was very much tempted to put an end to that scoundrel," said Von Koren, "but you shouted close by, and I missed my aim. The whole procedure is revolting to any one who is not used to it, and it has exhausted me, deacon. I feel awfully tired. Come along. . . ."

"No, you must let me walk back. I must get dry, for I am wet and cold."

"Well, as you like," said the zoologist, in a weary tone, feeling dispirited, and, getting into the carriage, he closed his eyes. "As you like. . . ."

While they were moving about the carriages and taking their seats, Kerbalay stood in the road, and, laying his hands on his stomach, he bowed low, showing his teeth; he imagined that the gentry had come to enjoy the beauties of nature and drink tea, and could not understand why they were getting into the carriages. The party set off in complete silence and only the deacon was left by the *duhan*.

"Come to the *duhan*, drink tea," he said to Kerbalay. "Me wants to eat."

Kerbalay spoke good Russian, but the deacon imagined that the Tatar would understand him better if he talked to him in broken Russian. "Cook omelette, give cheese. . . ."

"Come, come, father," said Kerbalay, bowing. "I'll give you everything . . . . I've cheese and wine. . . . Eat what you like."

"What is 'God' in Tatar?" asked the deacon, going into the *duhan*.

"Your God and my God are the same," said Kerbalay, not understanding him. "God is the same for all men, only men are different. Some are Russian, some are Turks, some are English—there are many sorts of men, but God is one."

"Very good. If all men worship the same God, why do you Mohammedans look upon Christians as your everlasting enemies?"

"Why are you angry?" said Kerbalay, laying both hands on his stomach. "You are a priest; I am a Mussulman: you say, 'I want to eat'—I give it you. . . . Only the rich man distinguishes your God from my God; for the poor man it is all the same. If you please, it is ready."

While this theological conversation was taking place at the *duhan*, Laevsky was driving home thinking how dreadful it had been driving there at daybreak, when the roads, the rocks, and the mountains were wet and dark, and the uncertain future seemed like a terrible abyss, of which one could not see the bottom; while now the raindrops hanging on the grass and on the stones were sparkling in the sun like diamonds, nature was smiling joyfully, and the terrible future was left behind. He looked at Sheshkovsky's sullen, tear-stained face, and at the two carriages ahead of them in which Von Koren, his seconds, and the doctor were sitting, and it seemed to him as though they were all coming back from a graveyard in which a wearisome, insufferable man who was a burden to others had just been buried.

"Everything is over," he thought of his past, cautiously touching his neck with his fingers.

On the right side of his neck was a small swelling, of the length and breadth of his little finger, and he felt a pain, as though some one had passed a hot iron over his neck. The bullet had bruised it.

Afterwards, when he got home, a strange, long, sweet day began for him, misty as forgetfulness. Like a man released from prison or from hospital, he stared at the long-familiar objects and wondered that the tables, the windows, the chairs, the light, and the sea stirred in him a keen, childish delight such as he had not known for long, long years. Nadyezhda Fyodorovna, pale and haggard, could not understand his gentle voice and strange movements; she made haste to tell him everything that had happened to her. . . . It seemed to her that very likely he scarcely heard and did not understand her, and that if he did know everything he would curse her and kill her, but he listened to her, stroked her face and hair, looked into her eyes and said:

"I have nobody but you. . . ."

Then they sat a long while in the garden, huddled close together, saying nothing, or dreaming aloud of their happy life in the future, in brief, broken sentences, while it seemed to him that he had never spoken at such length or so eloquently.

XXI

More than three months had passed.

The day came that Von Koren had fixed on for his departure. A cold, heavy rain had been falling from early morning, a north-east wind was blowing, and the waves were high on the sea. It was said that the steamer would hardly be able to come into the harbour in such weather. By the time-table it should have arrived at ten o'clock in the morning, but Von Koren, who had gone on to the sea-front at midday and again after dinner, could see nothing through the field-glass but grey waves and rain covering the horizon.

Towards the end of the day the rain ceased and the wind began to drop perceptibly. Von Koren had already made up his mind that he would not be able to get off that day, and had settled down to play chess with Samoylenko; but after dark the orderly announced that there were lights on the sea and that a rocket had been seen.

Von Koren made haste. He put his satchel over his shoulder, and kissed Samoylenko and the deacon. Though there was not the slightest necessity, he went through the rooms again, said good-bye to the orderly and the cook, and went out into the street, feeling that he had left something behind, either at the doctor's or his lodging. In the street he walked beside Samoylenko, behind them came the deacon with a box, and last of all the orderly with two portmanteaus. Only Samoylenko and the orderly could distinguish the dim lights on the sea. The others gazed into the darkness and saw nothing. The steamer had stopped a long way from the coast.

"Make haste, make haste," Von Koren hurried them. "I am afraid it will set off."

As they passed the little house with three windows, into which Laevsky had moved soon after the duel, Von Koren could not resist peeping in at the window. Laevsky was sitting, writing, bent over the table, with his back to the window.

"I wonder at him!" said the zoologist softly. "What a screw he has put on himself!"

"Yes, one may well wonder," said Samoylenko. "He sits from morning till night, he's always at work. He works to pay off his debts. And he lives, brother, worse than a beggar!"

Half a minute of silence followed. The zoologist, the doctor, and the deacon stood at the window and went on looking at Laevsky.

"So he didn't get away from here, poor fellow," said Samoylenko.

"Do you remember how hard he tried?"

"Yes, he has put a screw on himself," Von Koren repeated. "His marriage, the way he works all day long for his daily bread, a new expression in his face, and even in his walk—it's all so extraordinary that I don't know what to call it."

The zoologist took Samoylenko's sleeve and went on with emotion in his voice:

"You tell him and his wife that when I went away I was full of admiration for them and wished them all happiness . . . and I beg him, if he can, not to remember evil against me. He knows me. He knows that if I could have foreseen this change, then I might have become his best friend."

"Go in and say good-bye to him."

"No, that wouldn't do."

"Why? God knows, perhaps you'll never see him again."

The zoologist reflected, and said:

"That's true."

Samoylenko tapped softly at the window. Laevsky started and looked round.

"Vanya, Nikolay Vassilitch wants to say goodbye to you," said Samoylenko. "He is just going away."

Laevsky got up from the table, and went into the passage to open the door. Samoylenko, the zoologist, and the deacon went into the house.

"I can only come for one minute," began the zoologist, taking off his goloshes in the passage, and already wishing he had not given way to his feelings and come in, uninvited. "It is as though I were forcing myself on him," he thought, "and that's stupid."

"Forgive me for disturbing you," he said as he went into the room with Laevsky, "but I'm just going away, and I had an impulse to see you. God knows whether we shall ever meet again."

"I am very glad to see you. . . . Please come in," said Laevsky, and he awkwardly set chairs for his visitors as though he wanted to bar their way, and stood in the middle of the room, rubbing his hands.

"I should have done better to have left my audience in the street," thought Von Koren, and he said firmly: "Don't remember evil against me, Ivan Andreitch. To forget the past is, of course, impossible it is too painful, and I've not come here to apologise or to declare that I was not to blame. I acted sincerely, and I have not changed my convictions since then. . . . It is true that I see, to my great delight, that I was mistaken in regard to you, but it's easy to make a false step even on a smooth road, and, in fact, it's the natural human lot: if one is not mistaken in the main, one is mistaken in the details. Nobody knows the real truth."

"No, no one knows the truth," said Laevsky.

"Well, good-bye. . . . God give you all happiness."

Von Koren gave Laevsky his hand; the latter took it and bowed.

"Don't remember evil against me," said Von Koren. "Give my greetings to your wife, and say I am very sorry not to say good-bye to her."

"She is at home."

Laevsky went to the door of the next room, and said:

"Nadya, Nikolay Vassilitch wants to say goodbye to you."

Nadyezhda Fyodorovna came in; she stopped near the doorway and looked shyly at the visitors. There was a look of guilt and dismay on her face, and she held her hands like a schoolgirl receiving a scolding.

"I'm just going away, Nadyezhda Fyodorovna," said Von Koren, "and have come to say good-bye."

She held out her hand uncertainly, while Laevsky bowed.

"What pitiful figures they are, though!" thought Von Koren. "The life they are living does not come easy to them. I shall be in Moscow and Petersburg; can I send you anything?" he asked.

"Oh!" said Nadyezhda Fyodorovna, and she looked anxiously at her husband. "I don't think there's anything. . . ."

"No, nothing . . ." said Laevsky, rubbing his hands. "Our greetings."

Von Koren did not know what he could or ought to say, though as he went in he thought he would say a very great deal that would be warm and good and important. He shook hands with Laevsky and his wife in silence, and left them with a depressed feeling.

"What people!" said the deacon in a low voice, as he walked behind them. "My God, what people! Of a truth, the right hand of God has planted this vine! Lord! Lord! One man vanquishes thousands and another tens of thousands. Nikolay Vassilitch," he said ecstatically, "let me tell you that to-day you have conquered the greatest of man's enemies—pride."

"Hush, deacon! Fine conquerors we are! Conquerors ought to look like eagles, while he's a pitiful figure, timid, crushed; he bows like a Chinese idol, and I, I am sad. . . ."

They heard steps behind them. It was Laevsky, hurrying after them to see him off. The orderly was standing on the quay with the two portmanteaus, and at a little distance stood four boatmen.

"There is a wind, though. . . . Brrr!" said Samoylenko. "There must be a pretty stiff storm on the sea now! You are not going off at a nice time, Koyla."

"I'm not afraid of sea-sickness."

"That's not the point. . . . I only hope these rascals won't upset you. You ought to have crossed in the agent's sloop. Where's the agent's sloop?" he shouted to the boatmen.

"It has gone, Your Excellency."

"And the Customs-house boat?"

"That's gone, too."

"Why didn't you let us know," said Samoylenko angrily. "You dolts!"

"It's all the same, don't worry yourself . . ." said Von Koren.

"Well, good-bye. God keep you."

Samoylenko embraced Von Koren and made the sign of the cross over him three times.

"Don't forget us, Kolya. . . . Write. . . . We shall look out for you next spring."

"Good-bye, deacon," said Von Koren, shaking hands with the deacon.
"Thank you for your company and for your pleasant conversation.
Think about the expedition."

"Oh Lord, yes! to the ends of the earth," laughed the deacon. "I've nothing against it."

Von Koren recognised Laevsky in the darkness, and held out his hand without speaking. The boatmen were by now below, holding the boat, which was beating against the piles, though the breakwater screened it from the breakers. Von Koren went down the ladder, jumped into the boat, and sat at the helm.

"Write!" Samoylenko shouted to him. "Take care of yourself."

"No one knows the real truth," thought Laevsky, turning up the collar of his coat and thrusting his hands into his sleeves.

The boat turned briskly out of the harbour into the open sea. It vanished in the waves, but at once from a deep hollow glided up onto a high breaker, so that they could distinguish the men and even the oars. The boat moved three yards forward and was sucked two yards back.

"Write!" shouted Samoylenko; "it's devilish weather for you to go in."

"Yes, no one knows the real truth . . ." thought Laevsky, looking wearily at the dark, restless sea.

"It flings the boat back," he thought; "she makes two steps forward and one step back; but the boatmen are stubborn, they work the oars unceasingly, and are not afraid of the high waves. The boat goes on and on. Now she is out of sight, but in half an hour the boatmen will see the steamer lights distinctly, and within an hour they will be by the steamer ladder. So it is in life. . . . In the search for truth man makes two steps forward and one step back. Suffering, mistakes, and weariness of life thrust them back, but the thirst for truth and stubborn will drive them on and on. And who knows? Perhaps they will reach the real truth at last."

"Go—o—od-by—e," shouted Samoylenko.

"There's no sight or sound of them," said the deacon. "Good luck on the journey!"

It began to spot with rain.

EXCELLENT PEOPLE

ONCE upon a time there lived in Moscow a man called Vladimir Semyonitch Liadovsky. He took his degree at the university in the faculty of law and had a post on the board of management of some railway; but if you had asked him what his work was, he would look candidly and openly at you with his large bright eyes through his gold pincenez, and would answer in a soft, velvety, lisping baritone:

"My work is literature."

After completing his course at the university, Vladimir Semyonitch had had a paragraph of theatrical criticism accepted by a newspaper. From this paragraph he passed on to reviewing, and a year later he had advanced to writing a weekly article on literary matters for the same paper. But it does not follow from these facts that he was an amateur, that his literary work was of an ephemeral, haphazard character. Whenever I saw his neat spare figure, his high forehead and long mane of hair, when I listened to his speeches, it always seemed to me that his writing, quite apart from what and how he wrote, was something organically part of him, like the beating of his heart, and that his whole literary programme must have been an integral part of his brain while he was a baby in his mother's womb. Even in his walk, his gestures, his manner of shaking off the ash from his cigarette, I could read this whole programme from A to Z, with all its claptrap, dulness, and honourable sentiments. He was a literary man all over when with an inspired face he laid a wreath on the coffin of some celebrity, or with a grave and solemn face collected signatures for some address; his passion for making the acquaintance of distinguished literary men, his faculty for finding talent even where it was absent, his perpetual enthusiasm, his pulse that went at one hundred and twenty a minute, his ignorance of life, the genuinely feminine flutter with which he threw himself into concerts and literary evenings for the benefit of destitute students, the way in which he gravitated towards the young—all this would have created for him the reputation of a writer even if he had not written his articles.

He was one of those writers to whom phrases like, "We are but few," or "What would life be without strife? Forward!" were pre-eminently becoming, though he never strove with any one and never did go forward. It did not even sound mawkish when he fell to discoursing of ideals. Every anniversary of the university, on St. Tatiana's Day, he got drunk, chanted *Gaudeamus* out of tune, and his beaming and perspiring countenance seemed to say: "See, I'm drunk; I'm keeping it up!" But even that suited him.

Vladimir Semyonitch had genuine faith in his literary vocation and his whole programme. He had no doubts, and was evidently very well pleased with himself. Only one thing grieved him—the paper for which he worked had a limited circulation and was not very influential. But Vladimir Semyonitch believed that sooner or later he would succeed in getting on to a solid magazine where he would have scope and could display himself—and what little distress he felt on this score was pale beside the brilliance of his hopes.

Visiting this charming man, I made the acquaintance of his sister, Vera Semyonovna, a woman doctor. At first sight, what struck me about this woman was her look of exhaustion and extreme ill-health. She was young, with a good figure and regular, rather large features, but in comparison with her agile, elegant, and talkative brother she seemed angular, listless, slovenly, and sullen. There was something strained, cold, apathetic in her movements, smiles, and words; she was not liked, and was thought proud and not very intelligent.

In reality, I fancy, she was resting.

"My dear friend," her brother would often say to me, sighing and flinging back his hair in his picturesque literary way, "one must never judge by appearances! Look at this book: it has long ago been read. It is warped, tattered, and lies in the dust uncared for; but open it, and it will make you weep and turn pale. My sister is like that book. Lift the cover and peep into her soul, and you will be horror-stricken. Vera passed in some three months through experiences that would have been ample for a whole lifetime!"

Vladimir Semyonitch looked round him, took me by the sleeve, and began to whisper:

"You know, after taking her degree she married, for love, an architect. It's a complete tragedy! They had hardly been married a month when—whew—her husband died of typhus. But that was not all. She caught typhus from him, and when, on her recovery, she learnt that her Ivan was dead, she took a good dose of morphia. If it had not been for vigorous measures taken by her friends, my Vera would have been by now in Paradise. Tell me, isn't it a tragedy? And is not my sister like an *ingenue*, who has played already all the five acts of her life? The audience may stay for the farce, but the *ingenue* must go home to rest."

After three months of misery Vera Semyonovna had come to live with her brother. She was not fitted for the practice of medicine, which exhausted her and did not satisfy her; she did not give one the impression of knowing her subject, and I never once heard her say anything referring to her medical studies.

She gave up medicine, and, silent and unoccupied, as though she were a prisoner, spent the remainder of her youth in colourless apathy, with bowed head and hanging hands. The only thing to which she was not completely indifferent, and which brought some brightness into the twilight of her life, was the presence of her brother, whom she loved. She loved him himself and his programme, she was full of reverence for his articles; and when she was asked what her brother was doing, she would answer in a subdued voice as though afraid of waking or distracting him: "He is writing. . . ." Usually when he was at his work she used to sit beside him, her eyes fixed on his writing hand. She used at such moments to look like a sick animal warming itself in the sun. . . .

One winter evening Vladimir Semyonitch was sitting at his table writing a critical article for his newspaper: Vera Semyonovna was sitting beside him, staring as usual at his writing hand. The critic wrote rapidly, without erasures or corrections. The pen scratched and squeaked. On the table near the writing hand there lay open a freshly-cut volume of a thick magazine, containing a story of peasant life, signed with two initials. Vladimir Semyonitch was enthusiastic; he thought the author was admirable in his handling of the subject, suggested Turgenev in his descriptions of nature, was truthful, and had an excellent knowledge of the life of the peasantry. The critic himself knew nothing of peasant life except from books and hearsay, but his feelings and his inner convictions forced him to believe the story. He foretold a brilliant future for the author, assured him he should await the conclusion of the story with great impatience, and so on.

"Fine story!" he said, flinging himself back in his chair and closing his eyes with pleasure. "The tone is extremely good."

Vera Semyonovna looked at him, yawned aloud, and suddenly asked an unexpected question. In the evening she had a habit of yawning nervously and asking short, abrupt questions, not always relevant.

"Volodya," she asked, "what is the meaning of non-resistance to evil?"

"Non-resistance to evil!" repeated her brother, opening his eyes.

"Yes. What do you understand by it?"

"You see, my dear, imagine that thieves or brigands attack you, and you, instead of . . ."

"No, give me a logical definition."

"A logical definition? Um! Well." Vladimir Semyonitch pondered. "Non-resistance to evil means an attitude of non-interference with regard to all that in the sphere of mortality is called evil."

Saying this, Vladimir Semyonitch bent over the table and took up a novel. This novel, written by a woman, dealt with the painfulness of the irregular position of a society lady who was living under the same roof with her lover and her illegitimate child. Vladimir Semyonitch was pleased with the excellent tendency of the story, the plot and the presentation of it. Making a brief summary of the novel, he selected the best passages and added to them in his account: "How true to reality, how living, how picturesque! The author is not merely an artist; he is also a subtle psychologist who can see into the hearts of his characters. Take, for example, this vivid description of the emotions of the heroine on meeting her husband," and so on.

"Volodya," Vera Semyonovna interrupted his critical effusions, "I've been haunted by a strange idea since yesterday. I keep wondering where we should all be if human life were ordered on the basis of non-resistance to evil?

"In all probability, nowhere. Non-resistance to evil would give the full rein to the criminal will, and, to say nothing of civilisation, this would leave not one stone standing upon another anywhere on earth."

"What would be left?"

"Bashi-Bazouke and brothels. In my next article I'll talk about that perhaps. Thank you for reminding me."

And a week later my friend kept his promise. That was just at the period—in the eighties—when people were beginning to talk and write of non-resistance, of the right to judge, to punish, to make war; when some people in our set were beginning to do without servants, to retire into the country, to work on the land, and to renounce animal food and carnal love.

After reading her brother's article, Vera Semyonovna pondered and hardly perceptibly shrugged her shoulders.

"Very nice!" she said. "But still there's a great deal I don't understand. For instance, in Leskov's story 'Belonging to the Cathedral' there is a queer gardener who sows for the benefit of all—for customers, for beggars, and any who care to steal. Did he behave sensibly?"

From his sister's tone and expression Vladimir Semyonitch saw that she did not like his article, and, almost for the first time in his life, his vanity as an author sustained a shock. With a shade of irritation he answered:

"Theft is immoral. To sow for thieves is to recognise the right of thieves to existence. What would you think if I were to establish a newspaper and, dividing it into sections, provide for blackmailing as well as for liberal ideas? Following the example of that gardener, I ought, logically, to provide a section for blackmailers, the intellectual scoundrels? Yes."

Vera Semyonovna made no answer. She got up from the table, moved languidly to the sofa and lay down.

"I don't know, I know nothing about it," she said musingly. "You are probably right, but it seems to me, I feel somehow, that there's something false in our resistance to evil, as though there were something concealed or unsaid. God knows, perhaps our methods of resisting evil belong to the category of prejudices which have become so deeply rooted in us, that we are incapable of parting with them, and therefore cannot form a correct judgment of them."

"How do you mean?"

"I don't know how to explain to you. Perhaps man is mistaken in thinking that he is obliged to resist evil and has a right to do so, just as he is mistaken in thinking, for instance, that the heart looks like an ace of hearts. It is very possible in resisting evil we ought not to use force, but to use what is the very opposite of force—if you, for instance, don't want this picture stolen from you, you ought to give it away rather than lock it up. . . ."

"That's clever, very clever! If I want to marry a rich, vulgar woman, she ought to prevent me from such a shabby action by hastening to make me an offer herself!"

The brother and sister talked till midnight without understanding each other. If any outsider had overheard them he would hardly have been able to make out what either of them was driving at.

They usually spent the evening at home. There were no friends' houses to which they could go, and they felt no need for friends; they only went to the theatre when there was a new play—such was the custom in literary circles—they did not go to concerts, for they did not care for music.

"You may think what you like," Vera Semyonovna began again the next day, "but for me the question is to a great extent settled. I am firmly convinced that I have no grounds for resisting evil directed against me personally. If they want to kill me, let them. My defending myself will not make the murderer better. All I have now to decide is the second half of the question: how I ought to behave to evil directed against my neighbours?"

"Vera, mind you don't become rabid!" said Vladimir Semyonitch, laughing. "I see non-resistance is becoming your *idee fixe*!"

He wanted to turn off these tedious conversations with a jest, but somehow it was beyond a jest; his smile was artificial and sour. His sister gave up sitting beside his table and gazing reverently at his writing hand, and he felt every evening that behind him on the sofa lay a person who did not agree with him. And his back grew stiff and numb, and there was a chill in his soul. An author's vanity is vindictive, implacable, incapable of forgiveness, and his sister was the first and only person who had laid bare and disturbed that uneasy feeling, which is like a big box of crockery, easy to unpack but impossible to pack up again as it was before.

Weeks and months passed by, and his sister clung to her ideas, and did not sit down by the table. One spring evening Vladimir Semyonitch was sitting at his table writing an article. He was reviewing a novel which described how a village schoolmistress refused the man whom she loved and who loved her, a man both wealthy and intellectual, simply because marriage made her work as a schoolmistress impossible. Vera Semyonovna lay on the sofa and brooded.

"My God, how slow it is!" she said, stretching. "How insipid and empty life is! I don't know what to do with myself, and you are wasting your best years in goodness knows what. Like some alchemist, you are rummaging in old rubbish that nobody wants. My God!"

Vladimir Semyonitch dropped his pen and slowly looked round at his sister.

"It's depressing to look at you!" said his sister. "Wagner in 'Faust' dug up worms, but he was looking for a treasure, anyway, and you are looking for worms for the sake of the worms."

"That's vague!"

"Yes, Volodya; all these days I've been thinking, I've been thinking painfully for a long time, and I have come to the conclusion that you are hopelessly reactionary and conventional. Come, ask yourself what is the object of your zealous, conscientious work? Tell me, what is it? Why, everything has long ago been extracted that can be extracted from that rubbish in which you are always rummaging. You may pound water in a mortar and analyse it as long as you like, you'll make nothing more of it than the chemists have made already. . . ."

"Indeed!" drawled Vladimir Semyonitch, getting up. "Yes, all this is old rubbish because these ideas are eternal; but what do you consider new, then?"

"You undertake to work in the domain of thought; it is for you to think of something new. It's not for me to teach you."

"Me—an alchemist!" the critic cried in wonder and indignation, screwing up his eyes ironically. "Art, progress—all that is alchemy?"

"You see, Volodya, it seems to me that if all you thinking people had set yourselves to solving great problems, all these little questions that you fuss about now would solve themselves by the way. If you go up in a balloon to see a town, you will incidentally, without any effort, see the fields and the villages and the rivers as well. When stearine is manufactured, you get glycerine as a by-product. It seems to me that contemporary thought has settled on one spot and stuck to it. It is prejudiced, apathetic, timid, afraid to take a wide titanic flight, just as you and I are afraid to climb on a high mountain; it is conservative."

Such conversations could not but leave traces. The relations of the brother and sister grew more and more strained every day. The brother became unable to work in his sister's presence, and grew irritable when he knew his sister was lying on the sofa, looking at his back; while the sister frowned nervously and stretched when, trying to bring back the past, he attempted to share his enthusiasms with her. Every evening she complained of being bored, and talked about independence of mind and those who are in the rut of tradition. Carried away by her new ideas, Vera Semyonovna proved that the work that her brother was so engrossed in was conventional, that it was a vain effort of conservative minds to preserve what had already served its turn and was vanishing from the scene of action. She made no end of comparisons. She compared her brother at one time to an alchemist, then to a musty old Believer who would sooner die than listen to reason. By degrees there was a perceptible change in her manner of life, too. She was capable of lying on the sofa all day long doing nothing but think, while her face wore a cold, dry expression such as one sees in one-sided people of strong faith. She began to refuse the attentions of the servants, swept and tidied her own room, cleaned her own boots and brushed her own clothes. Her brother could not help looking with irritation and even hatred at her cold face when she went about her menial work. In that work, which was always performed with a certain solemnity, he saw something strained and false, he saw something both pharisaical and affected. And knowing he could not touch her by persuasion, he carped at her and teased her like a schoolboy.

"You won't resist evil, but you resist my having servants!" he taunted her. "If servants are an evil, why do you oppose it? That's inconsistent!"

He suffered, was indignant and even ashamed. He felt ashamed when his sister began doing odd things before strangers.

"It's awful, my dear fellow," he said to me in private, waving his hands in despair. "It seems that our *ingenue* has remained to play a part in the farce, too. She's become morbid to the marrow of her bones! I've washed my hands of her, let her think as she likes; but why does she talk, why does she excite me? She ought to think what it means for me to listen to her. What I feel when in my presence she has the effrontery to support her errors by blasphemously quoting the teaching of Christ! It chokes me! It makes me hot all over to hear my sister propounding her doctrines and trying to distort the Gospel to suit her, when she purposely refrains from mentioning how the moneychangers were driven out of the Temple. That's, my dear fellow, what comes of being half educated, undeveloped! That's what comes of medical studies which provide no general culture!"

One day on coming home from the office, Vladimir Semyonitch found his sister crying. She was sitting on the sofa with her head bowed, wringing her hands, and tears were flowing freely down her cheeks. The critic's good heart throbbed with pain. Tears fell from his eyes, too, and he longed to pet his sister, to forgive her, to beg her forgiveness, and to live as they used to before. . . . He knelt down and kissed her head, her hands, her shoulders. . . . She smiled, smiled bitterly, unaccountably, while he with a cry of joy jumped up, seized the magazine from the table and said warmly:

"Hurrah! We'll live as we used to, Verotchka! With God's blessing! And I've such a surprise for you here! Instead of celebrating the occasion with champagne, let us read it together! A splendid, wonderful thing!"

"Oh, no, no!" cried Vera Semyonovna, pushing away the book in alarm.

"I've read it already! I don't want it, I don't want it!"

"When did you read it?"

"A year . . . two years ago. . . I read it long ago, and I know it, I know it!"

"H'm! . . . You're a fanatic!" her brother said coldly, flinging the magazine on to the table.

"No, you are a fanatic, not I! You!" And Vera Semyonovna dissolved into tears again. Her brother stood before her, looked at her quivering shoulders, and thought. He thought, not of the agonies of loneliness endured by any one who begins to think in a new way of their own, not of the inevitable sufferings of a genuine spiritual revolution, but of the outrage of his programme, the outrage to his author's vanity.

From this time he treated his sister coldly, with careless irony, and he endured her presence in the room as one endures the presence of old women that are dependent on one. For her part, she left off disputing with him and met all his arguments, jeers, and attacks with a condescending silence which irritated him more than ever.

One summer morning Vera Semyonovna, dressed for travelling with a satchel over her shoulder, went in to her brother and coldly kissed him on the forehead.

"Where are you going?" he asked with surprise.

"To the province of N. to do vaccination work." Her brother went out into the street with her.

"So that's what you've decided upon, you queer girl," he muttered.

"Don't you want some money?"

"No, thank you. Good-bye."

The sister shook her brother's hand and set off.

"Why don't you have a cab?" cried Vladimir Semyonitch.

She did not answer. Her brother gazed after her, watched her rusty-looking waterproof, the swaying of her figure as she slouched along, forced himself to sigh, but did not succeed in rousing a feeling of regret. His sister had become a stranger to him. And he was a stranger to her. Anyway, she did not once look round.

Going back to his room, Vladimir Semyonitch at once sat down to the table and began to work at his article.

I never saw Vera Semyonovna again. Where she is now I do not know. And Vladimir Semyonitch went on writing his articles, laying wreaths on coffins, singing *Gaudeamus*, busying himself over the Mutual Aid Society of Moscow Journalists.

He fell ill with inflammation of the lungs; he was ill in bed for three months—at first at home, and afterwards in the Golitsyn Hospital. An abscess developed in his knee. People said he ought to be sent to the Crimea, and began getting up a collection for him. But he did not go to the Crimea—he died. We buried him in the Vagankovsky Cemetery, on the left side, where artists and literary men are buried.

One day we writers were sitting in the Tatars' restaurant. I mentioned that I had lately been in the Vagankovsky Cemetery and had seen Vladimir Semyonitch's grave there. It was utterly neglected and almost indistinguishable from the rest of the ground, the cross had fallen; it was necessary to collect a few roubles to put it in order.

But they listened to what I said unconcernedly, made no answer, and I could not collect a farthing. No one remembered Vladimir Semyonitch. He was utterly forgotten.

MIRE

I

GRACEFULLY swaying in the saddle, a young man wearing the snow-white tunic of an officer rode into the great yard of the vodka distillery belonging to the heirs of M. E. Rothstein. The sun smiled carelessly on the lieutenant's little stars, on the white trunks of the birch-trees, on the heaps of broken glass scattered here and there in the yard. The radiant, vigorous beauty of a summer day lay over everything, and nothing hindered the snappy young green leaves from dancing gaily and winking at the clear blue sky. Even the dirty and soot-begrimed appearance of the bricksheds and the stifling fumes of the distillery did not spoil the general good impression. The lieutenant sprang gaily out of the saddle, handed over his horse to a man who ran up, and stroking with his finger his delicate black moustaches, went in at the front door. On the top step of the old but light and softly carpeted staircase he was met by a maidservant with a haughty, not very youthful face. The lieutenant gave her his card without speaking.

As she went through the rooms with the card, the maid could see on it the name "Alexandr Grigoryevitch Sokolsky." A minute later she came back and told the lieutenant that her mistress could not see him, as she was not feeling quite well. Sokolsky looked at the ceiling and thrust out his lower lip.

"How vexatious!" he said. "Listen, my dear," he said eagerly. "Go and tell Susanna Moiseyevna, that it is very necessary for me to speak to her—very. I will only keep her one minute. Ask her to excuse me."

The maid shrugged one shoulder and went off languidly to her mistress.

"Very well!" she sighed, returning after a brief interval. "Please walk in!"

The lieutenant went with her through five or six large, luxuriously furnished rooms and a corridor, and finally found himself in a large and lofty square room, in which from the first step he was impressed by the abundance of flowers and plants and the sweet, almost revoltingly heavy fragrance of jasmine. Flowers were trained to trellis-work along the walls, screening the windows, hung from the ceiling, and were wreathed over the corners, so that the room was more like a greenhouse than a place to live in. Tits, canaries, and goldfinches chirruped among the green leaves and fluttered against the window-panes.

"Forgive me for receiving you here," the lieutenant heard in a mellow feminine voice with a burr on the letter *r* which was not without charm. "Yesterday I had a sick headache, and I'm trying to keep still to prevent its coming on again. What do you want?"

Exactly opposite the entrance, he saw sitting in a big low chair, such as old men use, a woman in an expensive Chinese dressing-gown, with her head wrapped up, leaning back on a pillow. Nothing could be seen behind the woollen shawl in which she was muffled but a pale, long, pointed, somewhat aquiline nose, and one large dark eye. Her ample dressing-gown concealed her figure, but judging from her beautiful hand, from her voice, her nose, and her eye, she might be twenty-six or twenty-eight.

"Forgive me for being so persistent . . ." began the lieutenant, clinking his spurs. "Allow me to introduce myself: Sokolsky! I come with a message from my cousin, your neighbour, Alexey Ivanovitch Kryukov, who . . ."

"I know!" interposed Susanna Moiseyevna. "I know Kryukov. Sit down;

I don't like anything big standing before me."

"My cousin charges me to ask you a favour," the lieutenant went on, clinking his spurs once more and sitting down. "The fact is, your late father made a purchase of oats from my cousin last winter, and a small sum was left owing. The payment only becomes due next week, but my cousin begs you most particularly to pay him—if possible, to-day."

As the lieutenant talked, he stole side-glances about him.

"Surely I'm not in her bedroom?" he thought.

In one corner of the room, where the foliage was thickest and tallest, under a pink awning like a funeral canopy, stood a bed not yet made, with the bedclothes still in disorder. Close by on two arm-chairs lay heaps of crumpled feminine garments.

Petticoats and sleeves with rumpled lace and flounces were trailing on the carpet, on which here and there lay bits of white tape, cigarette-ends, and the papers of caramels. . . . Under the bed the toes, pointed and square, of slippers of all kinds peeped out in a long row. And it seemed to the lieutenant that the scent of the jasmine came not from the flowers, but from the bed and the slippers.

"And what is the sum owing?" asked Susanna Moiseyevna.

"Two thousand three hundred."

"Oho!" said the Jewess, showing another large black eye. "And you call that—a small sum! However, it's just the same paying it to-day or paying it in a week, but I've had so many payments to make in the last two months since my father's death. . . . Such a lot of stupid business, it makes my head go round! A nice idea! I want to go abroad, and they keep forcing me to attend to these silly things. Vodka, oats . . ." she muttered, half closing her eyes, "oats, bills, percentages, or, as my head-clerk says, 'percentage.' . . . It's awful. Yesterday I simply turned the excise officer out. He pesters me with his Tralles. I said to him: 'Go to the devil with your Tralles! I can't see any one!' He kissed my hand and went away. I tell you what: can't your cousin wait two or three months?"

"A cruel question!" laughed the lieutenant. "My cousin can wait a year, but it's I who cannot wait! You see, it's on my own account I'm acting, I ought to tell you. At all costs I must have money, and by ill-luck my cousin hasn't a rouble to spare. I'm forced to ride about and collect debts. I've just been to see a peasant, our tenant; here I'm now calling on you; from here I shall go on to somewhere else, and keep on like that until I get together five thousand roubles. I need money awfully!"

"Nonsense! What does a young man want with money? Whims, mischief. Why, have you been going in for dissipation? Or losing at cards? Or are you getting married?"

"You've guessed!" laughed the lieutenant, and rising slightly from his seat, he clinked his spurs. "I really am going to be married."

Susanna Moiseyevna looked intently at her visitor, made a wry face, and sighed.

"I can't make out what possesses people to get married!" she said, looking about her for her pocket-handkerchief. "Life is so short, one has so little freedom, and they must put chains on themselves!"

"Every one has his own way of looking at things. . . ."

"Yes, yes, of course; every one has his own way of looking at things . . . . But, I say, are you really going to marry some one poor? Are you passionately in love? And why must you have five thousand? Why won't four do, or three?"

"What a tongue she has!" thought the lieutenant, and answered: "The difficulty is that an officer is not allowed by law to marry till he is twenty-eight; if you choose to marry, you have to leave the Service or else pay a deposit of five thousand."

"Ah, now I understand. Listen. You said just now that every one has his own way of looking at things. . . . Perhaps your fiancee is some one special and remarkable, but . . . but I am utterly unable to understand how any decent man can live with a woman. I can't for the life of me understand it. I have lived, thank the Lord, twenty-seven years, and I have never yet seen an endurable woman. They're all affected minxes, immoral, liars. . . . The only ones I can put up with are cooks and housemaids, but so-called ladies I won't let come within shooting distance of me. But, thank God, they hate me and don't force themselves on me! If one of them wants money she sends her husband, but nothing will induce her to come herself, not from pride—no, but from cowardice; she's afraid of my making a scene. Oh, I understand their hatred very well! Rather! I openly display what they do their very utmost to conceal from God and man. How can they help hating me? No doubt you've heard bushels of scandal about me already. . . ."

"I only arrived here so lately . . ."

"Tut, tut, tut! . . . I see from your eyes! But your brother's wife, surely she primed you for this expedition? Think of letting a young man come to see such an awful woman without warning him—how could she? Ha, ha! . . . But tell me, how is your brother? He's a fine fellow, such a handsome man! . . . I've seen him several times at mass. Why do you look at me like that? I very often go to church! We all have the same God. To an educated person externals matter less than the idea. . . . That's so, isn't it?"

"Yes, of course . . ." smiled the lieutenant.

"Yes, the idea. . . . But you are not a bit like your brother. You are handsome, too, but your brother is a great deal better-looking. There's wonderfully little likeness!"

"That's quite natural; he's not my brother, but my cousin."

"Ah, to be sure! So you must have the money to-day? Why to-day?"

"My furlough is over in a few days."

"Well, what's to be done with you!" sighed Susanna Moiseyevna. "So be it. I'll give you the money, though I know you'll abuse me for it afterwards. You'll quarrel with your wife after you are married, and say: 'If that mangy Jewess hadn't given me the money, I should perhaps have been as free as a bird to-day!' Is your fiancee pretty?"

"Oh yes. . . ."

"H'm! . . . Anyway, better something, if it's only beauty, than nothing. Though however beautiful a woman is, it can never make up to her husband for her silliness."

"That's original!" laughed the lieutenant. "You are a woman yourself, and such a woman-hater!"

"A woman . . ." smiled Susanna. "It's not my fault that God has cast me into this mould, is it? I'm no more to blame for it than you are for having moustaches. The violin is not responsible for the choice of its case. I am very fond of myself, but when any one reminds me that I am a woman, I begin to hate myself. Well, you can go away, and I'll dress. Wait for me in the drawing-room."

The lieutenant went out, and the first thing he did was to draw a deep breath, to get rid of the heavy scent of jasmine, which had begun to irritate his throat and to make him feel giddy.

"What a strange woman!" he thought, looking about him. "She talks fluently, but . . . far too much, and too freely. She must be neurotic."

The drawing-room, in which he was standing now, was richly furnished, and had pretensions to luxury and style. There were dark bronze dishes with patterns in relief, views of Nice and the Rhine on the tables, old-fashioned sconces, Japanese statuettes, but all this striving after luxury and style only emphasised the lack of taste which was glaringly apparent in the gilt cornices, the gaudy wall-paper, the bright velvet table-cloths, the common oleographs in heavy frames. The bad taste of the general effect was the more complete from the lack of finish and the overcrowding of the room, which gave one a feeling that something was lacking, and that a great deal should have been thrown away. It was evident that the furniture had not been bought all at once, but had been picked up at auctions and other favourable opportunities.

Heaven knows what taste the lieutenant could boast of, but even he noticed one characteristic peculiarity about the whole place, which no luxury or style could efface—a complete absence of all trace of womanly, careful hands, which, as we all know, give a warmth, poetry, and snugness to the furnishing of a room. There was a chilliness about it such as one finds in waiting-rooms at stations, in clubs, and foyers at the theatres.

There was scarcely anything in the room definitely Jewish, except, perhaps, a big picture of the meeting of Jacob and Esau. The lieutenant looked round about him, and, shrugging his shoulders, thought of his strange, new acquaintance, of her free-and-easy manners, and her way of talking. But then the door opened, and in the doorway appeared the lady herself, in a long black dress, so slim and tightly laced that her figure looked as though it had been turned in a lathe. Now the lieutenant saw not only the nose and eyes, but also a thin white face, a head black and as curly as lamb's-wool. She did not attract him, though she did not strike him as ugly. He had a prejudice against un-Russian faces in general, and he considered, too, that the lady's white face, the whiteness of which for some reason suggested the cloying scent of jasmine, did not go well with her little black curls and thick eyebrows; that her nose and ears were astoundingly white, as though they belonged to a corpse, or had been moulded out of transparent wax. When she smiled she showed pale gums as well as her teeth, and he did not like that either.

"Anaemic debility . . ." he thought; "she's probably as nervous as a turkey."

"Here I am! Come along!" she said, going on rapidly ahead of him and pulling off the yellow leaves from the plants as she passed.

"I'll give you the money directly, and if you like I'll give you some lunch. Two thousand three hundred roubles! After such a good stroke of business you'll have an appetite for your lunch. Do you like my rooms? The ladies about here declare that my rooms always smell of garlic. With that culinary gibe their stock of wit is exhausted. I hasten to assure you that I've no garlic even in the cellar. And one day when a doctor came to see me who smelt of garlic, I asked him to take his hat and go and spread his fragrance elsewhere. There is no smell of garlic here, but the place does smell of drugs. My father lay paralyzed for a year and a half, and the whole house smelt of medicine. A year and a half! I was sorry to lose him, but I'm glad he's dead: he suffered so!"

She led the officer through two rooms similar to the drawing-room, through a large reception hall, and came to a stop in her study, where there was a lady's writing-table covered with little knick-knacks. On the carpet near it several books lay strewn about, opened and folded back. Through a small door leading from the study he saw a table laid for lunch.

Still chatting, Susanna took out of her pocket a bunch of little keys and unlocked an ingeniously made cupboard with a curved, sloping lid. When the lid was raised the cupboard emitted a plaintive note which made the lieutenant think of an AEolian harp. Susanna picked out another key and clicked another lock.

"I have underground passages here and secret doors," she said, taking out a small morocco portfolio. "It's a funny cupboard, isn't it? And in this portfolio I have a quarter of my fortune. Look how podgy it is! You won't strangle me, will you?"

Susanna raised her eyes to the lieutenant and laughed good-naturedly.

The lieutenant laughed too.

"She's rather jolly," he thought, watching the keys flashing between her fingers.

"Here it is," she said, picking out the key of the portfolio. "Now, Mr. Creditor, trot out the IOU. What a silly thing money is really! How paltry it is, and yet how women love it! I am a Jewess, you know, to the marrow of my bones. I am passionately fond of Shmuls and Yankels, but how I loathe that passion for gain in our Semitic blood. They hoard and they don't know what they are hoarding for. One ought to live and enjoy oneself, but they're afraid of spending an extra farthing. In that way I am more like an hussar than a Shmul. I don't like money to be kept long in one place. And altogether I fancy I'm not much like a Jewess. Does my accent give me away much, eh?"

"What shall I say?" mumbled the lieutenant. "You speak good Russian, but you do roll your *r's*."

Susanna laughed and put the little key in the lock of the portfolio. The lieutenant took out of his pocket a little roll of IOUs and laid them with a notebook on the table.

"Nothing betrays a Jew as much as his accent," Susanna went on, looking gaily at the lieutenant. "However much he twists himself into a Russian or a Frenchman, ask him to say 'feather' and he will say 'fedder' . . . but I pronounce it correctly: 'Feather! feather! feather!'"

Both laughed.

"By Jove, she's very jolly!" thought Sokolsky.

Susanna put the portfolio on a chair, took a step towards the lieutenant, and bringing her face close to his, went on gaily:

"Next to the Jews I love no people so much as the Russian and the French. I did not do much at school and I know no history, but it seems to me that the fate of the world lies in the hands of those two nations. I lived a long time abroad. . . . I spent six months in Madrid. . . . I've gazed my fill at the public, and the conclusion I've come to is that there are no decent peoples except the Russian and the French. Take the languages, for instance. . . . The German language is like the neighing of horses; as for the English . . . you can't imagine anything stupider. Fight—feet—foot! Italian is only pleasant when they speak it slowly. If you listen to Italians gabbling, you get the effect of the Jewish jargon. And the Poles? Mercy on us! There's no language so disgusting! 'Nie pieprz, Pietrze, pieprzem wieprza bo mozeoz przepieprzye wieprza pieprzem.' That means: 'Don't pepper a sucking pig with pepper, Pyotr, or perhaps you'll over-pepper the sucking pig with pepper.' Ha, ha, ha!"

Susanna Moiseyevna rolled her eyes and broke into such a pleasant, infectious laugh that the lieutenant, looking at her, went off into a loud and merry peal of laughter. She took the visitor by the button, and went on:

"You don't like Jews, of course . . . they've many faults, like all nations. I don't dispute that. But are the Jews to blame for it? No, it's not the Jews who are to blame, but the Jewish women! They are narrow-minded, greedy; there's no sort of poetry about them, they're dull. . . . You have never lived with a Jewess, so you don't know how charming it is!" Susanna Moiseyevna pronounced the last words with deliberate emphasis and with no eagerness or laughter. She paused as though frightened at her own openness, and her face was suddenly distorted in a strange, unaccountable way. Her eyes stared at the lieutenant without blinking, her lips parted and showed clenched teeth. Her whole face, her throat, and even her bosom, seemed quivering with a spiteful, catlike expression. Still keeping her eyes fixed on her visitor, she rapidly bent to one side, and swiftly, like a cat, snatched something from the table. All this was the work of a few seconds. Watching her movements, the lieutenant saw five fingers crumple up his IOUs and caught a glimpse of the white rustling paper as it disappeared in her clenched fist. Such an extraordinary transition from good-natured laughter to crime so appalled him that he turned pale and stepped back. . . .

And she, still keeping her frightened, searching eyes upon him, felt along her hip with her clenched fist for her pocket. Her fist struggled convulsively for the pocket, like a fish in the net, and could not find the opening. In another moment the IOUs would have vanished in the recesses of her feminine garments, but at that point the lieutenant uttered a faint cry, and, moved more by instinct than reflection, seized the Jewess by her arm above the clenched fist. Showing her teeth more than ever, she struggled with all her might and pulled her hand away. Then Sokolsky put his right arm firmly round her waist, and the other round her chest and a struggle followed. Afraid of outraging her sex or hurting her, he tried only to prevent her moving, and to get hold of the fist with the IOUs; but she wriggled like an eel in his arms with her supple, flexible body, struck him in the chest with her elbows, and scratched him, so that he could not help touching her all over, and was forced to hurt her and disregard her modesty.

"How unusual this is! How strange!" he thought, utterly amazed, hardly able to believe his senses, and feeling rather sick from the scent of jasmine.

In silence, breathing heavily, stumbling against the furniture, they moved about the room. Susanna was carried away by the struggle. She flushed, closed her eyes, and forgetting herself, once even pressed her face against the face of the lieutenant, so that there was a sweetish taste left on his lips. At last he caught hold of her clenched hand. . . . Forcing it open, and not finding the papers in it, he let go the Jewess. With flushed faces and dishevelled hair, they looked at one another, breathing hard. The spiteful, catlike expression on the Jewess's face was gradually replaced by a good-natured smile. She burst out laughing, and turning on one foot, went towards the room where lunch was ready. The lieutenant moved slowly after her. She sat down to the table, and, still flushed and breathing hard, tossed off half a glass of port.

"Listen"—the lieutenant broke the silence—"I hope you are joking?"

"Not a bit of it," she answered, thrusting a piece of bread into her mouth.

"H'm! . . . How do you wish me to take all this?"

"As you choose. Sit down and have lunch!"

"But . . . it's dishonest!"

"Perhaps. But don't trouble to give me a sermon; I have my own way of looking at things."

"Won't you give them back?"

"Of course not! If you were a poor unfortunate man, with nothing to eat, then it would be a different matter. But—he wants to get married!"

"It's not my money, you know; it's my cousin's!"

"And what does your cousin want with money? To get fashionable clothes for his wife? But I really don't care whether your *belle-soeur* has dresses or not."

The lieutenant had ceased to remember that he was in a strange house with an unknown lady, and did not trouble himself with decorum. He strode up and down the room, scowled and nervously fingered his waistcoat. The fact that the Jewess had lowered herself in his eyes by her dishonest action, made him feel bolder and more free-and-easy.

"The devil knows what to make of it!" he muttered. "Listen. I shan't go away from here until I get the IOUs!"

"Ah, so much the better," laughed Susanna. "If you stay here for good, it will make it livelier for me."

Excited by the struggle, the lieutenant looked at Susanna's laughing, insolent face, at her munching mouth, at her heaving bosom, and grew bolder and more audacious. Instead of thinking about the IOU he began for some reason recalling with a sort of relish his cousin's stories of the Jewess's romantic adventures, of her free way of life, and these reminiscences only provoked him to greater audacity. Impulsively he sat down beside the Jewess and thinking no more of the IOUs began to eat. . . .

"Will you have vodka or wine?" Susanna asked with a laugh. "So you will stay till you get the IOUs? Poor fellow! How many days and nights you will have to spend with me, waiting for those IOUs! Won't your fiancee have something to say about it?"

II

Five hours had passed. The lieutenant's cousin, Alexey Ivanovitch Kryukov was walking about the rooms of his country-house in his dressing-gown and slippers, and looking impatiently out of window. He was a tall, sturdy man, with a large black beard and a manly face; and as the Jewess had truly said, he was handsome, though he had reached the age when men are apt to grow too stout, puffy, and bald. By mind and temperament he was one of those natures in which the Russian intellectual classes are so rich: warm-hearted, good-natured, well-bred, having some knowledge of the arts and sciences, some faith, and the most chivalrous notions about honour, but indolent and lacking in depth. He was fond of good eating and drinking, was an ideal whist-player, was a connoisseur in women and horses, but in other things he was apathetic and sluggish as a seal, and to rouse him from his lethargy something extraordinary and quite revolting was needed, and then he would forget everything in the world and display intense activity; he would fume and talk of a duel, write a petition of seven pages to a Minister, gallop at breakneck speed about the district, call some one publicly "a scoundrel," would go to law, and so on.

"How is it our Sasha's not back yet?" he kept asking his wife, glancing out of window. "Why, it's dinner-time!"

After waiting for the lieutenant till six o'clock, they sat down to dinner. When supper-time came, however, Alexey Ivanovitch was listening to every footstep, to every sound of the door, and kept shrugging his shoulders.

"Strange!" he said. "The rascally dandy must have stayed on at the tenant's."

As he went to bed after supper, Kryukov made up his mind that the lieutenant was being entertained at the tenant's, where after a festive evening he was staying the night.

Alexandr Grigoryevitch only returned next morning. He looked extremely crumpled and confused.

"I want to speak to you alone . . ." he said mysteriously to his cousin.

They went into the study. The lieutenant shut the door, and he paced for a long time up and down before he began to speak.

"Something's happened, my dear fellow," he began, "that I don't know how to tell you about. You wouldn't believe it . . ."

And blushing, faltering, not looking at his cousin, he told what had happened with the IOUs. Kryukov, standing with his feet wide apart and his head bent, listened and frowned.

"Are you joking?" he asked.

"How the devil could I be joking? It's no joking matter!"

"I don't understand!" muttered Kryukov, turning crimson and flinging up his hands. "It's positively . . . immoral on your part. Before your very eyes a hussy is up to the devil knows what, a serious crime, plays a nasty trick, and you go and kiss her!"

"But I can't understand myself how it happened!" whispered the lieutenant, blinking guiltily. "Upon my honour, I don't understand it! It's the first time in my life I've come across such a monster! It's not her beauty that does for you, not her mind, but that . . . you understand . . . insolence, cynicism. . . ."

"Insolence, cynicism . . . it's unclean! If you've such a longing for insolence and cynicism, you might have picked a sow out of the mire and have devoured her alive. It would have been cheaper, anyway! Instead of two thousand three hundred!"

"You do express yourself elegantly!" said the lieutenant, frowning.

"I'll pay you back the two thousand three hundred!"

"I know you'll pay it back, but it's not a question of money! Damn the money! What revolts me is your being such a limp rag . . . such filthy feebleness! And engaged! With a fiancee!"

"Don't speak of it . . ." said the lieutenant, blushing. "I loathe myself as it is. I should like to sink into the earth. It's sickening and vexatious that I shall have to bother my aunt for that five thousand. . . ."

Kryukov continued for some time longer expressing his indignation and grumbling, then, as he grew calmer, he sat down on the sofa and began to jeer at his cousin.

"You young officers!" he said with contemptuous irony. "Nice bridegrooms."

Suddenly he leapt up as though he had been stung, stamped his foot, and ran about the study.

"No, I'm not going to leave it like that!" he said, shaking his fist. "I will have those IOUs, I will! I'll give it her! One doesn't beat women, but I'll break every bone in her body. . . . I'll pound her to a jelly! I'm not a lieutenant! You won't touch me with insolence or cynicism! No-o-o, damn her! Mishka!" he shouted, "run and tell them to get the racing droshky out for me!"

Kryukov dressed rapidly, and, without heeding the agitated lieutenant, got into the droshky, and with a wave of his hand resolutely raced off to Susanna Moiseyevna. For a long time the lieutenant gazed out of window at the clouds of dust that rolled after his cousin's droshky, stretched, yawned, and went to his own room. A quarter of an hour later he was sound asleep.

At six o'clock he was waked up and summoned to dinner.

"How nice this is of Alexey!" his cousin's wife greeted him in the dining-room. "He keeps us waiting for dinner."

"Do you mean to say he's not come back yet?" yawned the lieutenant.

"H'm! . . . he's probably gone round to see the tenant."

But Alexey Ivanovitch was not back by supper either. His wife and Sokolsky decided that he was playing cards at the tenant's and would most likely stay the night there. What had happened was not what they had supposed, however.

Kryukov returned next morning, and without greeting any one, without a word, dashed into his study.

"Well?" whispered the lieutenant, gazing at him round-eyed.

Kryukov waved his hand and gave a snort.

"Why, what's the matter? What are you laughing at?"

Kryukov flopped on the sofa, thrust his head in the pillow, and shook with suppressed laughter. A minute later he got up, and looking at the surprised lieutenant, with his eyes full of tears from laughing, said:

"Close the door. Well . . . she *is* a fe-e-male, I beg to inform you!"

"Did you get the IOUs?"

Kryukov waved his hand and went off into a peal of laughter again.

"Well! she is a female!" he went on. "Merci for the acquaintance, my boy! She's a devil in petticoats. I arrived; I walked in like such an avenging Jove, you know, that I felt almost afraid of myself . . . . I frowned, I scowled, even clenched my fists to be more awe-inspiring. . . . 'Jokes don't pay with me, madam!' said I, and more in that style. And I threatened her with the law and with the Governor. To begin with she burst into tears, said she'd been joking with you, and even took me to the cupboard to give me the money. Then she began arguing that the future of Europe lies in the hands of the French, and the Russians, swore at women. . . . Like you, I listened, fascinated, ass that I was. . . . She kept singing the praises of my beauty, patted me on the arm near the shoulder, to see how strong I was, and . . . and as you see, I've only just got away from her! Ha, ha! She's enthusiastic about you!"

"You're a nice fellow!" laughed the lieutenant. "A married man! highly respected. . . . Well, aren't you ashamed? Disgusted? Joking apart though, old man, you've got your Queen Tamara in your own neighbourhood. . . ."

"In my own neighbourhood! Why, you wouldn't find another such chameleon in the whole of Russia! I've never seen anything like it in my life, though I know a good bit about women, too. I have known regular devils in my time, but I never met anything like this. It is, as you say, by insolence and cynicism she gets over you. What is so attractive in her is the diabolical suddenness, the quick transitions, the swift shifting hues. . . . Brrr! And the IOU— phew! Write it off for lost. We are both great sinners, we'll go halves in our sin. I shall put down to you not two thousand three hundred, but half of it. Mind, tell my wife I was at the tenant's."

Kryukov and the lieutenant buried their heads in the pillows, and broke into laughter; they raised their heads, glanced at one another, and again subsided into their pillows.

"Engaged! A lieutenant!" Kryukov jeered.

"Married!" retorted Sokolsky. "Highly respected! Father of a family!"

At dinner they talked in veiled allusions, winked at one another, and, to the surprise of the others, were continually gushing with laughter into their dinner-napkins. After dinner, still in the best of spirits, they dressed up as Turks, and, running after one another with guns, played at soldiers with the children. In the evening they had a long argument. The lieutenant maintained that it was mean and contemptible to accept a dowry with your wife, even when there was passionate love on both sides. Kryukov thumped the table with his fists and declared that this was absurd, and that a husband who did not like his wife to have property of her own was an egoist and a despot. Both shouted, boiled over, did not understand each other, drank a good deal, and in the end, picking up the skirts of their dressing-gowns, went to their bedrooms. They soon fell asleep and slept soundly.

Life went on as before, even, sluggish and free from sorrow. The shadows lay on the earth, thunder pealed from the clouds, from time to time the wind moaned plaintively, as though to prove that nature, too, could lament, but nothing troubled the habitual tranquillity of these people. Of Susanna Moiseyevna and the IOUs they said nothing. Both of them felt, somehow, ashamed to speak of the incident aloud. Yet they remembered it and thought of it with pleasure, as of a curious farce, which life had unexpectedly and casually played upon them, and which it would be pleasant to recall in old age.

On the sixth or seventh day after his visit to the Jewess, Kryukov was sitting in his study in the morning writing a congratulatory letter to his aunt. Alexandr Grigoryevitch was walking to and fro near the table in silence. The lieutenant had slept badly that night; he woke up depressed, and now he felt bored. He paced up and down, thinking of the end of his furlough, of his fiancee, who was expecting him, of how people could live all their lives in the country without feeling bored. Standing at the window, for a long time he stared at the trees, smoked three cigarettes one after another, and suddenly turned to his cousin.

"I have a favour to ask you, Alyosha," he said. "Let me have a saddle-horse for the day. . . ."

Kryukov looked searchingly at him and continued his writing with a frown.

"You will, then?" asked the lieutenant.

Kryukov looked at him again, then deliberately drew out a drawer in the table, and taking out a thick roll of notes, gave it to his cousin.

"Here's five thousand . . ." he said. "Though it's not my money, yet, God bless you, it's all the same. I advise you to send for post-horses at once and go away. Yes, really!"

The lieutenant in his turn looked searchingly at Kryukov and laughed.

"You've guessed right, Alyosha," he said, reddening. "It was to her I meant to ride. Yesterday evening when the washerwoman gave me that damned tunic, the one I was wearing then, and it smelt of jasmine, why . . . I felt I must go!"

"You must go away."

"Yes, certainly. And my furlough's just over. I really will go to-day! Yes, by Jove! However long one stays, one has to go in the end. . . . I'm going!"

The post-horses were brought after dinner the same day; the lieutenant said good-bye to the Kryukovs and set off, followed by their good wishes.

Another week passed. It was a dull but hot and heavy day. From early morning Kryukov walked aimlessly about the house, looking out of window, or turning over the leaves of albums, though he was sick of the sight of them already. When he came across his wife or children, he began grumbling crossly. It seemed to him, for some reason that day, that his children's manners were revolting, that his wife did not know how to look after the servants, that their expenditure was quite disproportionate to their income. All this meant that "the master" was out of humour.

After dinner, Kryukov, feeling dissatisfied with the soup and the roast meat he had eaten, ordered out his racing droshky. He drove slowly out of the courtyard, drove at a walking pace for a quarter of a mile, and stopped.

"Shall I . . . drive to her . . . that devil?" he thought, looking at the leaden sky.

And Kryukov positively laughed, as though it were the first time that day he had asked himself that question. At once the load of boredom was lifted from his heart, and there rose a gleam of pleasure in his lazy eyes. He lashed the horse. . . .

All the way his imagination was picturing how surprised the Jewess would be to see him, how he would laugh and chat, and come home feeling refreshed. . . .

"Once a month one needs something to brighten one up . . . something out of the common round," he thought, "something that would give the stagnant organism a good shaking up, a reaction . . . whether it's a drinking bout, or . . . Susanna. One can't get on without it."

It was getting dark when he drove into the yard of the vodka distillery. From the open windows of the owner's house came sounds of laughter and singing:

"'Brighter than lightning, more burning than flame. . . .'"

sang a powerful, mellow, bass voice.

"Aha! she has visitors," thought Kryukov.

And he was annoyed that she had visitors.

"Shall I go back?" he thought with his hand on the bell, but he rang all the same, and went up the familiar staircase. From the entry he glanced into the reception hall. There were about five men there—all landowners and officials of his acquaintance; one, a tall, thin gentleman, was sitting at the piano, singing, and striking the keys with his long, thin fingers. The others were listening and grinning with enjoyment. Kryukov looked himself up and down in the looking-glass, and was about to go into the hall, when Susanna Moiseyevna herself darted into the entry, in high spirits and wearing the same black dress. . . . Seeing Kryukov, she was petrified for an instant, then she uttered a little scream and beamed with delight.

"Is it you?" she said, clutching his hand. "What a surprise!"

"Here she is!" smiled Kryukov, putting his arm round her waist. "Well! Does the destiny of Europe still lie in the hands of the French and the Russians?"

"I'm so glad," laughed the Jewess, cautiously removing his arm. "Come, go into the hall; they're all friends there. . . . I'll go and tell them to bring you some tea. Your name's Alexey, isn't it? Well, go in, I'll come directly. . . ."

She blew him a kiss and ran out of the entry, leaving behind her the same sickly smell of jasmine. Kryukov raised his head and walked into the hall. He was on terms of friendly intimacy with all the men in the room, but scarcely nodded to them; they, too, scarcely responded, as though the places in which they met were not quite decent, and as though they were in tacit agreement with one another that it was more suitable for them not to recognise one another.

From the hall Kryukov walked into the drawing-room, and from it into a second drawing-room. On the way he met three or four other guests, also men whom he knew, though they barely recognised him. Their faces were flushed with drink and merriment. Alexey Ivanovitch glanced furtively at them and marvelled that these men, respectable heads of families, who had known sorrow and privation, could demean themselves to such pitiful, cheap gaiety! He shrugged his shoulders, smiled, and walked on.

"There are places," he reflected, "where a sober man feels sick, and a drunken man rejoices. I remember I never could go to the operetta or the gipsies when I was sober: wine makes a man more good-natured and reconciles him with vice. . . ."

Suddenly he stood still, petrified, and caught hold of the door-post with both hands. At the writing-table in Susanna's study was sitting Lieutenant Alexandr Grigoryevitch. He was discussing something in an undertone with a fat, flabby-looking Jew, and seeing his cousin, flushed crimson and looked down at an album.

The sense of decency was stirred in Kryukov and the blood rushed to his head. Overwhelmed with amazement, shame, and anger, he walked up to the table without a word. Sokolsky's head sank lower than ever. His face worked with an expression of agonising shame.

"Ah, it's you, Alyosha!" he articulated, making a desperate effort to raise his eyes and to smile. "I called here to say good-bye, and, as you see. . . . But to-morrow I am certainly going."

"What can I say to him? What?" thought Alexey Ivanovitch. "How can I judge him since I'm here myself?"

And clearing his throat without uttering a word, he went out slowly.

"'Call her not heavenly, and leave her on earth. . . .'"

The bass was singing in the hall. A little while after, Kryukov's racing droshky was bumping along the dusty road.

NEIGHBOURS

PYOTR MIHALITCH IVASHIN was very much out of humour: his sister, a young girl, had gone away to live with Vlassitch, a married man. To shake off the despondency and depression which pursued him at home and in the fields, he called to his aid his sense of justice, his genuine and noble ideas—he had always defended free-love! but this was of no avail, and he always came back to the same conclusion as their foolish old nurse, that his sister had acted wrongly and that Vlassitch had abducted his sister. And that was distressing.

His mother did not leave her room all day long; the old nurse kept sighing and speaking in whispers; his aunt had been on the point of taking her departure every day, and her trunks were continually being brought down to the hall and carried up again to her room. In the house, in the yard, and in the garden it was as still as though there were some one dead in the house. His aunt, the servants, and even the peasants, so it seemed to Pyotr Mihalitch, looked at him enigmatically and with perplexity, as though they wanted to say "Your sister has been seduced; why are you doing nothing?" And he reproached himself for inactivity, though he did not know precisely what action he ought to have taken.

So passed six days. On the seventh—it was Sunday afternoon—a messenger on horseback brought a letter. The address was in a familiar feminine handwriting: "Her Excy. Anna Nikolaevna Ivashin." Pyotr Mihalitch fancied that there was something defiant, provocative, in the handwriting and in the abbreviation "Excy." And advanced ideas in women are obstinate, ruthless, cruel.

"She'd rather die than make any concession to her unhappy mother, or beg her forgiveness," thought Pyotr Mihalitch, as he went to his mother with the letter.

His mother was lying on her bed, dressed. Seeing her son, she rose impulsively, and straightening her grey hair, which had fallen from under her cap, asked quickly:

"What is it? What is it?"

"This has come . . ." said her son, giving her the letter.

Zina's name, and even the pronoun "she" was not uttered in the house. Zina was spoken of impersonally: "this has come," "Gone away," and so on. . . . The mother recognised her daughter's handwriting, and her face grew ugly and unpleasant, and her grey hair escaped again from her cap.

"No!" she said, with a motion of her hands, as though the letter scorched her fingers. "No, no, never! Nothing would induce me!"

The mother broke into hysterical sobs of grief and shame; she evidently longed to read the letter, but her pride prevented her. Pyotr Mihalitch realised that he ought to open the letter himself and read it aloud, but he was overcome by anger such as he had never felt before; he ran out into the yard and shouted to the messenger:

"Say there will be no answer! There will be no answer! Tell them that, you beast!"

And he tore up the letter; then tears came into his eyes, and feeling that he was cruel, miserable, and to blame, he went out into the fields.

He was only twenty-seven, but he was already stout. He dressed like an old man in loose, roomy clothes, and suffered from asthma. He already seemed to be developing the characteristics of an elderly country bachelor. He never fell in love, never thought of marriage, and loved no one but his mother, his sister, his old nurse, and the gardener, Vassilitch. He was fond of good fare, of his nap after dinner, and of talking about politics and exalted subjects. He had in his day taken his degree at the university, but he now looked upon his studies as though in them he had discharged a duty incumbent upon young men between the ages of eighteen and twenty-five; at any rate, the ideas which now strayed every day through his mind had nothing in common with the university or the subjects he had studied there.

In the fields it was hot and still, as though rain were coming. It was steaming in the wood, and there was a heavy fragrant scent from the pines and rotting leaves. Pyotr Mihalitch stopped several times and wiped his wet brow. He looked at his winter corn and his spring oats, walked round the clover-field, and twice drove away a partridge with its chicks which had strayed in from the wood. And all the while he was thinking that this insufferable state of things could not go on for ever, and that he must end it one way or another. End it stupidly, madly, but he must end it.

"But how? What can I do?" he asked himself, and looked imploringly at the sky and at the trees, as though begging for their help.

But the sky and the trees were mute. His noble ideas were no help, and his common sense whispered that the agonising question could have no solution but a stupid one, and that to-day's scene with the messenger was not the last one of its kind. It was terrible to think what was in store for him!

As he returned home the sun was setting. By now it seemed to him that the problem was incapable of solution. He could not accept the accomplished fact, and he could not refuse to accept it, and there was no intermediate course. When, taking off his hat and fanning himself with his handkerchief, he was walking along the road, and had only another mile and a half to go before he would reach home, he heard bells behind him. It was a very choice and successful combination of bells, which gave a clear crystal note. No one had such bells on his horses but the police captain, Medovsky, formerly an officer in the hussars, a man in broken-down health, who had been a great rake and spendthrift, and was a distant relation of Pyotr Mihalitch. He was like one of the family at the Ivashins' and had a tender, fatherly affection for Zina, as well as a great admiration for her.

"I was coming to see you," he said, overtaking Pyotr Mihalitch.

"Get in; I'll give you a lift."

He was smiling and looked cheerful. Evidently he did not yet know that Zina had gone to live with Vlassitch; perhaps he had been told of it already, but did not believe it. Pyotr Mihalitch felt in a difficult position.

"You are very welcome," he muttered, blushing till the tears came into his eyes, and not knowing how to lie or what to say. "I am delighted," he went on, trying to smile, "but . . . Zina is away and mother is ill."

"How annoying!" said the police captain, looking pensively at Pyotr Mihalitch. "And I was meaning to spend the evening with you. Where has Zinaida Mihalovna gone?"

"To the Sinitskys', and I believe she meant to go from there to the monastery. I don't quite know."

The police captain talked a little longer and then turned back. Pyotr Mihalitch walked home, and thought with horror what the police captain's feelings would be when he learned the truth. And Pyotr Mihalitch imagined his feelings, and actually experiencing them himself, went into the house.

"Lord help us," he thought, "Lord help us!"

At evening tea the only one at the table was his aunt. As usual, her face wore the expression that seemed to say that though she was a weak, defenceless woman, she would allow no one to insult her. Pyotr Mihalitch sat down at the other end of the table (he did not like his aunt) and began drinking tea in silence.

"Your mother has had no dinner again to-day," said his aunt. "You ought to do something about it, Petrusha. Starving oneself is no help in sorrow."

It struck Pyotr Mihalitch as absurd that his aunt should meddle in other people's business and should make her departure depend on Zina's having gone away. He was tempted to say something rude to her, but restrained himself. And as he restrained himself he felt the time had come for action, and that he could not bear it any longer. Either he must act at once or fall on the ground, and scream and bang his head upon the floor. He pictured Vlassitch and Zina, both of them progressive and self-satisfied, kissing each other somewhere under a maple tree, and all the anger and bitterness that had been accumulating in him for the last seven days fastened upon Vlassitch.

"One has seduced and abducted my sister," he thought, "another will come and murder my mother, a third will set fire to the house and sack the place. . . . And all this under the mask of friendship, lofty ideas, unhappiness!"

"No, it shall not be!" Pyotr Mihalitch cried suddenly, and he brought his fist down on the table.

He jumped up and ran out of the dining-room. In the stable the steward's horse was standing ready saddled. He got on it and galloped off to Vlassitch.

There was a perfect tempest within him. He felt a longing to do something extraordinary, startling, even if he had to repent of it all his life afterwards. Should he call Vlassitch a blackguard, slap him in the face, and then challenge him to a duel? But Vlassitch was not one of those men who do fight duels; being called a blackguard and slapped in the face would only make him more unhappy, and would make him shrink into himself more than ever. These unhappy, defenceless people are the most insufferable, the most tiresome creatures in the world. They can do anything with impunity. When the luckless man responds to well-deserved reproach by looking at you with eyes full of deep and guilty feeling, and with a sickly smile bends his head submissively, even justice itself could not lift its hand against him.

"No matter. I'll horsewhip him before her eyes and tell him what I think of him," Pyotr Mihalitch decided.

He was riding through his wood and waste land, and he imagined Zina would try to justify her conduct by talking about the rights of women and individual freedom, and about there being no difference between legal marriage and free union. Like a woman, she would argue about what she did not understand. And very likely at the end she would ask, "How do you come in? What right have you to interfere?"

"No, I have no right," muttered Pyotr Mihalitch. "But so much the better. . . . The harsher I am, the less right I have to interfere, the better."

It was sultry. Clouds of gnats hung over the ground and in the waste places the peewits called plaintively. Everything betokened rain, but he could not see a cloud in the sky. Pyotr Mihalitch crossed the boundary of his estate and galloped over a smooth, level field. He often went along this road and knew every bush, every hollow in it. What now in the far distance looked in the dusk like a dark cliff was a red church; he could picture it all down to the smallest detail, even the plaster on the gate and the calves that were always grazing in the church enclosure. Three-quarters of a mile to the right of the church there was a copse like a dark blur—it was Count Koltonovitch's. And beyond the church Vlassitch's estate began.

From behind the church and the count's copse a huge black storm-cloud was rising, and there were ashes of white lightning.

"Here it is!" thought Pyotr Mihalitch. "Lord help us, Lord help us!"

The horse was soon tired after its quick gallop, and Pyotr Mihalitch was tired too. The storm-cloud looked at him angrily and seemed to advise him to go home. He felt a little scared.

"I will prove to them they are wrong," he tried to reassure himself. "They will say that it is free-love, individual freedom; but freedom means self-control and not subjection to passion. It's not liberty but license!"

He reached the count's big pond; it looked dark blue and frowning under the cloud, and a smell of damp and slime rose from it. Near the dam, two willows, one old and one young, drooped tenderly towards one another. Pyotr Mihalitch and Vlassitch had been walking near this very spot only a fortnight before, humming a students' song:

"'Youth is wasted, life is nought, when the heart is cold and loveless.'"

A wretched song!

It was thundering as Pyotr Mihalitch rode through the copse, and the trees were bending and rustling in the wind. He had to make haste. It was only three-quarters of a mile through a meadow from the copse to Vlassitch's house. Here there were old birch-trees on each side of the road. They had the same melancholy and unhappy air as their owner Vlassitch, and looked as tall and lanky as he. Big drops of rain pattered on the birches and on the grass; the wind had suddenly dropped, and there was a smell of wet earth and poplars. Before him he saw Vlassitch's fence with a row of yellow acacias, which were tall and lanky too; where the fence was broken he could see the neglected orchard.

Pyotr Mihalitch was not thinking now of the horsewhip or of a slap in the face, and did not know what he would do at Vlassitch's. He felt nervous. He felt frightened on his own account and on his sister's, and was terrified at the thought of seeing her. How would she behave with her brother? What would they both talk about? And had he not better go back before it was too late? As he made these reflections, he galloped up the avenue of lime-trees to the house, rode round the big clumps of lilacs, and suddenly saw Vlassitch.

Vlassitch, wearing a cotton shirt, and top-boots, bending forward, with no hat on in the rain, was coming from the corner of the house to the front door. He was followed by a workman with a hammer and a box of nails. They must have been mending a shutter which had been banging in the wind. Seeing Pyotr Mihalitch, Vlassitch stopped.

"It's you!" he said, smiling. "That's nice."

"Yes, I've come, as you see," said Pyotr Mihalitch, brushing the rain off himself with both hands.

"Well, that's capital! I'm very glad," said Vlassitch, but he did not hold out his hand: evidently he did not venture, but waited for Pyotr Mihalitch to hold out his. "It will do the oats good," he said, looking at the sky.

"Yes."

They went into the house in silence. To the right of the hall was a door leading to another hall and then to the drawing-room, and on the left was a little room which in winter was used by the steward. Pyotr Mihalitch and Vlassitch went into this little room.

"Where were you caught in the rain?"

"Not far off, quite close to the house."

Pyotr Mihalitch sat down on the bed. He was glad of the noise of the rain and the darkness of the room. It was better: it made it less dreadful, and there was no need to see his companion's face. There was no anger in his heart now, nothing but fear and vexation with himself. He felt he had made a bad beginning, and that nothing would come of this visit.

Both were silent for some time and affected to be listening to the rain.

"Thank you, Petrusha," Vlassitch began, clearing his throat. "I am very grateful to you for coming. It's generous and noble of you. I understand it, and, believe me, I appreciate it. Believe me."

He looked out of the window and went on, standing in the middle of the room:

"Everything happened so secretly, as though we were concealing it all from you. The feeling that you might be wounded and angry has been a blot on our happiness all these days. But let me justify myself. We kept it secret not because we did not trust you. To begin with, it all happened suddenly, by a kind of inspiration; there was no time to discuss it. Besides, it's such a private, delicate matter, and it was awkward to bring a third person in, even some one as intimate as you. Above all, in all this we reckoned on your generosity. You are a very noble and generous person. I am infinitely grateful to you. If you ever need my life, come and take it."

Vlassitch talked in a quiet, hollow bass, always on the same droning note; he was evidently agitated. Pyotr Mihalitch felt it was his turn to speak, and that to listen and keep silent would really mean playing the part of a generous and noble simpleton, and that had not been his idea in coming. He got up quickly and said, breathlessly in an undertone:

"Listen, Grigory. You know I liked you and could have desired no better husband for my sister; but what has happened is awful! It's terrible to think of it!"

"Why is it terrible?" asked Vlassitch, with a quiver in his voice.

"It would be terrible if we had done wrong, but that isn't so."

"Listen, Grigory. You know I have no prejudices; but, excuse my frankness, to my mind you have both acted selfishly. Of course, I shan't say so to my sister—it will distress her; but you ought to know: mother is miserable beyond all description."

"Yes, that's sad," sighed Vlassitch. "We foresaw that, Petrusha, but what could we have done? Because one's actions hurt other people, it doesn't prove that they are wrong. What's to be done! Every important step one takes is bound to distress somebody. If you went to fight for freedom, that would distress your mother, too. What's to be done! Any one who puts the peace of his family before everything has to renounce the life of ideas completely."

There was a vivid flash of lightning at the window, and the lightning seemed to change the course of Vlassitch's thoughts. He sat down beside Pyotr Mihalitch and began saying what was utterly beside the point.

"I have such a reverence for your sister, Petrusha," he said. "When I used to come and see you, I felt as though I were going to a holy shrine, and I really did worship Zina. Now my reverence for her grows every day. For me she is something higher than a wife—yes, higher!" Vlassitch waved his hands. "She is my holy of holies. Since she is living with me, I enter my house as though it were a temple. She is an extraordinary, rare, most noble woman!"

"Well, he's off now!" thought Pyotr Mihalitch; he disliked the word "woman."

"Why shouldn't you be married properly?" he asked. "How much does your wife want for a divorce?"

"Seventy-five thousand."

"It's rather a lot. But if we were to negotiate with her?"

"She won't take a farthing less. She is an awful woman, brother," sighed Vlassitch. "I've never talked to you about her before—it was unpleasant to think of her; but now that the subject has come up, I'll tell you about her. I married her on the impulse of the moment—a fine, honourable impulse. An officer in command of a battalion of our regiment—if you care to hear the details—had an affair with a girl of eighteen; that is, to put it plainly, he seduced her, lived with her for two months, and abandoned her. She was in an awful position, brother. She was ashamed to go home to her parents; besides, they wouldn't have received her. Her lover had abandoned her; there was nothing left for her but to go to the barracks and sell herself. The other officers in the regiment were indignant. They were by no means saints themselves, but the baseness of it was so striking. Besides, no one in the regiment could endure the man. And to spite him, you understand, the indignant lieutenants and ensigns began getting up a subscription for the unfortunate girl. And when we subalterns met together and began to subscribe five or ten roubles each, I had a sudden inspiration. I felt it was an opportunity to do something fine. I hastened to the girl and warmly expressed my sympathy. And while I was on my way to her, and while I was talking to her, I loved her fervently as a woman insulted and injured. Yes. . . . Well, a week later I made her an offer. The colonel and my comrades thought my marriage out of keeping with the dignity of an officer. That roused me more than ever. I wrote a long letter, do you know, in which I proved that my action ought to be inscribed in the annals of the regiment in letters of gold, and so on. I sent the letter to my colonel and copies to my comrades. Well, I was excited, and, of course, I could not avoid being rude. I was asked to leave the regiment. I have a rough copy of it put away somewhere; I'll give it to you to read sometime. It was written with great feeling. You will see what lofty and noble sentiments I was experiencing. I resigned my commission and came here with my wife. My father had left a few debts, I had no money, and from the first day my wife began making acquaintances, dressing herself smartly, and playing cards, and I was obliged to mortgage the estate. She led a bad life, you understand, and you are the only one of the neighbours who hasn't been her lover. After two years I gave her all I had to set me free and she went off to town. Yes. . . . And now I pay her twelve hundred roubles a year. She is an awful woman! There is a fly, brother, which lays an egg in the back of a spider so that the spider can't shake it off: the grub fastens upon the spider and drinks its heart's blood. That was how this woman fastened upon me and sucks the blood of my heart. She hates and despises me for being so stupid; that is, for marrying a woman like her. My chivalry seems to her despicable. 'A wise man cast me off,' she says, 'and a fool picked me up.' To her thinking no one but a pitiful idiot could have behaved as I did. And that is insufferably bitter to me, brother. Altogether, I may say in parenthesis, fate has been hard upon me, very hard."

Pyotr Mihalitch listened to Vlassitch and wondered in perplexity what it was in this man that had so charmed his sister. He was not young—he was forty-one—lean and lanky, narrow-chested, with a long nose, and grey hairs in his beard. He talked in a droning voice, had a sickly smile, and waved his hands awkwardly as he talked. He had neither health, nor pleasant, manly manners, nor *savoir-faire*, nor gaiety, and in all his exterior there was something colourless and indefinite. He dressed without taste, his surroundings were depressing, he did not care for poetry or painting because "they have no answer to give to the questions of the day" that is, he did not understand them; music did not touch him. He was a poor farmer.

His estate was in a wretched condition and was mortgaged; he was paying twelve percent on the second mortgage and owed ten thousand on personal securities as well. When the time came to pay the interest on the mortgage or to send money to his wife, he asked every one to lend him money with as much agitation as though his house were on fire, and, at the same time losing his head, he would sell the whole of his winter store of fuel for five roubles and a stack of straw for three roubles, and then have his garden fence or old cucumber-frames chopped up to heat his stoves. His meadows were ruined by pigs, the peasants' cattle strayed in the undergrowth in his woods, and every year the old trees were fewer and fewer: beehives and rusty pails lay about in his garden and kitchen-garden. He had neither talents nor abilities, nor even ordinary capacity for living like other people. In practical life he was a weak, naive man, easy to deceive and to cheat, and the peasants with good reason called him "simple."

He was a Liberal, and in the district was regarded as a "Red," but even his progressiveness was a bore. There was no originality nor moving power about his independent views: he was revolted, indignant, and delighted always on the same note; it was always spiritless and ineffective. Even in moments of strong enthusiasm he never raised his head or stood upright. But the most tiresome thing of all was that he managed to express even his best and finest ideas so that they seemed in him commonplace and out of date. It reminded one of something old one had read long ago, when slowly and with an air of profundity he would begin discoursing of his noble, lofty moments, of his best years; or when he went into raptures over the younger generation, which has always been, and still is, in advance of society; or abused Russians for donning their dressing-gowns at thirty and forgetting the principles of their *alma mater*. If you stayed the night with him, he would put Pissarev or Darwin on your bedroom table; if you said you had read it, he would go and bring Dobrolubov.

In the district this was called free-thinking, and many people looked upon this free-thinking as an innocent and harmless eccentricity; it made him profoundly unhappy, however. It was for him the maggot of which he had just been speaking; it had fastened upon him and was sucking his life-blood. In his past there had been the strange marriage in the style of Dostoevsky; long letters and copies written in a bad, unintelligible hand-writing, but with great feeling, endless misunderstandings, explanations, disappointments, then debts, a second mortgage, the allowance to his wife, the monthly borrowing of money—and all this for no benefit to any one, either himself or others. And in the present, as in the past, he was still in a nervous flurry, on the lookout for heroic actions, and poking his nose into other people's affairs; as before, at every favourable opportunity there were long letters and copies, wearisome, stereotyped conversations about the village community, or the revival of handicrafts or the establishment of cheese factories—conversations as like one another as though he had prepared them, not in his living brain, but by some mechanical process. And finally this scandal with Zina of which one could not see the end!

And meanwhile Zina was young—she was only twenty-two—good-looking, elegant, gay; she was fond of laughing, chatter, argument, a passionate musician; she had good taste in dress, in furniture, in books, and in her own home she would not have put up with a room like this, smelling of boots and cheap vodka. She, too, had advanced ideas, but in her free-thinking one felt the overflow of energy, the vanity of a young, strong, spirited girl, passionately eager to be better and more original than others. . . . How had it happened that she had fallen in love with Vlassitch?

"He is a Quixote, an obstinate fanatic, a maniac," thought Pyotr Mihalitch, "and she is as soft, yielding, and weak in character as I am. . . . She and I give in easily, without resistance. She loves him; but, then, I, too, love him in spite of everything."

Pyotr Mihalitch considered Vlassitch a good, straightforward man, but narrow and one-sided. In his perturbations and his sufferings, and in fact in his whole life, he saw no lofty aims, remote or immediate; he saw nothing but boredom and incapacity for life. His self-sacrifice and all that Vlassitch himself called heroic actions or noble impulses seemed to him a useless waste of force, unnecessary blank shots which consumed a great deal of powder. And Vlassitch's fanatical belief in the extraordinary loftiness and faultlessness of his own way of thinking struck him as naive and even morbid; and the fact that Vlassitch all his life had contrived to mix the trivial with the exalted, that he had made a stupid marriage and looked upon it as an act of heroism, and then had affairs with other women and regarded that as a triumph of some idea or other was simply incomprehensible.

Nevertheless, Pyotr Mihalitch was fond of Vlassitch; he was conscious of a sort of power in him, and for some reason he had never had the heart to contradict him.

Vlassitch sat down quite close to him for a talk in the dark, to the accompaniment of the rain, and he had cleared his throat as a prelude to beginning on something lengthy, such as the history of his marriage. But it was intolerable for Pyotr Mihalitch to listen to him; he was tormented by the thought that he would see his sister directly.

"Yes, you've had bad luck," he said gently; "but, excuse me, we've been wandering from the point. That's not what we are talking about."

"Yes, yes, quite so. Well, let us come back to the point," said Vlassitch, and he stood up. "I tell you, Petrusha, our conscience is clear. We are not married, but there is no need for me to prove to you that our marriage is perfectly legitimate. You are as free in your ideas as I am, and, happily, there can be no disagreement between us on that point. As for our future, that ought not to alarm you. I'll work in the sweat of my brow, I'll work day and night— in fact, I will strain every nerve to make Zina happy. Her life will be a splendid one! You may ask, am I able to do it. I am, brother! When a man devotes every minute to one thought, it's not difficult for him to attain his object. But let us go to Zina; it will be a joy to her to see you."

Pyotr Mihalitch's heart began to beat. He got up and followed Vlassitch into the hall, and from there into the drawing-room. There was nothing in the huge gloomy room but a piano and a long row of old chairs ornamented with bronze, on which no one ever sat. There was a candle alight on the piano. From the drawing-room they went in silence into the dining-room. This room, too, was large and comfortless; in the middle of the room there was a round table with two leaves with six thick legs, and only one candle. A clock in a large mahogany case like an ikon stand pointed to half-past two.

Vlassitch opened the door into the next room and said:

"Zina, here is Petrusha come to see us!"

At once there was the sound of hurried footsteps and Zina came into the dining-room. She was tall, plump, and very pale, and, just as when he had seen her for the last time at home, she was wearing a black skirt and a red blouse, with a large buckle on her belt. She flung one arm round her brother and kissed him on the temple.

"What a storm!" she said. "Grigory went off somewhere and I was left quite alone in the house."

She was not embarrassed, and looked at her brother as frankly and candidly as at home; looking at her, Pyotr Mihalitch, too, lost his embarrassment.

"But you are not afraid of storms," he said, sitting down at the table.

"No," she said, "but here the rooms are so big, the house is so old, and when there is thunder it all rattles like a cupboard full of crockery. It's a charming house altogether," she went on, sitting down opposite her brother. "There's some pleasant memory in every room. In my room, only fancy, Grigory's grandfather shot himself."

"In August we shall have the money to do up the lodge in the garden," said Vlassitch.

"For some reason when it thunders I think of that grandfather," Zina went on. "And in this dining-room somebody was flogged to death."

"That's an actual fact," said Vlassitch, and he looked with wide-open eyes at Pyotr Mihalitch. "Sometime in the forties this place was let to a Frenchman called Olivier. The portrait of his daughter is lying in an attic now—a very pretty girl. This Olivier, so my father told me, despised Russians for their ignorance and treated them with cruel derision. Thus, for instance, he insisted on the priest walking without his hat for half a mile round his house, and on the church bells being rung when the Olivier family drove through the village. The serfs and altogether the humble of this world, of course, he treated with even less ceremony. Once there came along this road one of the simple-hearted sons of wandering Russia, somewhat after the style of Gogol's divinity student, Homa Brut. He asked for a night's lodging, pleased the bailiffs, and was given a job at the office of the estate. There are many variations of the story. Some say the divinity student stirred up the peasants, others that Olivier's daughter fell in love with him. I don't know which is true, only one fine evening Olivier called him in here and cross-examined him, then ordered him to be beaten. Do you know, he sat here at this table drinking claret while the stable-boys beat the man. He must have tried to wring something out of him. Towards morning the divinity student died of the torture and his body was hidden. They say it was thrown into Koltovitch's pond. There was an inquiry, but the Frenchman paid some thousands to some one in authority and went away to Alsace. His lease was up just then, and so the matter ended."

"What scoundrels!" said Zina, shuddering.

"My father remembered Olivier and his daughter well. He used to say she was remarkably beautiful and eccentric. I imagine the divinity student had done both— stirred up the peasants and won the daughter's heart. Perhaps he wasn't a divinity student at all, but some one travelling incognito."

Zina grew thoughtful; the story of the divinity student and the beautiful French girl had evidently carried her imagination far away. It seemed to Pyotr Mihalitch that she had not changed in the least during the last week, except that she was a little paler. She looked calm and just as usual, as though she had come with her brother to visit Vlassitch. But Pyotr Mihalitch felt that some change had taken place in himself. Before, when she was living at home, he could have spoken to her about anything, and now he did not feel equal to asking her the simple question, "How do you like being here?" The question seemed awkward and unnecessary. Probably the same change had taken place in her. She was in no haste to turn the conversation to her mother, to her home, to her relations with Vlassitch; she did not defend herself, she did not say that free unions are better than marriages in the church; she was not agitated, and calmly brooded over the story of Olivier. . . . And why had they suddenly begun talking of Olivier?

"You are both of you wet with the rain," said Zina, and she smiled joyfully; she was touched by this point of resemblance between her brother and Vlassitch.

And Pyotr Mihalitch felt all the bitterness and horror of his position. He thought of his deserted home, the closed piano, and Zina's bright little room into which no one went now; he thought there were no prints of little feet on the garden-paths, and that before tea no one went off, laughing gaily, to bathe. What he had clung to more and more from his childhood upwards, what he had loved thinking about when he used to sit in the stuffy class-room or the lecture theatre—brightness, purity, and joy, everything that filled the house with life and light, had gone never to return, had vanished, and was mixed up with a coarse, clumsy story of some battalion officer, a chivalrous lieutenant, a depraved woman and a grandfather who had shot himself. . . . And to begin to talk about his mother or to think that the past could ever return would mean not understanding what was clear.

Pyotr Mihalitch's eyes filled with tears and his hand began to tremble as it lay on the table. Zina guessed what he was thinking about, and her eyes, too, glistened and looked red.

"Grigory, come here," she said to Vlassitch.

They walked away to the window and began talking of something in a whisper. From the way that Vlassitch stooped down to her and the way she looked at him, Pyotr Mihalitch realised again that everything was irreparably over, and that it was no use to talk of anything. Zina went out of the room.

"Well, brother!" Vlassitch began, after a brief silence, rubbing his hands and smiling. "I called our life happiness just now, but that was, so to speak, poetical license. In reality, there has not been a sense of happiness so far. Zina has been thinking all the time of you, of her mother, and has been worrying; looking at her, I, too, felt worried. Hers is a bold, free nature, but, you know, it's difficult when you're not used to it, and she is young, too. The servants call her 'Miss'; it seems a trifle, but it upsets her.

There it is, brother."

Zina brought in a plateful of strawberries. She was followed by a little maidservant, looking crushed and humble, who set a jug of milk on the table and made a very low bow: she had something about her that was in keeping with the old furniture, something petrified and dreary.

The sound of the rain had ceased. Pyotr Mihalitch ate strawberries while Vlassitch and Zina looked at him in silence. The moment of the inevitable but useless conversation was approaching, and all three felt the burden of it. Pyotr Mihalitch's eyes filled with tears again; he pushed away his plate and said that he must be going home, or it would be getting late, and perhaps it would rain again. The time had come when common decency required Zina to speak of those at home and of her new life.

"How are things at home?" she asked rapidly, and her pale face quivered. "How is mother?"

"You know mother . . ." said Pyotr Mihalitch, not looking at her.

"Petrusha, you've thought a great deal about what has happened," she said, taking hold of her brother's sleeve, and he knew how hard it was for her to speak. "You've thought a great deal: tell me, can we reckon on mother's accepting Grigory . . . and the whole position, one day?"

She stood close to her brother, face to face with him, and he was astonished that she was so beautiful, and that he seemed not to have noticed it before. And it seemed to him utterly absurd that his sister, so like his mother, pampered, elegant, should be living with Vlassitch and in Vlassitch's house, with the petrified servant, and the table with six legs—in the house where a man had been flogged to death, and that she was not going home with him, but was staying here to sleep.

"You know mother," he said, not answering her question. "I think you ought to have . . . to do something, to ask her forgiveness or something. . . ."

"But to ask her forgiveness would mean pretending we had done wrong.

I'm ready to tell a lie to comfort mother, but it won't lead anywhere. I know mother. Well, what will be, must be!" said Zina, growing more cheerful now that the most unpleasant had been said. "We'll wait for five years, ten years, and be patient, and then God's will be done."

She took her brother's arm, and when she walked through the dark hall she squeezed close to him. They went out on the steps. Pyotr Mihalitch said good-bye, got on his horse, and set off at a walk;

Zina and Vlassitch walked a little way with him. It was still and warm, with a delicious smell of hay; stars were twinkling brightly between the clouds. Vlassitch's old garden, which had seen so many gloomy stories in its time, lay slumbering in the darkness, and for some reason it was mournful riding through it.

"Zina and I to-day after dinner spent some really exalted moments," said Vlassitch. "I read aloud to her an excellent article on the question of emigration. You must read it, brother! You really must. It's remarkable for its lofty tone. I could not resist writing a letter to the editor to be forwarded to the author. I wrote only a single line: 'I thank you and warmly press your noble hand.'"

Pyotr Mihalitch was tempted to say, "Don't meddle in what does not concern you," but he held his tongue.

Vlassitch walked by his right stirrup and Zina by the left; both seemed to have forgotten that they had to go home. It was damp, and they had almost reached Koltovitch's copse. Pyotr Mihalitch felt that they were expecting something from him, though they hardly knew what it was, and he felt unbearably sorry for them. Now as they walked by the horse with submissive faces, lost in thought, he had a deep conviction that they were unhappy, and could not be happy, and their love seemed to him a melancholy, irreparable mistake. Pity and the sense that he could do nothing to help them reduced him to that state of spiritual softening when he was ready to make any sacrifice to get rid of the painful feeling of sympathy.

"I'll come over sometimes for a night," he said.

But it sounded as though he were making a concession, and did not satisfy him. When they stopped near Koltovitch's copse to say good-bye, he bent down to Zina, touched her shoulder, and said:

"You are right, Zina! You have done well." To avoid saying more and bursting into tears, he lashed his horse and galloped into the wood. As he rode into the darkness, he looked round and saw Vlassitch and Zina walking home along the road—he taking long strides, while she walked with a hurried, jerky step beside him—talking eagerly about something.

"I am an old woman!" thought Pyotr Mihalitch. "I went to solve the question and I have only made it more complicated—there it is!"

He was heavy at heart. When he got out of the copse he rode at a walk and then stopped his horse near the pond. He wanted to sit and think without moving. The moon was rising and was reflected in a streak of red on the other side of the pond. There were low rumbles of thunder in the distance. Pyotr Mihalitch looked steadily at the water and imagined his sister's despair, her martyr-like pallor, the tearless eyes with which she would conceal her humiliation from others. He imagined her with child, imagined the death of their mother, her funeral, Zina's horror. . . . The proud, superstitious old woman would be sure to die of grief. Terrible pictures of the future rose before him on the background of smooth, dark water, and among pale feminine figures he saw himself, a weak, cowardly man with a guilty face.

A hundred paces off on the right bank of the pond, something dark was standing motionless: was it a man or a tall post? Pyotr Mihalitch thought of the divinity student who had been killed and thrown into the pond.

"Olivier behaved inhumanly, but one way or another he did settle the question, while I have settled nothing and have only made it worse," he thought, gazing at the dark figure that looked like a ghost. "He said and did what he thought right while I say and do what I don't think right; and I don't know really what I do think. . . ."

He rode up to the dark figure: it was an old rotten post, the relic of some shed.

From Koltovitch's copse and garden there came a strong fragrant scent of lilies of the valley and honey-laden flowers. Pyotr Mihalitch rode along the bank of the pond and looked mournfully into the water. And thinking about his life, he came to the conclusion he had never said or acted upon what he really thought, and other people had repaid him in the same way. And so the whole of life seemed to him as dark as this water in which the night sky was reflected and water-weeds grew in a tangle. And it seemed to him that nothing could ever set it right.

AT HOME

I

THE Don railway. A quiet, cheerless station, white and solitary in the steppe, with its walls baking in the sun, without a speck of shade, and, it seems, without a human being. The train goes on after leaving one here; the sound of it is scarcely audible and dies away at last. Outside the station it is a desert, and there are no horses but one's own. One gets into the carriage—which is so pleasant after the train—and is borne along the road through the steppe, and by degrees there are unfolded before one views such as one does not see near Moscow—immense, endless, fascinating in their monotony. The steppe, the steppe, and nothing more; in the distance an ancient barrow or a windmill; ox-waggons laden with coal trail by. . . . Solitary birds fly low over the plain, and a drowsy feeling comes with the monotonous beat of their wings. It is hot. Another hour or so passes, and still the steppe, the steppe, and still in the distance the barrow. The driver tells you something, some long unnecessary tale, pointing into the distance with his whip. And tranquillity takes possession of the soul; one is loth to think of the past. . . .

A carriage with three horses had been sent to fetch Vera Ivanovna Kardin. The driver put in her luggage and set the harness to rights.

"Everything just as it always has been," said Vera, looking about her. "I was a little girl when I was here last, ten years ago. I remember old Boris came to fetch me then. Is he still living, I wonder?"

The driver made no reply, but, like a Little Russian, looked at her angrily and clambered on to the box.

It was a twenty-mile drive from the station, and Vera, too, abandoned herself to the charm of the steppe, forgot the past, and thought only of the wide expanse, of the freedom. Healthy, clever, beautiful, and young—she was only three-and-twenty—she had hitherto lacked nothing in her life but just this space and freedom.

The steppe, the steppe. . . . The horses trotted, the sun rose higher and higher; and it seemed to Vera that never in her childhood had the steppe been so rich, so luxuriant in June; the wild flowers were green, yellow, lilac, white, and a fragrance rose from them and from the warmed earth; and there were strange blue birds along the roadside. . . . Vera had long got out of the habit of praying, but now, struggling with drowsiness, she murmured:

"Lord, grant that I may be happy here."

And there was peace and sweetness in her soul, and she felt as though she would have been glad to drive like that all her life, looking at the steppe.

Suddenly there was a deep ravine overgrown with oak saplings and alder-trees; there was a moist feeling in the air—there must have been a spring at the bottom. On the near side, on the very edge of the ravine, a covey of partridges rose noisily. Vera remembered that in old days they used to go for evening walks to this ravine; so it must be near home! And now she could actually see the poplars, the barn, black smoke rising on one side—they were burning old straw. And there was Auntie Dasha coming to meet her and waving her handkerchief; grandfather was on the terrace. Oh dear, how happy she was!

"My darling, my darling!" cried her aunt, shrieking as though she were in hysterics. "Our real mistress has come! You must understand you are our mistress, you are our queen! Here everything is yours! My darling, my beauty, I am not your aunt, but your willing slave!"

Vera had no relations but her aunt and her grandfather; her mother had long been dead; her father, an engineer, had died three months before at Kazan, on his way from Siberia. Her grandfather had a big grey beard. He was stout, red-faced, and asthmatic, and walked leaning on a cane and sticking his stomach out. Her aunt, a lady of forty-two, drawn in tightly at the waist and fashionably dressed with sleeves high on the shoulder, evidently tried to look young and was still anxious to be charming; she walked with tiny steps with a wriggle of her spine.

"Will you love us?" she said, embracing Vera, "You are not proud?"

At her grandfather's wish there was a thanksgiving service, then they spent a long while over dinner—and Vera's new life began. She was given the best room. All the rugs in the house had been put in it, and a great many flowers; and when at night she lay down in her snug, wide, very soft bed and covered herself with a silk quilt that smelt of old clothes long stored away, she laughed with pleasure. Auntie Dasha came in for a minute to wish her good-night.

"Here you are home again, thank God," she said, sitting down on the bed. "As you see, we get along very well and have everything we want. There's only one thing: your grandfather is in a poor way! A terribly poor way! He is short of breath and he has begun to lose his memory. And you remember how strong, how vigorous, he used to be! There was no doing anything with him. . . . In old days, if the servants didn't please him or anything else went wrong, he would jump up at once and shout: 'Twenty-five strokes! The birch!' But now he has grown milder and you never hear him. And besides, times are changed, my precious; one mayn't beat them nowadays. Of course, they oughtn't to be beaten, but they need looking after."

"And are they beaten now, auntie?" asked Vera.

"The steward beats them sometimes, but I never do, bless their hearts! And your grandfather sometimes lifts his stick from old habit, but he never beats them."

Auntie Dasha yawned and crossed herself over her mouth and her right ear.

"It's not dull here?" Vera inquired.

"What shall I say? There are no landowners living here now, but there have been works built near, darling, and there are lots of engineers, doctors, and mine managers. Of course, we have theatricals and concerts, but we play cards more than anything.

They come to us, too. Dr. Neshtchapov from the works comes to see us—such a handsome, interesting man! He fell in love with your photograph. I made up my mind: he is Verotchka's destiny, I thought. He's young, handsome, he has means—a good match, in fact. And of course you're a match for any one. You're of good family. The place is mortgaged, it's true, but it's in good order and not neglected; there is my share in it, but it will all come to you; I am your willing slave. And my brother, your father, left you fifteen thousand roubles. . . . But I see you can't keep your eyes open. Sleep, my child."

Next day Vera spent a long time walking round the house. The garden, which was old and unattractive, lying inconveniently upon the slope, had no paths, and was utterly neglected; probably the care of it was regarded as an unnecessary item in the management. There were numbers of grass-snakes. Hoopoes flew about under the trees calling "Oo-too-toot!" as though they were trying to remind her of something. At the bottom of the hill there was a river overgrown with tall reeds, and half a mile beyond the river was the village. From the garden Vera went out into the fields; looking into the distance, thinking of her new life in her own home, she kept trying to grasp what was in store for her. The space, the lovely peace of the steppe, told her that happiness was near at hand, and perhaps was here already; thousands of people, in fact, would have said: "What happiness to be young, healthy, well-educated, to be living on one's own estate!" And at the same time the endless plain, all alike, without one living soul, frightened her, and at moments it was clear to her that its peaceful green vastness would swallow up her life and reduce it to nothingness. She was very young, elegant, fond of life; she had finished her studies at an aristocratic boarding-school, had learnt three languages, had read a great deal, had travelled with her father—and could all this have been meant to lead to nothing but settling down in a remote country-house in the steppe, and wandering day after day from the garden into the fields and from the fields into the garden to while away the time, and then sitting at home listening to her grandfather's breathing? But what could she do? Where could she go? She could find no answer, and as she was returning home she doubted whether she would be happy here, and thought that driving from the station was far more interesting than living here.

Dr. Neshtchapov drove over from the works. He was a doctor, but three years previously he had taken a share in the works, and had become one of the partners; and now he no longer looked upon medicine as his chief vocation, though he still practised. In appearance he was a pale, dark man in a white waistcoat, with a good figure; but to guess what there was in his heart and his brain was difficult. He kissed Auntie Dasha's hand on greeting her, and was continually leaping up to set a chair or give his seat to some one. He was very silent and grave all the while, and, when he did speak, it was for some reason impossible to hear and understand his first sentence, though he spoke correctly and not in a low voice.

"You play the piano?" he asked Vera, and immediately leapt up, as she had dropped her handkerchief.

He stayed from midday to midnight without speaking, and Vera found him very unattractive. She thought that a white waistcoat in the country was bad form, and his elaborate politeness, his manners, and his pale, serious face with dark eyebrows, were mawkish; and it seemed to her that he was perpetually silent, probably because he was stupid. When he had gone her aunt said enthusiastically:

"Well? Isn't he charming?"

II

Auntie Dasha looked after the estate. Tightly laced, with jingling bracelets on her wrists, she went into the kitchen, the granary, the cattle-yard, tripping along with tiny steps, wriggling her spine; and whenever she talked to the steward or to the peasants, she used, for some reason, to put on a pince-nez. Vera's grandfather always sat in the same place, playing patience or dozing. He ate a very great deal at dinner and supper; they gave him the dinner cooked to-day and what was left from yesterday, and cold pie left from Sunday, and salt meat from the servants' dinner, and he ate it all greedily. And every dinner left on Vera such an impression, that when she saw afterwards a flock of sheep driven by, or flour being brought from the mill, she thought, "Grandfather will eat that." For the most part he was silent, absorbed in eating or in patience; but it sometimes happened at dinner that at the sight of Vera he would be touched and say tenderly:

"My only grandchild! Verotchka!"

And tears would glisten in his eyes. Or his face would turn suddenly crimson, his neck would swell, he would look with fury at the servants, and ask, tapping with his stick:

"Why haven't you brought the horse-radish?"

In winter he led a perfectly inactive existence; in summer he sometimes drove out into the fields to look at the oats and the hay; and when he came back he would flourish his stick and declare that everything was neglected now that he was not there to look after it.

"Your grandfather is out of humour," Auntie Dasha would whisper.

"But it's nothing now to what it used to be in the old days:

'Twenty-five strokes! The birch!'"

Her aunt complained that every one had grown lazy, that no one did anything, and that the estate yielded no profit. Indeed, there was no systematic farming; they ploughed and sowed a little simply from habit, and in reality did nothing and lived in idleness. Meanwhile there was a running to and fro, reckoning and worrying all day long; the bustle in the house began at five o'clock in the morning; there were continual sounds of "Bring it," "Fetch it," "Make haste," and by the evening the servants were utterly exhausted. Auntie Dasha changed her cooks and her housemaids every week; sometimes she discharged them for immorality; sometimes they went of their own accord, complaining that they were worked to death. None of the village people would come to the house as servants; Auntie Dasha had to hire them from a distance. There was only one girl from the village living in the house, Alyona, and she stayed because her whole family—old people and children—were living upon her wages. This Alyona, a pale, rather stupid little thing, spent the whole day turning out the rooms, waiting at table, heating the stoves, sewing, washing; but it always seemed as though she were only pottering about, treading heavily with her boots, and were nothing but a hindrance in the house. In her terror that she might be dismissed and sent home, she often dropped and broke the crockery, and they stopped the value of it out of her wages, and then her mother and grandmother would come and bow down at Auntie Dasha's feet.

Once a week or sometimes oftener visitors would arrive. Her aunt would come to Vera and say:

"You should sit a little with the visitors, or else they'll think that you are stuck up."

Vera would go in to the visitors and play *vint* with them for hours together, or play the piano for the visitors to dance; her aunt, in high spirits and breathless from dancing, would come up and whisper to her:

"Be nice to Marya Nikiforovna."

On the sixth of December, St. Nikolay's Day, a large party of about thirty arrived all at once; they played *vint* until late at night, and many of them stayed the night. In the morning they sat down to cards again, then they had dinner, and when Vera went to her room after dinner to rest from conversation and tobacco smoke, there were visitors there too, and she almost wept in despair. And when they began to get ready to go in the evening, she was so pleased they were going at last, that she said:

"Do stay a little longer."

She felt exhausted by the visitors and constrained by their presence; yet every day, as soon as it began to grow dark, something drew her out of the house, and she went out to pay visits either at the works or at some neighbours', and then there were cards, dancing, forfeits, suppers. . . .The young people in the works or in the mines sometimes sang Little Russian songs, and sang them very well. It made one sad to hear them sing. Or they all gathered together in one room and talked in the dusk of the mines, of the treasures that had once been buried in the steppes, of Saur's Grave. . . . Later on, as they talked, a shout of "Help!" sometimes reached them. It was a drunken man going home, or some one was being robbed by the pit near by. Or the wind howled in the chimneys, the shutters banged; then, soon afterwards, they would hear the uneasy church bell, as the snow-storm began.

At all the evening parties, picnics, and dinners, Auntie Dasha was invariably the most interesting woman and the doctor the most interesting man. There was very little reading either at the works or at the country-houses; they played only marches and polkas; and the young people always argued hotly about things they did not understand, and the effect was crude. The discussions were loud and heated, but, strange to say, Vera had nowhere else met people so indifferent and careless as these. They seemed to have no fatherland, no religion, no public interests. When they talked of literature or debated some abstract question, it could be seen from Dr. Neshtchapov's face that the question had no interest for him whatever, and that for long, long years he had read nothing and cared to read nothing. Serious and expressionless, like a badly painted portrait, for ever in his white waistcoat, he was silent and incomprehensible as before; but the ladies, young and old, thought him interesting and were enthusiastic over his manners. They envied Vera, who appeared to attract him very much. And Vera always came away from the visits with a feeling of vexation, vowing inwardly to remain at home; but the day passed, the evening came, and she hurried off to the works again, and it was like that almost all the winter.

She ordered books and magazines, and used to read them in her room. And she read at night, lying in bed. When the clock in the corridor struck two or three, and her temples were beginning to ache from reading, she sat up in bed and thought, "What am I to do? Where am I to go?" Accursed, importunate question, to which there were a number of ready-made answers, and in reality no answer at all.

Oh, how noble, how holy, how picturesque it must be to serve the people, to alleviate their sufferings, to enlighten them! But she, Vera, did not know the people. And how could she go to them? They were strange and uninteresting to her; she could not endure the stuffy smell of the huts, the pot-house oaths, the unwashed children, the women's talk of illnesses. To walk over the snow-drifts, to feel cold, then to sit in a stifling hut, to teach children she disliked—no, she would rather die! And to teach the peasants' children while Auntie Dasha made money out of the pot-houses and fined the peasants—it was too great a farce! What a lot of talk there was of schools, of village libraries, of universal education; but if all these engineers, these mine-owners and ladies of her acquaintance, had not been hypocrites, and really had believed that enlightenment was necessary, they would not have paid the schoolmasters fifteen roubles a month as they did now, and would not have let them go hungry. And the schools and the talk about ignorance—it was all only to stifle the voice of conscience because they were ashamed to own fifteen or thirty thousand acres and to be indifferent to the peasants' lot. Here the ladies said about Dr. Neshtchapov that he was a kind man and had built a school at the works. Yes, he had built a school out of the old bricks at the works for some eight hundred roubles, and they sang the prayer for "long life" to him when the building was opened, but there was no chance of his giving up his shares, and it certainly never entered his head that the peasants were human beings like himself, and that they, too, needed university teaching, and not merely lessons in these wretched schools.

And Vera felt full of anger against herself and every one else. She took up a book again and tried to read it, but soon afterwards sat down and thought again. To become a doctor? But to do that one must pass an examination in Latin; besides, she had an invincible repugnance to corpses and disease. It would be nice to become a mechanic, a judge, a commander of a steamer, a scientist; to do something into which she could put all her powers, physical and spiritual, and to be tired out and sleep soundly at night; to give up her life to something that would make her an interesting person, able to attract interesting people, to love, to have a real family of her own. . . . But what was she to do? How was she to begin?

One Sunday in Lent her aunt came into her room early in the morning to fetch her umbrella. Vera was sitting up in bed clasping her head in her hands, thinking.

"You ought to go to church, darling," said her aunt, "or people will think you are not a believer."

Vera made no answer.

"I see you are dull, poor child," said Auntie Dasha, sinking on her knees by the bedside; she adored Vera. "Tell me the truth, are you bored?"

"Dreadfully."

"My beauty, my queen, I am your willing slave, I wish you nothing but good and happiness. . . . Tell me, why don't you want to marry Nestchapov? What more do you want, my child? You must forgive me, darling; you can't pick and choose like this, we are not princes . . . . Time is passing, you are not seventeen. . . . And I don't understand it! He loves you, idolises you!"

"Oh, mercy!" said Vera with vexation. "How can I tell? He sits dumb and never says a word."

"He's shy, darling. . . . He's afraid you'll refuse him!"

And when her aunt had gone away, Vera remained standing in the middle of her room uncertain whether to dress or to go back to bed. The bed was hateful; if one looked out of the window there were the bare trees, the grey snow, the hateful jackdaws, the pigs that her grandfather would eat. . . .

"Yes, after all, perhaps I'd better get married!" she thought.

III

For two days Auntie Dasha went about with a tear-stained and heavily powdered face, and at dinner she kept sighing and looking towards the ikon. And it was impossible to make out what was the matter with her. But at last she made up her mind, went in to Vera, and said in a casual way:

"The fact is, child, we have to pay interest on the bank loan, and the tenant hasn't paid his rent. Will you let me pay it out of the fifteen thousand your papa left you?"

All day afterwards Auntie Dasha spent in making cherry jam in the garden. Alyona, with her cheeks flushed with the heat, ran to and from the garden to the house and back again to the cellar.

When Auntie Dasha was making jam with a very serious face as though she were performing a religious rite, and her short sleeves displayed her strong, little, despotic hands and arms, and when the servants ran about incessantly, bustling about the jam which they would never taste, there was always a feeling of martyrdom in the air. . . .

The garden smelt of hot cherries. The sun had set, the charcoal stove had been carried away, but the pleasant, sweetish smell still lingered in the air. Vera sat on a bench in the garden and watched a new labourer, a young soldier, not of the neighbourhood, who was, by her express orders, making new paths. He was cutting the turf with a spade and heaping it up on a barrow.

"Where were you serving?" Vera asked him.

"At Berdyansk."

"And where are you going now? Home?"

"No," answered the labourer. "I have no home."

"But where were you born and brought up?"

"In the province of Oryol. Till I went into the army I lived with my mother, in my step-father's house; my mother was the head of the house, and people looked up to her, and while she lived I was cared for. But while I was in the army I got a letter telling me my mother was dead. . . . And now I don't seem to care to go home. It's not my own father, so it's not like my own home."

"Then your father is dead?"

"I don't know. I am illegitimate."

At that moment Auntie Dasha appeared at the window and said:

"Il ne faut pas parler aux gens . . . . Go into the kitchen, my good man. You can tell your story there," she said to the soldier.

And then came as yesterday and every day supper, reading, a sleepless night, and endless thinking about the same thing. At three o'clock the sun rose; Alyona was already busy in the corridor, and Vera was not asleep yet and was trying to read. She heard the creak of the barrow: it was the new labourer at work in the garden. . . . Vera sat at the open window with a book, dozed, and watched the soldier making the paths for her, and that interested her. The paths were as even and level as a leather strap, and it was pleasant to imagine what they would be like when they were strewn with yellow sand.

She could see her aunt come out of the house soon after five o'clock, in a pink wrapper and curl-papers. She stood on the steps for three minutes without speaking, and then said to the soldier:

"Take your passport and go in peace. I can't have any one illegitimate in my house."

An oppressive, angry feeling sank like a stone on Vera's heart. She was indignant with her aunt, she hated her; she was so sick of her aunt that her heart was full of misery and loathing. But what was she to do? To stop her mouth? To be rude to her? But what would be the use? Suppose she struggled with her, got rid of her, made her harmless, prevented her grandfather from flourishing his stick— what would be the use of it? It would be like killing one mouse or one snake in the boundless steppe. The vast expanse, the long winters, the monotony and dreariness of life, instil a sense of helplessness; the position seems hopeless, and one wants to do nothing—everything is useless.

Alyona came in, and bowing low to Vera, began carrying out the arm-chairs to beat the dust out of them.

"You have chosen a time to clean up," said Vera with annoyance. "Go away."

Alyona was overwhelmed, and in her terror could not understand what was wanted of her. She began hurriedly tidying up the dressing-table.

"Go out of the room, I tell you," Vera shouted, turning cold; she had never had such an oppressive feeling before. "Go away!"

Alyona uttered a sort of moan, like a bird, and dropped Vera's gold watch on the carpet.

"Go away!" Vera shrieked in a voice not her own, leaping up and trembling all over. "Send her away; she worries me to death!" she went on, walking rapidly after Alyona down the passage, stamping her feet. "Go away! Birch her! Beat her!" Then suddenly she came to herself, and just as she was, unwashed, uncombed, in her dressing-gown and slippers, she rushed out of the house. She ran to the familiar ravine and hid herself there among the sloe-trees, so that she might see no one and be seen by no one. Lying there motionless on the grass, she did not weep, she was not horror-stricken, but gazing at the sky open-eyed, she reflected coldly and clearly that something had happened which she could never forget and for which she could never forgive herself all her life.

"No, I can't go on like this," she thought. "It's time to take myself in hand, or there'll be no end to it. . . . I can't go on like this. . . ."

At midday Dr. Neshtchapov drove by the ravine on his way to the house. She saw him and made up her mind that she would begin a new life, and that she would make herself begin it, and this decision calmed her. And following with her eyes the doctor's well-built figure, she said, as though trying to soften the crudity of her decision:

"He's a nice man. . . . We shall get through life somehow."

She returned home. While she was dressing, Auntie Dasha came into the room, and said:

"Alyona upset you, darling; I've sent her home to the village. Her mother's given her a good beating and has come here, crying."

"Auntie," said Vera quickly, "I'm going to marry Dr. Neshtchapov.

Only talk to him yourself . . . I can't."

And again she went out into the fields. And wandering aimlessly about, she made up her mind that when she was married she would look after the house, doctor the peasants, teach in the school, that she would do all the things that other women of her circle did. And this perpetual dissatisfaction with herself and every one else, this series of crude mistakes which stand up like a mountain before one whenever one looks back upon one's past, she would accept as her real life to which she was fated, and she would expect nothing better. . . . Of course there was nothing better! Beautiful nature, dreams, music, told one story, but reality another. Evidently truth and happiness existed somewhere outside real life. . . . One must give up one's own life and merge oneself into this luxuriant steppe, boundless and indifferent as eternity, with its flowers, its ancient barrows, and its distant horizon, and then it would be well with one. . . .

A month later Vera was living at the works.

EXPENSIVE LESSONS

FOR a cultivated man to be ignorant of foreign languages is a great inconvenience. Vorotov became acutely conscious of it when, after taking his degree, he began upon a piece of research work.

"It's awful," he said, breathing hard (although he was only twenty-six he was fat, heavy, and suffered from shortness of breath).

"It's awful! Without languages I'm like a bird without wings. I might just as well give up the work."

And he made up his mind at all costs to overcome his innate laziness, and to learn French and German; and began to look out for a teacher.

One winter noon, as Vorotov was sitting in his study at work, the servant told him that a young lady was inquiring for him.

"Ask her in," said Vorotov.

And a young lady elaborately dressed in the last fashion walked in. She introduced herself as a teacher of French, Alice Osipovna Enquete, and told Vorotov that she had been sent to him by one of his friends.

"Delighted! Please sit down," said Vorotov, breathing hard and putting his hand over the collar of his nightshirt (to breathe more freely he always wore a nightshirt at work instead of a stiff linen one with collar). "It was Pyotr Sergeitch sent you? Yes, yes . . . I asked him about it. Delighted!"

As he talked to Mdlle. Enquete he looked at her shyly and with curiosity. She was a genuine Frenchwoman, very elegant and still quite young. Judging from her pale, languid face, her short curly hair, and her unnaturally slim waist, she might have been eighteen; but looking at her broad, well-developed shoulders, the elegant lines of her back and her severe eyes, Vorotov thought that she was not less than three-and-twenty and might be twenty-five; but then again he began to think she was not more than eighteen. Her face looked as cold and business-like as the face of a person who has come to speak about money. She did not once smile or frown, and only once a look of perplexity flitted over her face when she learnt that she was not required to teach children, but a stout grown-up man.

"So, Alice Osipovna," said Vorotov, "we'll have a lesson every evening from seven to eight. As regards your terms—a rouble a lesson—I've nothing to say against that. By all means let it be a rouble. . . ."

And he asked her if she would not have some tea or coffee, whether it was a fine day, and with a good-natured smile, stroking the baize of the table, he inquired in a friendly voice who she was, where she had studied, and what she lived on.

With a cold, business-like expression, Alice Osipovna answered that she had completed her studies at a private school and had the diploma of a private teacher, that her father had died lately of scarlet fever, that her mother was alive and made artificial flowers; that she, Mdlle. Enquete, taught in a private school till dinnertime, and after dinner was busy till evening giving lessons in different good families.

She went away leaving behind her the faint fragrance of a woman's clothes. For a long time afterwards Vorotov could not settle to work, but, sitting at the table stroking its green baize surface, he meditated.

"It's very pleasant to see a girl working to earn her own living," he thought. "On the other hand, it's very unpleasant to think that poverty should not spare such elegant and pretty girls as Alice Osipovna, and that she, too, should have to struggle for existence. It's a sad thing!"

Having never seen virtuous Frenchwomen before, he reflected also that this elegantly dressed young lady with her well-developed shoulders and exaggeratedly small waist in all probability followed another calling as well as giving French lessons.

The next evening when the clock pointed to five minutes to seven, Mdlle. Enquete appeared, rosy from the frost. She opened Margot, which she had brought with her, and without introduction began:

"French grammar has twenty-six letters. The first letter is called *A*, the second *B* . . ."

"Excuse me," Vorotov interrupted, smiling. "I must warn you, mademoiselle, that you must change your method a little in my case. You see, I know Russian, Greek, and Latin well. . . . I've studied comparative philology, and I think we might omit Margot and pass straight to reading some author."

And he explained to the French girl how grown-up people learn languages.

"A friend of mine," he said, "wanting to learn modern languages, laid before him the French, German, and Latin gospels, and read them side by side, carefully analysing each word, and would you believe it, he attained his object in less than a year. Let us do the same. We'll take some author and read him."

The French girl looked at him in perplexity. Evidently the suggestion seemed to her very naive and ridiculous. If this strange proposal had been made to her by a child, she would certainly have been angry and have scolded it, but as he was a grown-up man and very stout and she could not scold him, she only shrugged her shoulders hardly perceptibly and said:

"As you please."

Vorotov rummaged in his bookcase and picked out a dog's-eared French book.

"Will this do?"

"It's all the same," she said.

"In that case let us begin, and good luck to it! Let's begin with the title . . . 'Memoires.'"

"Reminiscences," Mdlle. Enquete translated.

With a good-natured smile, breathing hard, he spent a quarter of an hour over the word "Memoires," and as much over the word *de*, and this wearied the young lady. She answered his questions languidly, grew confused, and evidently did not understand her pupil well, and did not attempt to understand him. Vorotov asked her questions, and at the same time kept looking at her fair hair and thinking:

"Her hair isn't naturally curly; she curls it. It's a strange thing! She works from morning to night, and yet she has time to curl her hair."

At eight o'clock precisely she got up, and saying coldly and dryly, "Au revoir, monsieur," walked out of the study, leaving behind her the same tender, delicate, disturbing fragrance. For a long time again her pupil did nothing; he sat at the table meditating.

During the days that followed he became convinced that his teacher was a charming, conscientious, and precise young lady, but that she was very badly educated, and incapable of teaching grown-up people, and he made up his mind not to waste his time, to get rid of her, and to engage another teacher. When she came the seventh time he took out of his pocket an envelope with seven roubles in it, and holding it in his hand, became very confused and began:

"Excuse me, Alice Osipovna, but I ought to tell you . . . I'm under painful necessity . . ."

Seeing the envelope, the French girl guessed what was meant, and for the first time during their lessons her face quivered and her cold, business-like expression vanished. She coloured a little, and dropping her eyes, began nervously fingering her slender gold chain. And Vorotov, seeing her perturbation, realised how much a rouble meant to her, and how bitter it would be to her to lose what she was earning.

"I ought to tell you," he muttered, growing more and more confused, and quavering inwardly; he hurriedly stuffed the envelope into his pocket and went on: "Excuse me, I . . . I must leave you for ten minutes."

And trying to appear as though he had not in the least meant to get rid of her, but only to ask her permission to leave her for a short time, he went into the next room and sat there for ten minutes. And then he returned more embarrassed than ever: it struck him that she might have interpreted his brief absence in some way of her own, and he felt awkward.

The lessons began again. Yorotov felt no interest in them. Realising that he would gain nothing from the lessons, he gave the French girl liberty to do as she liked, asking her nothing and not interrupting her. She translated away as she pleased ten pages during a lesson, and he did not listen, breathed hard, and having nothing better to do, gazed at her curly head, or her soft white hands or her neck and sniffed the fragrance of her clothes. He caught himself thinking very unsuitable thoughts, and felt ashamed, or he was moved to tenderness, and then he felt vexed and wounded that she was so cold and business-like with him, and treated him as a pupil, never smiling and seeming afraid that he might accidentally touch her. He kept wondering how to inspire her with confidence and get to know her better, and to help her, to make her understand how badly she taught, poor thing.

One day Mdlle. Enquete came to the lesson in a smart pink dress, slightly *decollete*, and surrounded by such a fragrance that she seemed to be wrapped in a cloud, and, if one blew upon her, ready to fly away into the air or melt away like smoke. She apologised and said she could stay only half an hour for the lesson, as she was going straight from the lesson to a dance.

He looked at her throat and the back of her bare neck, and thought he understood why Frenchwomen had the reputation of frivolous creatures easily seduced; he was carried away by this cloud of fragrance, beauty, and bare flesh, while she, unconscious of his thoughts and probably not in the least interested in them, rapidly turned over the pages and translated at full steam:

"'He was walking the street and meeting a gentleman his friend and saying, "Where are you striving to seeing your face so pale it makes me sad."'"

The "Memoires" had long been finished, and now Alice was translating some other book. One day she came an hour too early for the lesson, apologizing and saying that she wanted to leave at seven and go to the Little Theatre. Seeing her out after the lesson, Vorotov dressed and went to the theatre himself. He went, and fancied that he was going simply for change and amusement, and that he was not thinking about Alice at all. He could not admit that a serious man, preparing for a learned career, lethargic in his habits, could fling up his work and go to the theatre simply to meet there a girl he knew very little, who was unintelligent and utterly unintellectual.

Yet for some reason his heart was beating during the intervals, and without realizing what he was doing, he raced about the corridors and foyer like a boy impatiently looking for some one, and he was disappointed when the interval was over. And when he saw the familiar pink dress and the handsome shoulders under the tulle, his heart quivered as though with a foretaste of happiness; he smiled joyfully, and for the first time in his life experienced the sensation of jealousy.

Alice was walking with two unattractive-looking students and an officer. She was laughing, talking loudly, and obviously flirting. Vorotov had never seen her like that. She was evidently happy, contented, warm, sincere. What for? Why? Perhaps because these men were her friends and belonged to her own circle. And Vorotov felt there was a terrible gulf between himself and that circle. He bowed to his teacher, but she gave him a chilly nod and walked quickly by; she evidently did not care for her friends to know that she had pupils, and that she had to give lessons to earn money.

After the meeting at the theatre Vorotov realised that he was in love. . . . During the subsequent lessons he feasted his eyes on his elegant teacher, and without struggling with himself, gave full rein to his imaginations, pure and impure. Mdlle. Enquete's face did not cease to be cold; precisely at eight o'clock every evening she said coldly,

"Au revoir, monsieur," and he felt she cared nothing about him, and never would care anything about him, and that his position was hopeless.

Sometimes in the middle of a lesson he would begin dreaming, hoping, making plans. He inwardly composed declarations of love, remembered that Frenchwomen were frivolous and easily won, but it was enough for him to glance at the face of his teacher for his ideas to be extinguished as a candle is blown out when you bring it into the wind on the verandah. Once, overcome, forgetting himself as though in delirium, he could not restrain himself, and barred her way as she was going from the study into the entry after the lesson, and, gasping for breath and stammering, began to declare his love:

"You are dear to me! I . . . I love you! Allow me to speak."

And Alice turned pale—probably from dismay, reflecting that after this declaration she could not come here again and get a rouble a lesson. With a frightened look in her eyes she said in a loud whisper:

"Ach, you mustn't! Don't speak, I entreat you! You mustn't!"

And Vorotov did not sleep all night afterwards; he was tortured by shame; he blamed himself and thought intensely. It seemed to him that he had insulted the girl by his declaration, that she would not come to him again.

He resolved to find out her address from the address bureau in the morning, and to write her a letter of apology. But Alice came without a letter. For the first minute she felt uncomfortable, then she opened a book and began briskly and rapidly translating as usual:

"'Oh, young gentleman, don't tear those flowers in my garden which I want to be giving to my ill daughter. . . .'"

She still comes to this day. Four books have already been translated, but Vorotov knows no French but the word "Memoires," and when he is asked about his literary researches, he waves his hand, and without answering, turns the conversation to the weather.

THE PRINCESS

A CARRIAGE with four fine sleek horses drove in at the big so-called Red Gate of the N--- Monastery. While it was still at a distance, the priests and monks who were standing in a group round the part of the hostel allotted to the gentry, recognised by the coachman and horses that the lady in the carriage was Princess Vera Gavrilovna, whom they knew very well.

An old man in livery jumped off the box and helped the princess to get out of the carriage. She raised her dark veil and moved in a leisurely way up to the priests to receive their blessing; then she nodded pleasantly to the rest of the monks and went into the hostel.

"Well, have you missed your princess?" she said to the monk who brought in her things. "It's a whole month since I've been to see you. But here I am; behold your princess. And where is the Father Superior? My goodness, I am burning with impatience! Wonderful, wonderful old man! You must be proud of having such a Superior."

When the Father Superior came in, the princess uttered a shriek of delight, crossed her arms over her bosom, and went up to receive his blessing.

"No, no, let me kiss your hand," she said, snatching it and eagerly kissing it three times. "How glad I am to see you at last, holy Father! I'm sure you've forgotten your princess, but my thoughts have been in your dear monastery every moment. How delightful it is here! This living for God far from the busy, giddy world has a special charm of its own, holy Father, which I feel with my whole soul although I cannot express it!"

The princess's cheeks glowed and tears came into her eyes. She talked incessantly, fervently, while the Father Superior, a grave, plain, shy old man of seventy, remained mute or uttered abruptly, like a soldier on duty, phrases such as:

"Certainly, Your Excellency. . . . Quite so. I understand."

"Has Your Excellency come for a long stay?" he inquired.

"I shall stay the night here, and to-morrow I'm going on to Klavdia Nikolaevna's— it's a long time since I've seen her—and the day after to-morrow I'll come back to you and stay three or four days. I want to rest my soul here among you, holy Father."

The princess liked being at the monastery at N---. For the last two years it had been a favourite resort of hers; she used to go there almost every month in the summer and stay two or three days, even sometimes a week. The shy novices, the stillness, the low ceilings, the smell of cypress, the modest fare, the cheap curtains on the windows—all this touched her, softened her, and disposed her to contemplation and good thoughts. It was enough for her to be half an hour in the hostel for her to feel that she, too, was timid and modest, and that she, too, smelt of cypress-wood. The past retreated into the background, lost its significance, and the princess began to imagine that in spite of her twenty-nine years she was very much like the old Father Superior, and that, like him, she was created not for wealth, not for earthly grandeur and love, but for a peaceful life secluded from the world, a life in twilight like the hostel.

It happens that a ray of light gleams in the dark cell of the anchorite absorbed in prayer, or a bird alights on the window and sings its song; the stern anchorite will smile in spite of himself, and a gentle, sinless joy will pierce through the load of grief over his sins, like water flowing from under a stone. The princess fancied she brought from the outside world just such comfort as the ray of light or the bird. Her gay, friendly smile, her gentle eyes, her voice, her jests, her whole personality in fact, her little graceful figure always dressed in simple black, must arouse in simple, austere people a feeling of tenderness and joy. Every one, looking at her, must think: "God has sent us an angel. . . ." And feeling that no one could help thinking this, she smiled still more cordially, and tried to look like a bird.

After drinking tea and resting, she went for a walk. The sun was already setting. From the monastery garden came a moist fragrance of freshly watered mignonette, and from the church floated the soft singing of men's voices, which seemed very pleasant and mournful in the distance. It was the evening service. In the dark windows where the little lamps glowed gently, in the shadows, in the figure of the old monk sitting at the church door with a collecting-box, there was such unruffled peace that the princess felt moved to tears.

Outside the gate, in the walk between the wall and the birch-trees where there were benches, it was quite evening. The air grew rapidly darker and darker. The princess went along the walk, sat on a seat, and sank into thought.

She thought how good it would be to settle down for her whole life in this monastery where life was as still and unruffled as a summer evening; how good it would be to forget the ungrateful, dissipated prince; to forget her immense estates, the creditors who worried her every day, her misfortunes, her maid Dasha, who had looked at her impertinently that morning. It would be nice to sit here on the bench all her life and watch through the trunks of the birch-trees the evening mist gathering in wreaths in the valley below; the rooks flying home in a black cloud like a veil far, far away above the forest; two novices, one astride a piebald horse, another on foot driving out the horses for the night and rejoicing in their freedom, playing pranks like little children; their youthful voices rang out musically in the still air, and she could distinguish every word. It is nice to sit and listen to the silence: at one moment the wind blows and stirs the tops of the birch-trees, then a frog rustles in last year's leaves, then the clock on the belfry strikes the quarter. . . . One might sit without moving, listen and think, and think. . . .

An old woman passed by with a wallet on her back. The princess thought that it would be nice to stop the old woman and to say something friendly and cordial to her, to help her. . . . But the old woman turned the corner without once looking round.

Not long afterwards a tall man with a grey beard and a straw hat came along the walk. When he came up to the princess, he took off his hat and bowed. From the bald patch on his head and his sharp, hooked nose the princess recognised him as the doctor, Mihail Ivanovitch, who had been in her service at Dubovki. She remembered that some one had told her that his wife had died the year before, and she wanted to sympathise with him, to console him.

"Doctor, I expect you don't recognise me?" she said with an affable smile.

"Yes, Princess, I recognised you," said the doctor, taking off his hat again.

"Oh, thank you; I was afraid that you, too, had forgotten your princess. People only remember their enemies, but they forget their friends. Have you, too, come to pray?"

"I am the doctor here, and I have to spend the night at the monastery every Saturday."

"Well, how are you?" said the princess, sighing. "I hear that you have lost your wife. What a calamity!"

"Yes, Princess, for me it is a great calamity."

"There's nothing for it! We must bear our troubles with resignation.

Not one hair of a man's head is lost without the Divine Will."

"Yes, Princess."

To the princess's friendly, gentle smile and her sighs the doctor responded coldly and dryly: "Yes, Princess." And the expression of his face was cold and dry.

"What else can I say to him?" she wondered.

"How long it is since we met!" she said. "Five years! How much water has flowed under the bridge, how many changes in that time; it quite frightens one to think of it! You know, I am married. . . . I am not a countess now, but a princess. And by now I am separated from my husband too."

"Yes, I heard so."

"God has sent me many trials. No doubt you have heard, too, that I am almost ruined. My Dubovki, Sofyino, and Kiryakovo have all been sold for my unhappy husband's debts. And I have only Baranovo and Mihaltsevo left. It's terrible to look back: how many changes and misfortunes of all kinds, how many mistakes!"

"Yes, Princess, many mistakes."

The princess was a little disconcerted. She knew her mistakes; they were all of such a private character that no one but she could think or speak of them. She could not resist asking:

"What mistakes are you thinking about?"

"You referred to them, so you know them . . ." answered the doctor, and he smiled. "Why talk about them!"

"No; tell me, doctor. I shall be very grateful to you. And please don't stand on ceremony with me. I love to hear the truth."

"I am not your judge, Princess."

"Not my judge! What a tone you take! You must know something about me. Tell me!"

"If you really wish it, very well. Only I regret to say I'm not clever at talking, and people can't always understand me."

The doctor thought a moment and began:

"A lot of mistakes; but the most important of them, in my opinion, was the general spirit that prevailed on all your estates. You see, I don't know how to express myself. I mean chiefly the lack of love, the aversion for people that was felt in absolutely everything. Your whole system of life was built upon that aversion. Aversion for the human voice, for faces, for heads, steps . . . in fact, for everything that makes up a human being. At all the doors and on the stairs there stand sleek, rude, and lazy grooms in livery to prevent badly dressed persons from entering the house; in the hall there are chairs with high backs so that the footmen waiting there, during balls and receptions, may not soil the walls with their heads; in every room there are thick carpets that no human step may be heard; every one who comes in is infallibly warned to speak as softly and as little as possible, and to say nothing that might have a disagreeable effect on the nerves or the imagination. And in your room you don't shake hands with any one or ask him to sit down— just as you didn't shake hands with me or ask me to sit down. . . ."

"By all means, if you like," said the princess, smiling and holding out her hand. "Really, to be cross about such trifles. . . ."

"But I am not cross," laughed the doctor, but at once he flushed, took off his hat, and waving it about, began hotly: "To be candid, I've long wanted an opportunity to tell you all I think. . . . That is, I want to tell you that you look upon the mass of mankind from the Napoleonic standpoint as food for the cannon. But Napoleon had at least some idea; you have nothing except aversion."

"I have an aversion for people?" smiled the princess, shrugging her shoulders in astonishment. "I have!"

"Yes, you! You want facts? By all means. In Mihaltsevo three former cooks of yours, who have gone blind in your kitchens from the heat of the stove, are living upon charity. All the health and strength and good looks that is found on your hundreds of thousands of acres is taken by you and your parasites for your grooms, your footmen, and your coachmen. All these two-legged cattle are trained to be flunkeys, overeat themselves, grow coarse, lose the 'image and likeness,' in fact. . . . Young doctors, agricultural experts, teachers, intellectual workers generally—think of it! are torn away from their honest work and forced for a crust of bread to take part in all sorts of mummeries which make every decent man feel ashamed! Some young men cannot be in your service for three years without becoming hypocrites, toadies, sneaks. . . . Is that a good thing? Your Polish superintendents, those abject spies, all those Kazimers and Kaetans, go hunting about on your hundreds of thousands of acres from morning to night, and to please you try to get three skins off one ox. Excuse me, I speak disconnectedly, but that doesn't matter. You don't look upon the simple people as human beings. And even the princes, counts, and bishops who used to come and see you, you looked upon simply as decorative figures, not as living beings. But the worst of all, the thing that most revolts me, is having a fortune of over a million and doing nothing for other people, nothing!"

The princess sat amazed, aghast, offended, not knowing what to say or how to behave. She had never before been spoken to in such a tone. The doctor's unpleasant, angry voice and his clumsy, faltering phrases made a harsh clattering noise in her ears and her head. Then she began to feel as though the gesticulating doctor was hitting her on the head with his hat.

"It's not true!" she articulated softly, in an imploring voice. "I've done a great deal of good for other people; you know it yourself!"

"Nonsense!" cried the doctor. "Can you possibly go on thinking of your philanthropic work as something genuine and useful, and not a mere mummery? It was a farce from beginning to end; it was playing at loving your neighbour, the most open farce which even children and stupid peasant women saw through! Take for instance your— what was it called? house for homeless old women without relations, of which you made me something like a head doctor, and of which you were the patroness. Mercy on us! What a charming institution it was! A house was built with parquet floors and a weathercock on the roof; a dozen old women were collected from the villages and made to sleep under blankets and sheets of Dutch linen, and given toffee to eat."

The doctor gave a malignant chuckle into his hat, and went on speaking rapidly and stammering:

"It was a farce! The attendants kept the sheets and the blankets under lock and key, for fear the old women should soil them—'Let the old devil's pepper-pots sleep on the floor.' The old women did not dare to sit down on the beds, to put on their jackets, to walk over the polished floors. Everything was kept for show and hidden away from the old women as though they were thieves, and the old women were clothed and fed on the sly by other people's charity, and prayed to God night and day to be released from their prison and from the canting exhortations of the sleek rascals to whose care you committed them. And what did the managers do? It was simply charming! About twice a week there would be thirty-five thousand messages to say that the princess— that is, you—were coming to the home next day. That meant that next day I had to abandon my patients, dress up and be on parade. Very good; I arrive. The old women, in everything clean and new, are already drawn up in a row, waiting. Near them struts the old garrison rat—the superintendent with his mawkish, sneaking smile. The old women yawn and exchange glances, but are afraid to complain. We wait. The junior steward gallops up. Half an hour later the senior steward; then the superintendent of the accounts' office, then another, and then another of them . . . they keep arriving endlessly. They all have mysterious, solemn faces. We wait and wait, shift from one leg to another, look at the clock—all this in monumental silence because we all hate each other like poison. One hour passes, then a second, and then at last the carriage is seen in the distance, and . . . and . . .”

The doctor went off into a shrill laugh and brought out in a shrill voice:

“You get out of the carriage, and the old hags, at the word of command from the old garrison rat, begin chanting: ‘The Glory of our Lord in Zion the tongue of man cannot express. . .’ A pretty scene, wasn't it?”

The doctor went off into a bass chuckle, and waved his hand as though to signify that he could not utter another word for laughing. He laughed heavily, harshly, with clenched teeth, as ill-natured people laugh; and from his voice, from his face, from his glittering, rather insolent eyes it could be seen that he had a profound contempt for the princess, for the home, and for the old women. There was nothing amusing or laughable in all that he described so clumsily and coarsely, but he laughed with satisfaction, even with delight.

“And the school?” he went on, panting from laughter. “Do you remember how you wanted to teach peasant children yourself? You must have taught them very well, for very soon the children all ran away, so that they had to be thrashed and bribed to come and be taught. And you remember how you wanted to feed with your own hands the infants whose mothers were working in the fields. You went about the village crying because the infants were not at your disposal, as the mothers would take them to the fields with them. Then the village foreman ordered the mothers by turns to leave their infants behind for your entertainment. A strange thing! They all ran away from your benevolence like mice from a cat! And why was it? It's very simple. Not because our people are ignorant and ungrateful, as you always explained it to yourself, but because in all your fads, if you'll excuse the word, there wasn't a ha'p'orth of love and kindness! There was nothing but the desire to amuse yourself with living puppets, nothing else. . . . A person who does not feel the difference between a human being and a lap-dog ought not to go in for philanthropy. I assure you, there's a great difference between human beings and lap-dogs!”

The princess's heart was beating dreadfully; there was a thudding in her ears, and she still felt as though the doctor were beating her on the head with his hat. The doctor talked quickly, excitedly, and uncouthly, stammering and gesticulating unnecessarily. All she grasped was that she was spoken to by a coarse, ill-bred, spiteful, and ungrateful man; but what he wanted of her and what he was talking about, she could not understand.

“Go away!” she said in a tearful voice, putting up her hands to protect her head from the doctor's hat; “go away!”

“And how you treat your servants!” the doctor went on, indignantly. “You treat them as the lowest scoundrels, and don't look upon them as human beings. For example, allow me to ask, why did you dismiss me? For ten years I worked for your father and afterwards for you, honestly, without vacations or holidays. I gained the love of all for more than seventy miles round, and suddenly one fine day I am informed that I am no longer wanted. What for? I've no idea to this day. I, a doctor of medicine, a gentleman by birth, a student of the Moscow University, father of a family—am such a petty, insignificant insect that you can kick me out without explaining the reason! Why stand on ceremony with me! I heard afterwards that my wife went without my knowledge three times to intercede with you for me—you wouldn't receive her. I am told she cried in your hall. And I shall never forgive her for it, never!"

The doctor paused and clenched his teeth, making an intense effort to think of something more to say, very unpleasant and vindictive. He thought of something, and his cold, frowning face suddenly brightened.

"Take your attitude to this monastery!" he said with avidity. "You've never spared any one, and the holier the place, the more chance of its suffering from your loving-kindness and angelic sweetness. Why do you come here? What do you want with the monks here, allow me to ask you? What is Hecuba to you or you to Hecuba? It's another farce, another amusement for you, another sacrilege against human dignity, and nothing more. Why, you don't believe in the monks' God; you've a God of your own in your heart, whom you've evolved for yourself at spiritualist seances. You look with condescension upon the ritual of the Church; you don't go to mass or vespers; you sleep till midday. . . . Why do you come here? . . . You come with a God of your own into a monastery you have nothing to do with, and you imagine that the monks look upon it as a very great honour. To be sure they do! You'd better ask, by the way, what your visits cost the monastery. You were graciously pleased to arrive here this evening, and a messenger from your estate arrived on horseback the day before yesterday to warn them of your coming. They were the whole day yesterday getting the rooms ready and expecting you. This morning your advance-guard arrived—an insolent maid, who keeps running across the courtyard, rustling her skirts, pestering them with questions, giving orders. . . . I can't endure it! The monks have been on the lookout all day, for if you were not met with due ceremony, there would be trouble! You'd complain to the bishop! 'The monks don't like me, your holiness; I don't know what I've done to displease them. It's true I'm a great sinner, but I'm so unhappy!' Already one monastery has been in hot water over you. The Father Superior is a busy, learned man; he hasn't a free moment, and you keep sending for him to come to your rooms. Not a trace of respect for age or for rank! If at least you were a bountiful giver to the monastery, one wouldn't resent it so much, but all this time the monks have not received a hundred roubles from you!"

Whenever people worried the princess, misunderstood her, or mortified her, and when she did not know what to say or do, she usually began to cry. And on this occasion, too, she ended by hiding her face in her hands and crying aloud in a thin treble like a child. The doctor suddenly stopped and looked at her. His face darkened and grew stern.

"Forgive me, Princess," he said in a hollow voice. "I've given way to a malicious feeling and forgotten myself. It was not right."

And coughing in an embarrassed way, he walked away quickly, without remembering to put his hat on.

Stars were already twinkling in the sky. The moon must have been rising on the further side of the monastery, for the sky was clear, soft, and transparent. Bats were flitting noiselessly along the white monastery wall.

The clock slowly struck three quarters, probably a quarter to nine. The princess got up and walked slowly to the gate. She felt wounded and was crying, and she felt that the trees and the stars and even the bats were pitying her, and that the clock struck musically only to express its sympathy with her. She cried and thought how nice it would be to go into a monastery for the rest of her life. On still summer evenings she would walk alone through the avenues, insulted, injured, misunderstood by people, and only God and the starry heavens would see the martyr's tears. The evening service was still going on in the church. The princess stopped and listened to the singing; how beautiful the singing sounded in the still darkness! How sweet to weep and suffer to the sound of that singing!

Going into her rooms, she looked at her tear-stained face in the glass and powdered it, then she sat down to supper. The monks knew that she liked pickled sturgeon, little mushrooms, Malaga and plain honey-cakes that left a taste of cypress in the mouth, and every time she came they gave her all these dishes. As she ate the mushrooms and drank the Malaga, the princess dreamed of how she would be finally ruined and deserted—how all her stewards, bailiffs, clerks, and maid-servants for whom she had done so much, would be false to her, and begin to say rude things; how people all the world over would set upon her, speak ill of her, jeer at her. She would renounce her title, would renounce society and luxury, and would go into a convent without one word of reproach to any one; she would pray for her enemies—and then they would all understand her and come to beg her forgiveness, but by that time it would be too late. . . .

After supper she knelt down in the corner before the ikon and read two chapters of the Gospel. Then her maid made her bed and she got into it. Stretching herself under the white quilt, she heaved a sweet, deep sigh, as one sighs after crying, closed her eyes, and began to fall asleep.

In the morning she waked up and glanced at her watch. It was half-past nine. On the carpet near the bed was a bright, narrow streak of sunlight from a ray which came in at the window and dimly lighted up the room. Flies were buzzing behind the black curtain at the window. "It's early," thought the princess, and she closed her eyes.

Stretching and lying snug in her bed, she recalled her meeting yesterday with the doctor and all the thoughts with which she had gone to sleep the night before: she remembered she was unhappy. Then she thought of her husband living in Petersburg, her stewards, doctors, neighbours, the officials of her acquaintance . . . a long procession of familiar masculine faces passed before her imagination. She smiled and thought, if only these people could see into her heart and understand her, they would all be at her feet.

At a quarter past eleven she called her maid.

"Help me to dress, Dasha," she said languidly. "But go first and tell them to get out the horses. I must set off for Klavdia Nikolaevna's."

Going out to get into the carriage, she blinked at the glaring daylight and laughed with pleasure: it was a wonderfully fine day! As she scanned from her half-closed eyes the monks who had gathered round the steps to see her off, she nodded graciously and said:

"Good-bye, my friends! Till the day after tomorrow."

It was an agreeable surprise to her that the doctor was with the monks by the steps. His face was pale and severe.

"Princess," he said with a guilty smile, taking off his hat, "I've been waiting here a long time to see you. Forgive me, for God's sake. . . . I was carried away yesterday by an evil, vindictive feeling and I talked . . . nonsense. In short, I beg your pardon."

The princess smiled graciously, and held out her hand for him to kiss. He kissed it, turning red.

Trying to look like a bird, the princess fluttered into the carriage and nodded in all directions. There was a gay, warm, serene feeling in her heart, and she felt herself that her smile was particularly soft and friendly. As the carriage rolled towards the gates, and afterwards along the dusty road past huts and gardens, past long trains of waggons and strings of pilgrims on their way to the monastery, she still screwed up her eyes and smiled softly. She was thinking there was no higher bliss than to bring warmth, light, and joy wherever one went, to forgive injuries, to smile graciously on one's enemies. The peasants she passed bowed to her, the carriage rustled softly, clouds of dust rose from under the wheels and floated over the golden rye, and it seemed to the princess that her body was swaying not on carriage cushions but on clouds, and that she herself was like a light, transparent little cloud. . . .

"How happy I am!" she murmured, shutting her eyes. "How happy I am!"

THE CHEMIST'S WIFE

THE little town of B----, consisting of two or three crooked streets, was sound asleep. There was a complete stillness in the motionless air. Nothing could be heard but far away, outside the town no doubt, the barking of a dog in a thin, hoarse tenor. It was close upon daybreak.

Everything had long been asleep. The only person not asleep was the young wife of Tchernomordik, a qualified dispenser who kept a chemist's shop at B----. She had gone to bed and got up again three times, but could not sleep, she did not know why. She sat at the open window in her nightdress and looked into the street. She felt bored, depressed, vexed . . . so vexed that she felt quite inclined to cry—again she did not know why. There seemed to be a lump in her chest that kept rising into her throat. . . . A few paces behind her Tchernomordik lay curled up close to the wall, snoring sweetly. A greedy flea was stabbing the bridge of his nose, but he did not feel it, and was positively smiling, for he was dreaming that every one in the town had a cough, and was buying from him the King of Denmark's cough-drops. He could not have been wakened now by pinpricks or by cannon or by caresses.

The chemist's shop was almost at the extreme end of the town, so that the chemist's wife could see far into the fields. She could see the eastern horizon growing pale by degrees, then turning crimson as though from a great fire. A big broad-faced moon peeped out unexpectedly from behind bushes in the distance. It was red (as a rule when the moon emerges from behind bushes it appears to be blushing).

Suddenly in the stillness of the night there came the sounds of footsteps and a jingle of spurs. She could hear voices.

"That must be the officers going home to the camp from the Police Captain's," thought the chemist's wife.

Soon afterwards two figures wearing officers' white tunics came into sight: one big and tall, the other thinner and shorter. . . . They slouched along by the fence, dragging one leg after the other and talking loudly together. As they passed the chemist's shop, they walked more slowly than ever, and glanced up at the windows.

"It smells like a chemist's," said the thin one. "And so it is! Ah, I remember. . . . I came here last week to buy some castor-oil. There's a chemist here with a sour face and the jawbone of an ass! Such a jawbone, my dear fellow! It must have been a jawbone like that Samson killed the Philistines with."

"M'yes," said the big one in a bass voice. "The pharmacist is asleep.

And his wife is asleep too. She is a pretty woman, Obtyosov."

"I saw her. I liked her very much. . . . Tell me, doctor, can she possibly love that jawbone of an ass? Can she?"

"No, most likely she does not love him," sighed the doctor, speaking as though he were sorry for the chemist. "The little woman is asleep behind the window, Obtyosov, what? Tossing with the heat, her little mouth half open . . . and one little foot hanging out of bed. I bet that fool the chemist doesn't realise what a lucky fellow he is. . . . No doubt he sees no difference between a woman and a bottle of carbolic!"

"I say, doctor," said the officer, stopping. "Let us go into the shop and buy something. Perhaps we shall see her."

"What an idea—in the night!"

"What of it? They are obliged to serve one even at night. My dear fellow, let us go in!"

"If you like. . . ."

The chemist's wife, hiding behind the curtain, heard a muffled ring. Looking round at her husband, who was smiling and snoring sweetly as before, she threw on her dress, slid her bare feet into her slippers, and ran to the shop.

On the other side of the glass door she could see two shadows. The chemist's wife turned up the lamp and hurried to the door to open it, and now she felt neither vexed nor bored nor inclined to cry, though her heart was thumping. The big doctor and the slender Obtyosov walked in. Now she could get a view of them. The doctor was corpulent and swarthy; he wore a beard and was slow in his movements. At the slightest motion his tunic seemed as though it would crack, and perspiration came on to his face. The officer was rosy, clean-shaven, feminine-looking, and as supple as an English whip.

"What may I give you? asked the chemist's wife, holding her dress across her bosom.

"Give us . . . er-er . . . four pennyworth of peppermint lozenges!"

Without haste the chemist's wife took down a jar from a shelf and began weighing out lozenges. The customers stared fixedly at her back; the doctor screwed up his eyes like a well-fed cat, while the lieutenant was very grave.

"It's the first time I've seen a lady serving in a chemist's shop," observed the doctor.

"There's nothing out of the way in it," replied the chemist's wife, looking out of the corner of her eye at the rosy-cheeked officer. "My husband has no assistant, and I always help him."

"To be sure. . . . You have a charming little shop! What a number of different . . . jars! And you are not afraid of moving about among the poisons? Brrr!"

The chemist's wife sealed up the parcel and handed it to the doctor.

Obtyosov gave her the money. Half a minute of silence followed. . . . The men exchanged glances, took a step towards the door, then looked at one another again.

"Will you give me two pennyworth of soda?" said the doctor.

Again the chemist's wife slowly and languidly raised her hand to the shelf.

"Haven't you in the shop anything . . . such as . . ." muttered Obtyosov, moving his fingers, "something, so to say, allegorical . . . revivifying . . . seltzer-water, for instance. Have you any seltzer-water?"

"Yes," answered the chemist's wife.

"Bravo! You're a fairy, not a woman! Give us three bottles!"

The chemist's wife hurriedly sealed up the soda and vanished through the door into the darkness.

"A peach!" said the doctor, with a wink. "You wouldn't find a pineapple like that in the island of Madeira! Eh? What do you say? Do you hear the snoring, though? That's his worship the chemist enjoying sweet repose."

A minute later the chemist's wife came back and set five bottles on the counter. She had just been in the cellar, and so was flushed and rather excited.

"Sh-sh! . . . quietly!" said Obtyosov when, after uncorking the bottles, she dropped the corkscrew. "Don't make such a noise; you'll wake your husband."

"Well, what if I do wake him?"

"He is sleeping so sweetly . . . he must be dreaming of you. . . .

To your health!"

"Besides," boomed the doctor, hiccupping after the seltzer-water, "husbands are such a dull business that it would be very nice of them to be always asleep. How good a drop of red wine would be in this water!"

"What an idea!" laughed the chemist's wife.

"That would be splendid. What a pity they don't sell spirits in chemist's shops! Though you ought to sell wine as a medicine. Have you any *vinum gallicum rubrum*?"

"Yes."

"Well, then, give us some! Bring it here, damn it!"

"How much do you want?"

"Quantum satis. . . . Give us an ounce each in the water, and afterwards we'll see. . . . Obtyosov, what do you say? First with water and afterwards *per se*. . . ."

The doctor and Obtyosov sat down to the counter, took off their caps, and began drinking the wine.

"The wine, one must admit, is wretched stuff! *Vinum nastissimum!* Though in the presence of . . . er . . . it tastes like nectar. You are enchanting, madam! In imagination I kiss your hand."

"I would give a great deal to do so not in imagination," said Obtyosov. "On my honour, I'd give my life."

"That's enough," said Madame Tchernomordik, flushing and assuming a serious expression.

"What a flirt you are, though!" the doctor laughed softly, looking slyly at her from under his brows. "Your eyes seem to be firing shot: piff-paff! I congratulate you: you've conquered! We are vanquished!"

The chemist's wife looked at their ruddy faces, listened to their chatter, and soon she, too, grew quite lively. Oh, she felt so gay! She entered into the conversation, she laughed, flirted, and even, after repeated requests from the customers, drank two ounces of wine.

"You officers ought to come in oftener from the camp," she said;

"it's awful how dreary it is here. I'm simply dying of it."

"I should think so!" said the doctor indignantly. "Such a peach, a miracle of nature, thrown away in the wilds! How well Griboyedov said, 'Into the wilds, to Saratov'! It's time for us to be off, though. Delighted to have made your acquaintance . . . very. How much do we owe you?"

The chemist's wife raised her eyes to the ceiling and her lips moved for some time.

"Twelve roubles forty-eight kopecks," she said.

Obtyosov took out of his pocket a fat pocket-book, and after fumbling for some time among the notes, paid.

"Your husband's sleeping sweetly . . . he must be dreaming," he muttered, pressing her hand at parting.

"I don't like to hear silly remarks. . . ."

"What silly remarks? On the contrary, it's not silly at all . . . even Shakespeare said: 'Happy is he who in his youth is young.'"

"Let go of my hand."

At last after much talk and after kissing the lady's hand at parting, the customers went out of the shop irresolutely, as though they were wondering whether they had not forgotten something.

She ran quickly into the bedroom and sat down in the same place. She saw the doctor and the officer, on coming out of the shop, walk lazily away a distance of twenty paces; then they stopped and began whispering together. What about? Her heart throbbed, there was a pulsing in her temples, and why she did not know. . . . Her heart beat violently as though those two whispering outside were deciding her fate.

Five minutes later the doctor parted from Obtyosov and walked on, while Obtyosov came back. He walked past the shop once and a second time. . . . He would stop near the door and then take a few steps again. At last the bell tinkled discreetly.

"What? Who is there?" the chemist's wife heard her husband's voice suddenly. "There's a ring at the bell, and you don't hear it," he said severely. "Is that the way to do things?"

He got up, put on his dressing-gown, and staggering, half asleep, flopped in his slippers to the shop.

"What . . . is it?" he asked Obtyosov.

"Give me . . . give me four pennyworth of peppermint lozenges."

Sniffing continually, yawning, dropping asleep as he moved, and knocking his knees against the counter, the chemist went to the shelf and reached down the jar.

Two minutes later the chemist's wife saw Obtyosov go out of the shop, and, after he had gone some steps, she saw him throw the packet of peppermints on the dusty road. The doctor came from behind a corner to meet him. . . . They met and, gesticulating, vanished in the morning mist.

"How unhappy I am!" said the chemist's wife, looking angrily at her husband, who was undressing quickly to get into bed again. "Oh, how unhappy I am!" she repeated, suddenly melting into bitter tears. "And nobody knows, nobody knows. . . ."

"I forgot fourpence on the counter," muttered the chemist, pulling the quilt over him. "Put it away in the till, please. . . ."

And at once he fell asleep again.

Anton Chekhov – A Biography

Anton Pavlovich Chekhov was born the third of six surviving children on 29th January 1860 in Taganrog, a port town on the Sea of Azov on the south coast of Russia. During his intense career he would make a name for himself as a playwright and author, though the whole time he practised as a physician. Indeed, he once wrote "medicine is my lawful wife, and literature is my mistress". This affair was an extended and colourful one, begun as a means of bolstering his income but developed as a form of artistic expression, through which he would make several key formal innovations which prevail in the writing of various authors who succeed him such as the method of stream-of-consciousness writing, heavily employed by the Irish novelist and poet James Joyce.

Chekhov's father Pavel Yegorovich, from whose Christian name Chekhov received his patronymic middle name, was the son of a former serf and ran a grocery store in Taganrog. As a devout orthodox Christian and director of the parish church choir in which Chekhov and his brothers sang, the stark contrast between this and his physically abusive attitude at home served as an example for many of Chekhov's portraits of hypocrisy, while also providing Chekhov with a model of how not to conduct himself in public and in private. This proved a valuable life lesson for him, for at every juncture Chekhov would treat those around him with dignity and respect. His mother, Yevgeniya, was a talented and passionate story-teller, and entertained the children with extensive stories about her travels across the entirety of Russia with her cloth merchant father. As his father provided character inspiration, his mother instilled in him a love of stories and a skill for telling them. He would later affirm that "our talents we got from our father, but our soul from our mother". The extent of the influence that this childhood had on him can be seen in his later chastisement of his elder brother Alexander, whose tyrannical treatment of his own wife and children reminded Chekhov all too painfully of their own fraught upbringing; he wrote, tentatively,

> Let me ask you to recall that it was despotism and lying that ruined your mother's youth. Despotism and lying so mutilated our childhood that it's sickening and frightening to think about it. Remember the horror and disgust we felt in those times when Father threw a tantrum at dinner over too much salt in the soup and called Mother a fool.

Between the ages of six and eight, he attended a Greek school in Taganrog, run by the Greek Church of Taganrog and funded by wealthy Greek merchants. Among the subjects taught were Greek language, God's law, mathematics, history, calligraphy and singing. Then, from 1868 he attended Taganrog gymnasium, the local grammar school, where he proved a distinctly average pupil. Despite being academically reserved and largely undemonstrative he nonetheless forged himself a reputation as a prankster, for making up humourous nicknames for his teachers and for being a reliable source of witty, satirical remarks. It soon became apparent that his interests lay away from academia for he became involved in amateur dramatics, frequently attending performances at the Taganrog Theatre. The first of these performances was Offenbach's operetta *Elena the Beautiful* which he saw when he was thirteen, and from then on he became an avid theatre attendee and spent much of his savings on visits, despite the theatre being out of bounds for Gymnasium students without special dispensation to visit; permission was rarely given, and mostly on weekends. So regular was he that he had a favourite seat, whose most attractive characteristic was its location; situated in the back gallery it was cheap, and being so far out of sight it proved an effective place to hide from the Gymnasium staff who would routinely check for unauthorised students. To further conceal themselves from these spot-checks, Anton and his schoolmates would disguise themselves with make-up, wigs and props such as spectacles and fake beards. Much of the savings which he spent at the theatre came from the annual 300 ruble grant he received from the Taganrog City Council after a failed assassination attempt on the then Tsar, Alexander II of Russia. Inspired by the drama he witnessed at the theatre, he tried his hand at writing short, amusing 'anecdotes' and stories. Alongside this he is known to have written a long, tragicomic play, entitled *Fatherless*, though he later destroyed it and no manuscript remains, and which his brother Alexander denounced as "an inexcusable though innocent fabrication".

His preoccupation with the theatre had a marked result on his school career, and the greatest blow came when he was fifteen and kept down a year for failing a Greek examination. During this time he sang under his Father's direction in the Greek orthodox ministry choir, a time which he would later recall as one of "suffering". A letter written in 1892 describes how "when my brothers and I used to stand in the middle of the church and sing the trio 'May my prayer be exalted', or 'The Archangel's Voice', everyone looked at us with emotion and envied our parents, but we at that moment felt like little convicts". The family gave an appearance of idyllic happiness and talent, though this contrast between this outward façade and the tyranny and despotism they experienced at home under Pavel's strict rule serves as another example of exactly the source of the picture of hypocrisy Chekhov paints in his work. When Chekhov was sixteen, Pavel mismanaged his own finances quite spectacularly during the process of building a new house which resulted in a declaration of bankruptcy and a subsequent fleeing to Moscow to avoid debtor's prison.

By now Chekhov's elder brothers Alexander and Nikolay were already studying at Moscow University so the majority of the family reunited there, living in poverty, a change of circumstance which left Yevgeniya in a state of emotional and physical infirmity. Chekhov, however, remained in Taganrog living with a man called Selivanov who, like Lopakhin in *The Cherry Orchard*, had bailed out the family for the price of their house, to complete his education. Although his board was free with Selivanov, he was left to pay for his schooling, covering the costs and surviving on a disparate income cobbled together from the selling off of family possessions and bolstered by private tutoring, catching and selling goldfinches, and by writing and selling short sketches to the newspapers. Every ruble he could spare from his education and his now less frequent theatre visits he sent to his family in Moscow, enclosed with humourous letters designed to cheer them up in their poverty and misery. He now began to take a more earnest interest in his education, reading extensively and analytically, including the works of Cervantes, Turgenev, Goncharov and Schopenhauer. Meanwhile he enjoyed a series of closeted love affairs, including one with the wife of one of his teachers. His schooling completed and a scholarship to Moscow University obtained, he moved there in 1879 and rejoined his family.

He now assumed responsibility for the family, supporting them by writing regular satirical sketches and vignettes of contemporary Russian lifestyle under pseudonyms such as 'Antosha Chekhonte' and 'Man Without a Spleen', and his prodigious output earned him first a reputation as a reputable chronicler and then, in 1882, a regular position writing for Oskolki, a journal owned by Nicolai Leykin, the most successful Russian publisher at the time. Although the wit and brevity of his work here prevails through much of his later writing, it was considerably harsher in tone, perhaps a reflection of the stressful position of poverty, study and patriarch in which he found himself. In 1884, he qualified as a physician and, although he earned little from the profession and often treated the poor free of charge, he considered this his principle profession. At this time and for the next two years he would regularly cough up blood, a symptom of tuberculosis with which he was all too familiar as a physician. However, not wishing to "submit himself to be sounded by his colleagues", he kept the condition to himself. The continued success of his periodical writing enabled him to move the family into progressively more comfortable accommodation, and then in 1886 he received an invitation to write for *Novoye Vremya* (*New Times*), owned and edited by the millionaire media magnate Alexey Suvorin. Paying double per line what Anton received from Leykin and being given three times the column inches he took the offer immediately and became close friends with Suvorin, a friendship which would last his lifetime.

His work at these periodicals was not the sole extent of his literary output, for in 1885 he published a short story, *The Huntsman*, which quickly attracted scholarly attention and recognition. The sixty-four year old celebrated writer Grigorovich wrote to him shortly after it first appeared on the shelves, saying "you have *real* talent—a talent which places you in the front rank among writers in the new generation." The letter continues in this effusive manner before resolving to offer Chekhov the practical advice to slow down, write less, and concentrate on literary quality. In reply, Chekhov admitted that he had been struck "like a thunderbolt" on reading the letter, confessing to hitherto writing his stories "the way reporters write up their notes about fires - mechanically, half-consciously, caring nothing about either the reader or myself." In making such an honest admission, Chekhov arguably undersold himself as a serious author, for despite the appearance of a nonchalant and casual approach, later analysis and comparison of early manuscripts reveals a huge extent of careful revision indicating a far more involved, authorial approach than he allows himself in correspondence with Grigorovich. Nonetheless, receiving such warm congratulation and encouragement along with such earnest advice from so respected an author caused Chekhov to sit up straight and approach his writing with far more serious, artistic ambition. Now twenty-six, and with the patronage of such a revered and loved author, his collection of short stories entitled *V Sumerkakh* (*At Dusk*) won him the much coveted Pushkin Prize, awarded "for the best literary production distinguished by high artistic worth".

Following this act of formal recognition and somewhat burnt out by the years of continued literary output his enduring success afforded him the time and the money to take a sabbatical, so he engaged in a journey to the Ukraine in 1887 whereupon he was reminded of the beauty of the Steppe. This excursion inspired the novella *The Steppe* which he started on his return, and which he described in a letter to Grigorovich as "something rather odd and much too original", and which was eventually published in *Severny Vestnik* (*The Northern Herald*). Later that year he was commissioned by a theatre manager to write a play, and a fortnight later Chekhov produced *Ivanov* which, though he considered the process "sickening" and described in a letter to his brother Alexander in the manner of a comic portrait, it was a huge success and was widely regarded as a work of excellent and noteworthy originality. Furthermore this period is considered the source of a literary device noted by Ilia Gurliand, who overheard it in conversation, as Chekhov's Gun; "if in act 1 you have a pistol hanging on the wall, then it must fire in the last act". Then, in 1889, his brother Nikolay died as a result of tuberculosis. Their brother Mikhail, who recorded Anton's depression during the period of mourning after the death, had been researching prisons as part of his studies in law, and Anton too became interested and eventually somewhat obsessed with the idea of prison reform.

This newfound interest in the humanitarian questions surrounding the prison system, combined with a conceivable yet subconscious desire to escape the close environment of mourning surrounding his brother's death, led Chekhov to journey to the penal colony Sakhalin, an island off the far East coast of Russia, where he spent three months interviewing convicts and settlers with the aim of compiling a census of the island. He made several now notorious remarks to his sister about what he witnessed (among others, a relatively lighthearted and blunt description of Tomsk, "a very dull town. To judge from the drunkards whose acquaintance I have made, and from the intellectual people who have come to the hotel to pay their respects to me, the inhabitants are very dull, too." [-the inhabitants of Tomsk later retaliated by erecting a mocking statue of Chekhov]). More seriously, though, many of the things he saw during this trip horrified him, writing that "there were times I felt that I saw before me the extreme limits of man's degradation." Among these was the plight of the children of the island, describing one such incident in his journals:

> On the Amur steamer going to Sakhalin, there was a convict who had murdered his wife and wore fetters on his legs. His daughter, a little girl of six, was with him. I noticed wherever the convict moved the little girl scrambled after him, holding on to his fetters. At night the child slept with the convicts and soldiers all in a heap together.

Concluding that the solution to this inhumanity lay not with charity and philanthropy, but with Government intervention and reform, he wrote *Ostrov Sakhalin* (*The Island of Sakhalin*), a work of social science which was praised, not for its literary brilliance, but for its steady and worthy informativeness, which was serialised and published in 1893-4. Though this initial work which stemmed from the trip was not literary in nature, the extended contact and expansive experience he received found itself expressed in *The Murder*, a story which, though longer than his others, is still considered short in nature.

In 1892 Chekhov had bought Melikhovo, a small country estate forty miles north of Moscow, which was his and his family's home until 1899. He joked about his residence there, quipping to his friend Ivan Leontyev that "it's nice to be a Lord" though this lighthearted remark belies the seriousness with which he undertook his responsibilities as a landlord. Within a few years of his taking residence there he had established his usefulness and sense of duty to the peasants, affording them relief from the 1892 outbreaks of cholera and bouts of famine, and building three schools, a fire station and a clinic, and offering his services as a physician to the peasantry of the surrounding countryside. Often he would find queues of patients lining up outside his door in the morning who had travelled by foot or by cart to receive treatment, and frequently he was called out to visit those too sick to travel. His brother Mikhail who resided with the family at Melikhovo recorded this honourable commitment to his role as estate physician, writing

> from the first day that Chekhov moved to Melikhovo, the sick began flocking to him from twenty miles around. They came on foot or were brought in carts, and often he was fetched to patients at a distance. Sometimes from early in the morning peasant women and children were standing before his door waiting.

Though these demanding hours left him with significantly less time for writing, they enriched his literary output for he was able to write informatively and genuinely about the peasantry and their living conditions, most notably in his short story *Peasants*. He did, however, visit those belonging to the upper-classes as well, though he was not enamoured by them, writing in his journal "Aristocrats? The same ugly bodies and physical uncleanliness, the same toothless old age and disgusting death, as with market-women".

He began to write arguably his most famous work, *The Seagull*, in 1894, in a lodge he had built himself in the orchard on the estate. Its first night on 17th October 1896 at the Alexandrinsky Theatre in Petersburg was something of a fiasco; it was booed by the audience, many of whom left, and this poor reception saw Chekhov fall out of love with the theatre. However, despite its poor reception by the play-going audience, it impressed the theatre director Vladimir Nemirovich-Danchenko so much that he proceeded to convince his colleague Constantin Stanislavski to take the play on and direct it in the innovative, progressive Moscow Art Theatre. This revival, in 1898, for the less-closeted Moscow audience was enormously well-received. Whereas the Petersburg performance had rendered the play literally and played down its more psychoanalytical aspects, Stanislavski payed far closer attention to the play's psychological realism and brought the deeply buried subtleties, lost on the Petersburg boards and on the audience's narrow-mindedness, to the surface. The play was such a success here that the Art Theatre commissioned further work from Chekhov, staging *Uncle Vanya* which he had completed in 1896. Furthermore, the positive critical reception had a restorative effect on Chekhov's interest in stage writing.

However, by now Chekhov's health condition was worsening, having suffered a major haemorrhage of the lungs in 1897 while visiting Moscow. His early reluctance to be seen by doctors prevailed and he protested to the notion of entering a clinic, though he eventually assented whereupon a formal diagnosis of the tuberculosis on the upper part of his lungs was reached, and the doctors ordered various changes in his lifestyle. His father then died in 1898, after which Chekhov bought a plot of land on the outskirts of Yalta and proceeded to build a villa, moving his mother and sister in with him the following year. Even though he pursued the enjoyment of gardening he had developed while at Melikhovo by planting trees and flowers, he kept dogs and tame cranes and regularly received highly regarded company such as Leo Tolstoy and Maxim Gorky, he spoke of a sense of relief upon each occasion of his leaving this "hot Siberia" for Moscow or to travel further afield. While here, he wrote two more plays for the Art Theatre, though these were composed with much greater difficulty; he remarked that unlike his youth when "[he] wrote serenely, the way [he eats] pancakes now". These two plays, *Three Sisters* and *The Cherry Orchard* took over a year each.

A quiet marriage to Olga Knipper on 25th May 1901 was performed in keeping with the position of suspicion he had always had towards weddings, with a small ceremony and little outside attention. Knipper was an actress whom he had met at the rehearsals for *The Seagull*, their marriage conformed to his stipulations;

> By all means I will be married if you wish it. But on these conditions: everything must be as it has been hitherto - that is, she must live in Moscow while I live in the country, and I will come and see her ... give me a wife who, like the moon, won't appear in my sky every day.

This proved convenient as Knipper remained in Moscow performing his work and that of contemporary playwrights, and their long-distance correspondence features various treasured pieces of writing, be they shared complaints about Stanislavski's method of direction or advice from Chekhov to Knipper as to her performances in his plays. Prior to the marriage, Chekhov had been considered "Russia's most elusive literary bachelor", preferring brief liaisons and dalliances with unknown women, or brothels, to commitment. Chekhov then wrote one of his most famous stories, *The Lady with the Dog*, depicting a casual encounter between two strangers who, despite their best efforts and risking the security, stability and respectability of their family lives, find themselves irrevocably drawn to one another.

Chekhov's tuberculosis was finally getting the better of him, and by May 1904 it was quite clear that his death was imminent. Despite this, Mikhail recorded that "everyone who saw him secretly thought the end was not far off, but the nearer [he] was to the end, the less he seemed to realise it". He set off for the German town Badenweiler on 3rd June, writing cheerful, witty letters to his sister describing variously the food and the surroundings, while assuring both her and his mother that his health was improving; his last letter contained a sardonic complaint about the German women's fashion. The circumstances of his death have become one of "the greatest set pieces of literary history", and are most accurately recorded in this, Knipper's own account from her diaries, written in 1908:

> Anton sat up unusually straight and said loudly and clearly (although he knew almost no German): *Ich sterbe* ("I'm dying"). The doctor calmed him, took a syringe, gave him an injection of camphor and ordered champagne. Anton took a full glass, examined it, smiled at me and said: 'It's a long time since I drank champagne.' He drained it, lay quietly on his left side, and I just had time to run to him and lean across the bed and call to him, but he had stopped breathing and was sleeping peacefully as a child.

His body, transferred to Moscow in a refrigerated railway car whose purpose was for fresh oysters, was then interred next to his father at Novodevichy Cemetery in Moscow. Although thousands of mourners mistakenly followed the pomp and circumstance of the military funeral procession for the also deceased General Keller, many hundreds of thousands of readers, writers and actors have followed correctly the path he pioneered for the short story and for twentieth century realism.

A Biography of Anton Chekov & List of His Most Famous Quotes

Anton Pavlovich Chekhov was born the third of six surviving children on 29th January 1860 in Taganrog, a port town on the Sea of Azov on the south coast of Russia. During his intense career he would make a name for himself as a playwright and author, though the whole time he practised as a physician. Indeed, he once wrote "medicine is my lawful wife, and literature is my mistress". This affair was an extended and colourful one, begun as a means of bolstering his income but developed as a form of artistic expression, through which he would make several key formal innovations which prevail in the writing of various authors who succeed him such as the method of stream-of-consciousness writing, heavily employed by the Irish novelist and poet James Joyce.

Chekhov's father Pavel Yegorovich, from whose Christian name Chekhov received his patronymic middle name, was the son of a former serf and ran a grocery store in Taganrog. As a devout orthodox Christian and director of the parish church choir in which Chekhov and his brothers sang, the stark contrast between this and his physically abusive attitude at home served as an example for many of Chekhov's portraits of hypocrisy, while also providing Chekhov with a model of how not to conduct himself in public and in private. This proved a valuable life lesson for him, for at every juncture Chekhov would treat those around him with dignity and respect. His mother, Yevgeniya, was a talented and passionate story-teller, and entertained the children with extensive stories about her travels across the entirety of Russia with her cloth merchant father. As his father provided character inspiration, his mother instilled in him a love of stories and a skill for telling them. He would later affirm that "our talents we got from our father, but our soul from our mother". The extent of the influence that this childhood had on him can be seen in his later chastisement of his elder brother Alexander, whose tyrannical treatment of his own wife and children reminded Chekhov all too painfully of their own fraught upbringing; he wrote, tentatively,

> Let me ask you to recall that it was despotism and lying that ruined your mother's youth. Despotism and lying so mutilated our childhood that it's sickening and frightening to think about it. Remember the horror and disgust we felt in those times when Father threw a tantrum at dinner over too much salt in the soup and called Mother a fool.

Between the ages of six and eight, he attended a Greek school in Taganrog, run by the Greek Church of Taganrog and funded by wealthy Greek merchants. Among the subjects taught were Greek language, God's law, mathematics, history, calligraphy and singing. Then, from 1868 he attended Taganrog gymnasium, the local grammar school, where he proved a distinctly average pupil. Despite being academically reserved and largely undemonstrative he nonetheless forged himself a reputation as a prankster, for making up humourous nicknames for his teachers and for being a reliable source of witty, satirical remarks. It soon became apparent that his interests lay away from academia for he became involved in amateur dramatics, frequently attending performances at the Taganrog Theatre. The first of these performances was Offenbach's operetta *Elena the Beautiful* which he saw when he was thirteen, and from then on he became an avid theatre attendee and spent much of his savings on visits, despite the theatre being out of bounds for Gymnasium students without special dispensation to visit; permission was rarely given, and mostly on weekends. So regular was he that he had a favourite seat, whose most attractive characteristic was its location; situated in the back gallery it was cheap, and being so far out of sight it proved an effective place to hide from the Gymnasium staff who would routinely check for unauthorised students. To further conceal themselves from these spot-checks, Anton and his schoolmates would disguise themselves with make-up, wigs and props such as spectacles and fake beards. Much of the savings which he spent at the theatre came from the annual 300 ruble grant he received from the Taganrog City Council after a failed assassination attempt on the then Tsar, Alexander II of Russia. Inspired by the drama he witnessed at the theatre, he tried his hand at writing short, amusing 'anecdotes' and stories. Alongside this he is known to have written a long, tragicomic play, entitled *Fatherless*, though he later destroyed it and no manuscript remains, and which his brother Alexander denounced as "an inexcusable though innocent fabrication".

His preoccupation with the theatre had a marked result on his school career, and the greatest blow came when he was fifteen and kept down a year for failing a Greek examination. During this time he sang under his Father's direction in the Greek orthodox ministry choir, a time which he would later recall as one of "suffering". A letter written in 1892 describes how "when my brothers and I used to stand in the middle of the church and sing the trio 'May my prayer be exalted', or 'The Archangel's Voice', everyone looked at us with emotion and envied our parents, but we at that moment felt like little convicts". The family gave an appearance of idyllic happiness and talent, though this contrast between this outward façade and the tyranny and despotism they experienced at home under Pavel's strict rule serves as another example of exactly the source of the picture of hypocrisy Chekhov paints in his work. When Chekhov was sixteen, Pavel mismanaged his own finances quite spectacularly during the process of building a new house which resulted in a declaration of bankruptcy and a subsequent fleeing to Moscow to avoid debtor's prison.

By now Chekhov's elder brothers Alexander and Nikolay were already studying at Moscow University so the majority of the family reunited there, living in poverty, a change of circumstance which left Yevgeniya in a state of emotional and physical infirmity. Chekhov, however, remained in Taganrog living with a man called Selivanov who, like Lopakhin in *The Cherry Orchard*, had bailed out the family for the price of their house, to complete his education. Although his board was free with Selivanov, he was left to pay for his schooling, covering the costs and surviving on a disparate income cobbled together from the selling off of family possessions and bolstered by private tutoring, catching and selling goldfinches, and by writing and selling short sketches to the newspapers. Every ruble he could spare from his education and his now less frequent theatre visits he sent to his family in Moscow, enclosed with humourous letters designed to cheer them up in their poverty and misery. He now began to take a more earnest interest in his education, reading extensively and analytically, including the works of Cervantes, Turgenev, Goncharov and Schopenhauer. Meanwhile he enjoyed a series of closeted love affairs, including one with the wife of one of his teachers. His schooling completed and a scholarship to Moscow University obtained, he moved there in 1879 and rejoined his family.

He now assumed responsibility for the family, supporting them by writing regular satirical sketches and vignettes of contemporary Russian lifestyle under pseudonyms such as 'Antosha Chekhonte' and 'Man Without a Spleen', and his prodigious output earned him first a reputation as a reputable chronicler and then, in 1882, a regular position writing for Oskolki, a journal owned by Nicolai Leykin, the most successful

Russian publisher at the time. Although the wit and brevity of his work here prevails through much of his later writing, it was considerably harsher in tone, perhaps a reflection of the stressful position of poverty, study and patriarch in which he found himself. In 1884, he qualified as a physician and, although he earned little from the profession and often treated the poor free of charge, he considered this his principle profession. At this time and for the next two years he would regularly cough up blood, a symptom of tuberculosis with which he was all too familiar as a physician. However, not wishing to "submit himself to be sounded by his colleagues", he kept the condition to himself. The continued success of his periodical writing enabled him to move the family into progressively more comfortable accommodation, and then in 1886 he received an invitation to write for *Novoye Vremya* (*New Times*), owned and edited by the millionaire media magnate Alexey Suvorin. Paying double per line what Anton received from Leykin and being given three times the column inches he took the offer immediately and became close friends with Suvorin, a friendship which would last his lifetime.

His work at these periodicals was not the sole extent of his literary output, for in 1885 he published a short story, *The Huntsman*, which quickly attracted scholarly attention and recognition. The sixty-four year old celebrated writer Grigorovich wrote to him shortly after it first appeared on the shelves, saying "you have *real* talent—a talent which places you in the front rank among writers in the new generation." The letter continues in this effusive manner before resolving to offer Chekhov the practical advice to slow down, write less, and concentrate on literary quality. In reply, Chekhov admitted that he had been struck "like a thunderbolt" on reading the letter, confessing to hitherto writing his stories "the way reporters write up their notes about fires - mechanically, half-consciously, caring nothing about either the reader or myself." In making such an honest admission, Chekhov arguably undersold himself as a serious author, for despite the appearance of a nonchalant and casual approach, later analysis and comparison of early manuscripts reveals a huge extent of careful revision indicating a far more involved, authorial approach than he allows himself in correspondence with Grigorovich. Nonetheless, receiving such warm congratulation and encouragement along with such earnest advice from so respected an author caused Chekhov to sit up straight and approach his writing with far more serious, artistic ambition. Now twenty-six, and with the patronage of such a revered and loved author, his collection of short stories entitled *V Sumerkakh* (*At Dusk*) won him the much coveted Pushkin Prize, awarded "for the best literary production distinguished by high artistic worth".

Following this act of formal recognition and somewhat burnt out by the years of continued literary output his enduring success afforded him the time and the money to take a sabbatical, so he engaged in a journey to the Ukraine in 1887 whereupon he was reminded of the beauty of the Steppe. This excursion inspired the novella *The Steppe* which he started on his return, and which he described in a letter to Grigorovich as "something rather odd and much too original", and which was eventually published in *Severny Vestnik* (*The Northern Herald*). Later that year he was commissioned by a theatre manager to write a play, and a fortnight later Chekhov produced *Ivanov* which, though he considered the process "sickening" and described in a letter to his brother Alexander in the manner of a comic portrait, it was a huge success and was widely regarded as a work of excellent and noteworthy originality. Furthermore this period is considered the source of a literary device noted by Ilia

Gurliand, who overheard it in conversation, as Chekhov's Gun; "if in act 1 you have a pistol hanging on the wall, then it must fire in the last act". Then, in 1889, his brother Nikolay died as a result of tuberculosis. Their brother Mikhail, who recorded Anton's depression during the period of mourning after the death, had been researching prisons as part of his studies in law, and Anton too became interested and eventually somewhat obsessed with the idea of prison reform.

This newfound interest in the humanitarian questions surrounding the prison system, combined with a conceivable yet subconscious desire to escape the close environment of mourning surrounding his brother's death, led Chekhov to journey to the penal colony Sakhalin, an island off the far East coast of Russia, where he spent three months interviewing convicts and settlers with the aim of compiling a census of the island. He made several now notorious remarks to his sister about what he witnessed (among others, a relatively lighthearted and blunt description of Tomsk, "a very dull town. To judge from the drunkards whose acquaintance I have made, and from the intellectual people who have come to the hotel to pay their respects to me, the inhabitants are very dull, too." [-the inhabitants of Tomsk later retaliated by erecting a mocking statue of Chekhov]). More seriously, though, many of the things he saw during this trip horrified him, writing that "there were times I felt that I saw before me the extreme limits of man's degradation." Among these was the plight of the children of the island, describing one such incident in his journals:

> On the Amur steamer going to Sakhalin, there was a convict who had murdered his wife and wore fetters on his legs. His daughter, a little girl of six, was with him. I noticed wherever the convict moved the little girl scrambled after him, holding on to his fetters. At night the child slept with the convicts and soldiers all in a heap together.

Concluding that the solution to this inhumanity lay not with charity and philanthropy, but with Government intervention and reform, he wrote *Ostrov Sakhalin* (*The Island of Sakhalin*), a work of social science which was praised, not for its literary brilliance, but for its steady and worthy informativeness, which was serialised and published in 1893-4. Though this initial work which stemmed from the trip was not literary in nature, the extended contact and expansive experience he received found itself expressed in *The Murder*, a story which, though longer than his others, is still considered short in nature.

In 1892 Chekhov had bought Melikhovo, a small country estate forty miles north of Moscow, which was his and his family's home until 1899. He joked about his residence there, quipping to his friend Ivan Leontyev that "it's nice to be a Lord" though this lighthearted remark belies the seriousness with which he undertook his responsibilities as a landlord. Within a few years of his taking residence there he had established his usefulness and sense of duty to the peasants, affording them relief from the 1892 outbreaks of cholera and bouts of famine, and building three schools, a fire station and a clinic, and offering his services as a physician to the peasantry of the surrounding countryside. Often he would find queues of patients lining up outside his door in the morning who had travelled by foot or by cart to receive treatment, and frequently he was called out to visit those too sick to travel. His brother Mikhail who resided with the family at Melikhovo recorded this honourable commitment to his role as estate physician, writing from the first day that Chekhov moved to Melikhovo, the sick began flocking to him from twenty miles around. They came on foot or were brought in carts, and often he was fetched to patients at a distance. Sometimes from early in the morning peasant women and children were standing before his door waiting.

Though these demanding hours left him with significantly less time for writing, they enriched his literary output for he was able to write informatively and genuinely about the peasantry and their living conditions, most notably in his short story *Peasants*. He did, however, visit those belonging to the upper-classes as well, though he was not enamoured by them, writing in his journal "Aristocrats? The same ugly bodies and physical uncleanliness, the same toothless old age and disgusting death, as with market-women".

He began to write arguably his most famous work, *The Seagull*, in 1894, in a lodge he had built himself in the orchard on the estate. Its first night on 17th October 1896 at the Alexandrinsky Theatre in Petersburg was something of a fiasco; it was booed by the audience, many of whom left, and this poor reception saw Chekhov fall out of love with the theatre. However, despite its poor reception by the play-going audience, it impressed the theatre director Vladimir Nemirovich-Danchenko so much that he proceeded to convince his colleague Constantin Stanislavski to take the play on and direct it in the innovative, progressive Moscow Art Theatre. This revival, in 1898, for the less-closeted Moscow audience was enormously well-received. Whereas the Petersburg performance had rendered the play literally and played down its more psychoanalytical aspects, Stanislavski payed far closer attention to the play's psychological realism and brought the deeply buried subtleties, lost on the Petersburg boards and on the audience's narrow-mindedness, to the surface. The play was such a success here that the Art Theatre commissioned further work from Chekhov, staging *Uncle Vanya* which he had completed in 1896. Furthermore, the positive critical reception had a restorative effect on Chekhov's interest in stage writing.

However, by now Chekhov's health condition was worsening, having suffered a major haemorrhage of the lungs in 1897 while visiting Moscow. His early reluctance to be seen by doctors prevailed and he protested to the notion of entering a clinic, though he eventually assented whereupon a formal diagnosis of the tuberculosis on the upper part of his lungs was reached, and the doctors ordered various changes in his lifestyle. His father then died in 1898, after which Chekhov bought a plot of land on the outskirts of Yalta and proceeded to build a villa, moving his mother and sister in with him the following year. Even though he pursued the enjoyment of gardening he had developed while at Melikhovo by planting trees and flowers, he kept dogs and tame cranes and regularly received highly regarded company such as Leo Tolstoy and Maxim Gorky, he spoke of a sense of relief upon each occasion of his leaving this "hot Siberia" for Moscow or to travel further afield. While here, he wrote two more plays for the Art Theatre, though these were composed with much greater difficulty; he remarked that unlike his youth when "[he] wrote serenely, the way [he eats] pancakes now". These two plays, *Three Sisters* and *The Cherry Orchard* took over a year each.

A quiet marriage to Olga Knipper on 25th May 1901 was performed in keeping with the position of suspicion he had always had towards weddings, with a small ceremony and little outside attention. Knipper was an actress whom he had met at the rehearsals for *The Seagull*, their marriage conformed to his stipulations;

> By all means I will be married if you wish it. But on these conditions: everything must be as it has been hitherto - that is, she must live in Moscow while I live in the country, and I will come and see her ... give me a wife who, like the moon, won't appear in my sky every day.

This proved convenient as Knipper remained in Moscow performing his work and that of contemporary playwrights, and their long-distance correspondence features various treasured pieces of writing, be they shared complaints about Stanislavski's method of direction or advice from Chekhov to Knipper as to her performances in his plays. Prior to the marriage, Chekhov had been considered "Russia's most elusive literary bachelor", preferring brief liaisons and dalliances with unknown women, or brothels, to commitment. Chekhov then wrote one of his most famous stories, *The Lady with the Dog*, depicting a casual encounter between two strangers who, despite their best efforts and risking the security, stability and respectability of their family lives, find themselves irrevocably drawn to one another.

Chekhov's tuberculosis was finally getting the better of him, and by May 1904 it was quite clear that his death was imminent. Despite this, Mikhail recorded that "everyone who saw him secretly thought the end was not far off, but the nearer [he] was to the end, the less he seemed to realise it". He set off for the German town Badenweiler on 3rd June, writing cheerful, witty letters to his sister describing variously the food and the surroundings, while assuring both her and his mother that his health was improving; his last letter contained a sardonic complaint about the German women's fashion. The circumstances of his death have become one of "the greatest set pieces of literary history", and are most accurately recorded in this, Knipper's own account from her diaries, written in 1908:

> Anton sat up unusually straight and said loudly and clearly (although he knew almost no German): *Ich sterbe* ("I'm dying"). The doctor calmed him, took a syringe, gave him an injection of camphor and ordered champagne. Anton took a full glass, examined it, smiled at me and said: 'It's a long time since I drank champagne.' He drained it, lay quietly on his left side, and I just had time to run to him and lean across the bed and call to him, but he had stopped breathing and was sleeping peacefully as a child.

His body, transferred to Moscow in a refrigerated railway car whose purpose was for fresh oysters, was then interred next to his father at Novodevichy Cemetery in Moscow. Although thousands of mourners mistakenly followed the pomp and circumstance of the military funeral procession for the also deceased General Keller, many hundreds of thousands of readers, writers and actors have followed correctly the path he pioneered for the short story and for twentieth century realism.

Quotes

Any idiot can face a crisis - it's day to day living that wears you out.

Medicine is my lawful wife and literature my mistress; when I get tired of one, I spend the night with the other.

People who lead a lonely existence always have something on their minds that they are eager to talk about.

Doctors are just the same as lawyers; the only difference is that lawyers merely rob you, whereas doctors rob you and kill you too.

If you are afraid of loneliness, do not marry.

Knowledge is of no value unless you put it into practice.

Don't tell me the moon is shining; show me the glint of light on broken glass.

I promise to be an excellent husband, but give me a wife who, like the moon, will not appear every day in my sky.

Let us learn to appreciate there will be times when the trees will be bare, and look forward to the time when we may pick the fruit.

Life does not agree with philosophy: There is no happiness that is not idleness, and only what is useless is pleasurable.

There is nothing new in art except talent.

A good upbringing means not that you won't spill sauce on the tablecloth, but that you won't notice it when someone else does.

Love, friendship and respect do not unite people as much as a common hatred for something.

The world perishes not from bandits and fires, but from hatred, hostility, and all these petty squabbles.

Advertising is the very essence of democracy.

Faith is an aptitude of the spirit. It is, in fact, a talent: you must be born with it.

People don't notice whether it's winter or summer when they're happy.

We shall find peace. We shall hear angels, we shall see the sky sparkling with diamonds.

You must trust and believe in people or life becomes impossible.

If you cry 'forward', you must without fail make plain in what direction to go.

No matter how corrupt and unjust a convict may be, he loves fairness more than anything else. If the people placed over him are unfair, from year to year he lapses into an embittered state characterized by an extreme lack of faith.

When you're thirsty and it seems that you could drink the entire ocean that's faith; when you start to drink and finish only a glass or two that's science.

All of life and human relations have become so incomprehensibly complex that, when you think about it, it becomes terrifying and your heart stands still.

How unbearable at times are people who are happy, people for whom everything works out.

Man is what he believes.

One must be a god to be able to tell successes from failures without making a mistake.

To advise is not to compel.

A fiancee is neither this nor that: he's left one shore, but not yet reached the other.

Money, like vodka, turns a person into an eccentric.

No psychologist should pretend to understand what he does not understand... Only fools and charlatans know everything and understand nothing.

Only entropy comes easy.

The more refined one is, the more unhappy.

The thirst for powerful sensations takes the upper hand both over fear and over compassion for the grief of others.

The University brings out all abilities, including incapability.

To judge between good or bad, between successful and unsuccessful would take the eye of a God.

We learn about life not from plusses alone, but from minuses as well.

When a woman isn't beautiful, people always say, 'You have lovely eyes, you have lovely hair.'

A writer is not a confectioner, a cosmetic dealer, or an entertainer.

Doctors are the same as lawyers; the only difference is that lawyers merely rob you, whereas doctors rob you and kill you too.

It's easier to write about Socrates than about a young woman or a cook.

Reason and justice tell me there's more love for humanity in electricity and steam than in chastity and vegetarianism.

The sea has neither meaning nor pity.

The wealthy are always surrounded by hangers-on; science and art are as well.

When a lot of remedies are suggested for a disease, that means it can't be cured.

When an actor has money he doesn't send letters, he sends telegrams.

About Us

We have many volumes of Chekhov available, together with other short story compilations, novels, essays and poetry from the most celebrated writers of all time. Use the search words 'miniature masterpieces' for other great short story compilations from incredible writers such as Arthur Conan Doyle, Joseph Conrad, Honore De Balzac, Robert Louis Stevenson and Rudyard Kipling among others. Use search words 'portable poetry' to find illuminating compositions by world renowned poets such as Rabindranth Tagore, Walt Whitman, Edgar Allan Poe, Thomas Hardy and Oscar Wilde among others. Use search words 'word to the wise' for some of the greatest novels, plays and essays ever written from history's very best including Jane Austen, Charles Dickens, Wilkie Collins, Elizabeth Gaskell, Anthony Trollope and Anthony Hope. Along with Anton Chekhov we offer many other foreign writers that have been translated to English such as Rumi, Henrik Ibsen, Miguel Cervantes, Dante Alighieri, Leo Tolstoy and Fyodor Dostoyevsky.

www.ingramcontent.com/pod-product-compliance
Lightning Source LLC
Chambersburg PA
CBHW051250170626
46809CB00004B/1576